Ivy

Eric knew what she was ~~~~~~
was becoming the type of woman that would
appeal to Kevin. There was nothing wrong in
that. He wished her luck. He liked her enough
to want her to have whatever would make her
happy.

Maybe he liked her too much.

It was true they spent a lot of time together,
and when they weren't together he found
himself thinking about her. He couldn't help
noticing how pretty she was, but mostly he
thought of her as a friend. A very good and
valued friend.

Over the years he had had several women
with whom he'd shared a friendship. But
there was something different, something
deeper about his feelings for Ivy. He felt a
bond with her that he hadn't felt with other
women. An easy companionship that was
becoming more important to him the longer
he knew her....

ABOUT THE AUTHOR

For Margaret St. George, writing fills a creative need, one she has been satisfying since she was sixteen years old. She starts writing with a single concept, asks the question "What if...?" then begins to formulate her characters. A full-time writer, Margaret uses this system for both her contemporary and historical romances.

She lives in her native Colorado with her own heart's desire—husband George.

Books by Margaret St. George

HARLEQUIN AMERICAN ROMANCE

142–WINTER MAGIC
159–CASTLES AND FAIRY TALES
203–THE HEART CLUB
231–WHERE THERE'S SMOKE...

Heart's
Desire
Margaret St. George

Harlequin Books

TORONTO • NEW YORK • LONDON
AMSTERDAM • PARIS • SYDNEY • HAMBURG
STOCKHOLM • ATHENS • TOKYO • MILAN

Published November 1988

First printing September 1988

ISBN 0-373-16272-3

Chapter One

"Are you nervous?" The woman in the blue dress moved to stand beside Ivy and peer out from the wings at the stage and the studio audience.

"Yes," Ivy Enders whispered. Her mouth was as dry as a cotton ball. She pressed her hands together and swallowed hard. Her palms were damp and her pulse fluttered.

On stage, Bob Barker, of *The Price Is Right* fame, was introducing the sweepstakes winners. With a flourish, he presented checks to those who had won the smaller amounts. Flashbulbs exploded, TV cameras whirred, and the audience applauded. Ivy bit the inside of her cheek and wondered frantically if she had chewed off her lipstick. What did her hair look like? And why hadn't she bought a new dress for this occasion? It was only the biggest, most exciting event of her life.

Sliding a glance toward the woman next to her, Ivy examined the blue dress. It was made of a silky material that clung to the woman's figure. Ivy wished she owned a clingy silk dress and had the figure to wear it. Instead, she wore a red linen jacket over a sensible, gray cotton with a gathered shirt and a white, Peter Pan collar. Practical, businesslike, but perhaps not the best choice for a television appearance. Compared to the blue silk, her outfit was drab. Moreover, she suddenly suspected that the red jacket her mother had given her might overwhelm her light brown hair and pale features. She should have worn a cocktail dress. Was there time to catch a taxi back to the hotel and change?

No. Bob Barker was working the audience, building excitement for the big winners.

"Imagine it, ladies and gentlemen—half a million dollars! That's what our next guest has won in the Celtex Sweepstakes! Let's have a nice round of applause for Mrs. Theresa Wykowski, a waitress from Brooklyn, New York!"

The woman in blue skipped on stage, ran up the red-carpeted steps to the dais and planted a moist kiss on Bob Barker's tanned cheek.

Ivy twisted her hands and closed her eyes. Butterflies the size of eagles fluttered in her stomach. Someone touched her arm, and she jumped and sucked in a breath.

"Didn't mean to startle you, dear." Jo Jo Martin patted Ivy's arm. Jo Jo headed the publicity department for Celtex Corporation. It had been she who had met Ivy at La-Guardia and escorted her to a waiting limo, then to the Plaza Hotel. A marvel of brisk efficiency, she had organized the dinner for the winners before the TV taping and had made certain they arrived at the studio on time.

Jo Jo leaned backward and studied Ivy. "The red is good," she muttered. "The gray? Well... We'll work around the white collar. Nose needs powdering. Billy? Billy, powder her nose." Jo Jo pushed back a strand from her short cap of black hair and frowned. "The glasses. The glasses have to go."

"I'm sorry, but I need my glasses."

Bob Barker was introducing a grinning man who had won the million-dollar prize in the sweepstakes. The audience applauded wildly as he shook Barker's hand and waved the check.

"Darling," said Jo Jo, "you have beautiful eyes. We don't want to hide them, now do we?" Jo Jo removed Ivy's glasses before Ivy realized what she intended to do.

Instantly the sharp angles of Jo Jo's face dissolved into a softly rounded, pale oval. "Jo Jo, please! This isn't going to work." Reaching blindly, Ivy tried to find Jo Jo's hands and her glasses. Panic dried her throat. "I can't see a thing."

"Better," Jo Jo said crisply. "Now we can see your pretty eyes." A round, fuzzy shape loomed out of the darkness and patted Ivy's nose. The powder. "Too bad about the Peter Pan collar," Jo Jo commented. "I suppose there's nothing we can do now."

"I've got to have my glasses!" Ivy's frantic plea was drowned in a rush of applause. "Jo Jo, you don't understand. I need my glasses!"

"You're next, dear. You'll be fine." Jo Jo hesitated before she spoke again. "How does it feel?" Her voice was a mixture of curiosity and envy that Ivy was beginning to recognize.

"It feels like I've gone blind!" Ivy said, though she knew that wasn't what Jo Jo meant. "Please, Jo Jo. I'm not exaggerating, I can't see a thing without—"

"Shhh. Bob's introducing you." A hand on Ivy's waist, presumably Jo Jo's, turned her toward the bright lights illuminating the stage.

"And now, ladies and gentlemen, what you've all been waiting for—the grand prize winner in the Celtex Sweepstakes. This little lady is a twenty-six-year-old secretary from Limon, Colorado. Please welcome our grand prize winner—Ivy Enders! Come on out, Ivy Enders!"

The hand in the middle of her back gave a little push, and Ivy stumbled onto the stage into a storm of applause. She directed a wobbly smile toward the sea of pale blobs that she guessed were faces of people in the audience. They were clapping for her. The realization was paralyzing, and she stopped, trying to get her bearings.

Bob Barker joked, "I'd have thought she would be in a hurry, wouldn't you?" and the audience laughed and applauded. Ivy could hear him, but the applause distorted her perspective, she wasn't sure where the dais was.

The audience was in front of her, a curtained backdrop behind her. She couldn't see a damned thing. Screwing up her face in a frantic expression, Ivy squinted to her left and released a breath when she saw a dark, blurred image that must be Bob Barker. Trying to smile, she walked toward him, remembering there were steps somewhere in front of her.

"Miss Enders? This way." Barker's amused call reached Ivy seconds before she walked into what she abruptly realized was a camera. The red eye winked on and she jerked her head back, more embarrassed than she'd ever been in her life. Feverish color burned on her cheeks, and nervous tears threatened behind her eyes.

To her immense relief a hand materialized at her elbow and steadied her. Bob Barker's voice addressed the audience over her head. "I think she's drunk with excitement, folks. Wouldn't you be? She's shaking like a leaf." Ivy felt like a fool. She wanted to drop through the stage floor and vanish.

Clinging to the host's arm, she moved forward, wanting to get it over with. And she tripped on the steps leading to the dais. If Bob Barker hadn't caught her, she would have fallen on her fanny. Desperately, she hoped the TV people would cut her entrance out of the tape. She felt near tears and knew her face was as scarlet as her jacket.

"Just relax," Bob Barker murmured, giving her arm an encouraging squeeze. To the cameras he said, "Miss Ivy Enders, ladies and gentlemen, the Celtex Sweepstakes Grand Prize winner of six million dollars!"

The applause rose like a tornado of sound, and Ivy blinked at the pale blobs in the audience. It was real, then. Or was this a sustained dream? She had thought tonight would finally make it seem real, that hearing Bob Barker announce her name and say the amount on TV would shatter her disbelief. But it didn't. She was still numb. She still felt as if at any minute someone would burst into laughter then reveal this was all a joke or a mistake. She hadn't really won six million dollars simply by returning three numbered cards that had arrived in the mail. No one actually won these sweepstakes things. Certainly not people Ivy knew. Certainly not her.

But she had. Six million dollars. She simply could not grasp an amount that high; it had to be a mistake.

Shaking, she clung to Bob Barker's arm and squinted up at him as he explained to the audience that Ivy would receive a check for three hundred thousand dollars once a year for the next twenty years.

"Well, Ivy Enders," he said, smiling the famed Bob Barker smile. At least she thought he was smiling, she couldn't be certain. "How does it feel to be rich? To be able to buy anything your heart desires?"

She didn't know how it felt, because she still didn't believe it. But she had to say something. "It feels fine." The banality emerged in a nervous whisper. After wetting her lips, she said it again in a stronger voice. "Fine, it feels just fine."

"I'll bet it does," Barker said with a laugh, and the audience laughed with him. "What do you plan to do with your first check"—he paused dramatically—"for three hundred thousand dollars?"

She had no idea. She hadn't dared to think about spending the money until she was convinced she had really won.

"Will you buy a house? A new car?" Barker tried to help her. "Diamonds? Furs?"

"I don't know. I'll pay my bills..." Damn, she sounded like an idiot. Twisting her hands, she swallowed and wondered which of the dark shapes were cameras and whether or not she was supposed to look at them. "I might buy a new car." Her old Chevy was coming apart at the seams.

"Or two or three," Barker said, giving the audience a broad wink. "One thing I'll bet you do is tell your boss he'll have to find himself a new secretary."

Ivy blinked as the audience laughed. She hadn't thought about it until now, but it did seem ridiculous to continue working for six dollars an hour when she had an automatic, guaranteed three hundred thousand dollars annually for the next twenty years.

"This is real," she whispered, staring at Bob Barker. She felt hot and cold, shaky inside and headachy. "This is really happening, isn't it?"

"She can't believe it, ladies and gentlemen. Maybe this will help." He extended something toward her and when she didn't react, Barker lifted her hand and closed her fingers around a check. She tried to take it, but Barker was holding on. "This is the first check for three hundred thousand dollars made out to you, Ivy Enders." In a lower voice he said kindly, "Smile for the people at home."

Blindly Ivy smiled toward what she hoped was a camera. At the same time she let go of the check, freshly embarrassed by a small tug of war with Barker. It drifted to the floor.

Bob Barker made a joke of it, reeling off half a dozen one-liners about throwing away money, while Ivy hastily knelt and felt around the floor by her feet. She wanted to die.

Her fingers groped across Bob Barker's shoes, then a microphone cord. He was talking above her head, closing the show for Celtex, his voice choked as if he were restraining a shout of laughter.

Then—finally, thankfully—it was over. The bright lights dimmed, the applause died away. Bob Barker bent, then pushed the check back into Ivy's hand. Someone kissed her cheek. It might have been Barker, or it might have been one of the dozens of people suddenly crowding the stage. Jo Jo appeared at her side and returned Ivy's glasses. Ivy pushed them hastily up her nose in time to watch a cluster of people following Bob Barker off the stage and into the wings.

Ivy sighed. She'd been so excited by the promise of seeing a TV celebrity up close, but it might as well not have happened. She didn't even know what color the man's eyes were. The whole thing had been a disaster. Every person in Limon, Colorado, was going to watch the tape of this show, and everyone she knew was going to see her make a prime fool of herself. Crimson flooded her cheeks as Jo Jo edged her toward the waiting group of Celtex sweepstakes winners.

"Limos are waiting downstairs to take us to Sardi's for a celebration," Jo Jo announced brightly. "You'll return to the Plaza for a nightcap, then tomorrow morning your drivers will take you to the airport for your flights home."

"When will the show air?" the woman in the blue dress asked.

"Friday at seven, Eastern Time. Check your local listings." Extending her arms, Jo Jo herded the group toward the elevator doors.

Still shaking, Ivy realized she didn't want to go to Sardi's. It was a great restaurant, she was sure, but she knew she wasn't dressed properly and her headache had settled into a steady pounding above her eyes. Now that reality was beginning to sink in, she badly wanted some time alone to think.

Resisting the urge to open her purse and verify the presence of the check, she cleared her throat and moved next to

Jo Jo. "If you don't mind, I think I'll skip Sardi's and go back to the hotel."

The elevator went silent and she was aware of the other winners listening. Jo Jo frowned. "We have a big celebration planned. The media will be there."

Ordinarily Jo Jo's words would have been enough to make Ivy crumble. Assertiveness wasn't her long suit and she lacked the confidence to go against what was expected of her. But she really did have a granddaddy of a headache and the idea of Sardi's was intimidating. She'd seen Sardi's in glamorous movies. No one had been wearing a gray dress with a white Peter Pan collar.

"I'm sorry," she whispered, looking down and twisting her purse straps. All her life she had daydreamed about places like Sardi's, had tried to imagine being in New York City. But in her dreams she was fifteen pounds lighter, she was dressed in something slinky and wonderful, and there was a handsome man on her arm. Someone like Richie Martin. In her dreams she frequented famous places like Sardi's and was comfortable going there. But in real life, she was just an unsophisticated woman from a small Colorado town, who was awed and not a little frightened by a city the size of New York. She lacked the polish for a place like Sardi's. She didn't belong.

"You're our big winner, our star," Jo Jo said persuasively. "You're the one the media will want to talk to."

The thought terrified her. What would she say to them? "I . . . I'm really sorry, but—"

"Well!" The woman in the blue dress lifted her chin and glared. "She's too good to be seen with small-timers like us, is that it? We're just small potatoes. None of us won six million dollars. I guess we aren't good enough for her."

Ivy stared at her, horrified. "That isn't it at all," she said anxiously. Dots of color burned in her cheeks.

"Oh?"

Ivy thought her shyness would have been painfully obvious. She had imagined everyone in the elevator would know at a glance that she didn't belong in a place like Sardi's, that the thought of a media interview appalled her. Instead they stared at her coldly, as if she'd betrayed them or snubbed them.

"You see..." The weight of their silent accusation squashed her resistance. "I...all right, I'll go." She hated herself for caving in.

The woman in the blue dress sniffed. "Hey, don't do us any favors."

Jo Jo pressed her arm as the elevator doors opened and everyone hurried toward the waiting limos. Once inside, Ivy leaned into the velvety luxury and cursed herself for lacking the confidence to say no.

Maybe now that she was rich, she'd gain more confidence. She certainly hoped so. Sitting very still as the limo glided through the streets of Manhattan, Ivy thought about what Jo Jo had told them at dinner. Their lives were going to change, especially hers. A person didn't win six million dollars and remain the same.

The inevitability was both frightening and exciting. Frightening because of the uncertainty, exciting because finally, finally, her life was going to begin. She could sense it out there, waiting for her.

"This is real!" she whispered, her eyes widening on Jo Jo. "I won six million dollars! Bob Barker said so on national television. It has to be true."

Jo Jo laughed and patted her arm. "Oh, it's true, all right. Are you just realizing it?"

"Yes." Slowly the elation built and sparkled in Ivy's eyes. "Six million dollars. I'm rich! Jo Jo, I'm rich!" Jo Jo grinned at her. "I can move if I want to. I can live anywhere. I can buy a new sewing machine. Or a fur coat. I'm rich!"

Dazed, she stared out of the window, only now letting herself really begin to believe it. She hadn't believed the letter from Celtex Corporation or the phone call from Celtex's president. But this was real. She was actually here, in New York City. She had been on TV, had met Bob Barker. She was going to Sardi's. And she had a check for three hundred thousand in her purse. While Jo Jo smiled at her, she blushed, then opened her purse and looked at the check. The zeros danced before her eyes.

Afterward she couldn't remember a thing about Sardi's. And that was a crushing disappointment, not to remember. But there were crowds of people, flashbulbs blinding her, a thousand questions. When she finally returned to her room at the Plaza, Ivy collapsed into a silk-covered chair and closed her eyes, trying to sort through the whirling impressions of the past three days. Her senses had overloaded hours ago and details were slipping away. She wished she weren't too tired to take notes. She had promised her mother and sister to remember every tiny detail.

After a shower, she washed her face with the floral-smelling hotel soap then climbed between crisp white sheets and folded her arms behind her head. Her life was going to change. It was already happening.

If she wanted to, she could stay at the Plaza again some time. She could afford the airfare to New York, a suite at the Plaza and dinner at Sardi's. She could make all her dreams become reality. Nothing was out of reach. The thought was so incredible she couldn't move past it to examine the dreams themselves. But eventually the numbed feeling would pass. Her dreams would be waiting.

"THE MAYOR IS GOING to give you the key to the city," Mary Enders said proudly. "Imagine that. My daughter getting the key to the city."

Ivy's parents and her sister and her sister's husband drove Ivy from the Denver airport to Limon. They plied her with questions during the two-hour drive, and she did her best to remember everything.

"They're giving *me* the key to the city?"

It was true. The mayor, the police chief and the fire chief were waiting on the steps of the Limon courthouse when Ivy's father turned into town. The high-school band played "Happy Days Are Here Again." The mayor gave a brief speech, the police chief made a few jokes, then the mayor thrust the microphone toward Ivy.

"How does it feel to be Limon's richest citizen?"

"It feels fine," Ivy whispered into the microphone.

She cast a shy glance toward the gathering of people smiling up at her from the bottom of the steps. Her boss, Mr. Batterson, had come. And her mother's friends from the D.A.R. She saw her best friend, Cass Myers. She wished Richie Martin could see her now. But Richie no longer lived in Limon. He had headed for Nashville an hour after he graduated high school ten years ago. The last Ivy heard, Richie was touring the States with his latest country-and-western hit. Limon claimed him as the town's most famous citizen, although Ivy suspected Richie Martin hadn't given Limon a single thought since he'd left it.

Actually Limon was a terrific little town that offered all the benefits of small-town living. Everything revolved around the high school, the Methodist church—and the seasons, of course, since Limon was primarily a farming community. It was a great place for settling down and raising a family away from the bustle and crime of a big city.

But it wasn't such a great place if you were twenty-six and single. This wasn't the first time Ivy had had such a thought. But it was the first time she'd been in a position to do something about it.

The mayor asked a few more questions, the fire chief exchanged jokes with the police chief, a reporter from the local paper interviewed Ivy, then the homecoming ceremony ended in a burst of good-natured applause.

The twelve-mile ride out to the farm was a repeat of the drive from Denver. Questions about being on TV, about meeting Bob Barker, about New York City. Ivy sat between her sister, Iris, and Iris's husband, Frank. It felt strange to be the center of attention. Iris was usually the one who claimed the honor. Iris was the pretty one. She had been a cheerleader in high school, and the prom queen during her senior year. She'd been the first to marry, the first to have a baby. Ivy had always imagined she would enjoy usurping the attention usually focused on Iris, but now that it was happening, she wasn't so sure.

After dinner she changed into a pair of faded jeans and a red plaid shirt and went outside to watch the sun drop over the fields of wheat and maize. The shoots were out of the ground now, marching toward the flat horizon in green lines of military precision.

A few minutes later her father crossed the yard and folded his arms on the top bar of the railing circling the corral. "Mind some company?" Ivy smiled and leaned her head on his shoulder. "Looks like it's going to be a good crop this year," her father commented.

Ivy hoped so. Sven Enders had been farming this ground for thirty years. He'd had his share of good crops and bad; most were poor to middling. The problem, as always with farming in arid land, was water.

"The first thing I want to do, Pop, is buy an irrigation system." She had thought about it during the flight home and had known immediately that's what she wanted.

Her father didn't answer at once. He was a quiet man, and proud, a man who loved his family and his land but who found it difficult to articulate those feelings. His large callused hand covered hers. "That's mighty generous, honey..."

"But?" she asked, hearing his hesitation.

"But the money is yours. It's your future," he said finally, gently. "I appreciate your offer, but the truth is, your mother and I have already saved up a down payment on an irrigation system." A smile pleated his sunburnt face. "You don't have to support us just yet." The sunset reflected in his large, dark eyes, so like her own.

"I didn't mean that. I just wanted to do something for you." Farming was a hard life and exhausting, but her father had always been there for her when she needed to talk. And during her growing-up years her parents had always found the money somehow to make sure that she and Iris had everything the other kids had.

A comfortable silence opened between them, then Sven Enders cleared his throat and touched her hair. "Do you want to talk about it, honey?" He had always known when she was troubled.

"I don't know, Pop. This is all so confusing...and scary. I guess everyone dreams about what they'd do if they won one of the big sweepstakes. But now that it's happened to me, I'm not sure what to do. Suddenly there are possibilities, choices that didn't exist before. Dozens of possibilities."

"Money opens doors—it does do that." Sven stroked her hand as they watched the sunset. "What is it you want out of life, honey?"

"The same thing everyone does," Ivy said after a minute. "A husband, a family, good friends, a happy life." When her father didn't speak, she said, "I know what you're thinking. You're thinking I could have those things without the sweepstakes money."

"Yes, but you have to learn that for yourself. Your mother and I have been worried about you, Ivy." He lifted her face so she could see he wasn't criticizing, so she could see how hard the words were to say. "You're too old to be living at home, sweetheart. We've been glad, blessed, to have you with us this long, but it's time you made a life of your own. A few weeks ago you didn't have much choice about living at home, or living here in Limon. Now you do."

"The things I want...I don't want them immediately, not all of them. Can you understand that, Pop?" She looked at him, wanting his approval. "I know you and Mom would like to see me married and settled down like Iris. But—" she shifted her gaze to the fields "—I've felt trapped for so long. Trapped in a small town, trapped in a going-nowhere job.... I just, I don't want to be trapped in a relationship. Not immediately. Not for a while. Does that make sense?"

"You want to kick up your heels a bit." Her father smiled. "It's about time."

"You don't think that's wrong? Or silly?"

"I'd rather see you enjoy yourself now than see you hurry into something and have regrets later. Wish you'd had more time on your own first." He was silent for a moment. "One thing about small towns, Ivy. Most are family centered. This means most girls look at marriage as the most desirable goal. The sooner the better. I know you've been feeling certain pressures, and it hasn't been easy at times."

"Sometimes I think everybody is looking at me and wondering why I haven't settled down. And all the time I'm feeling like my life hasn't started yet. There are so many things I want to do and experience first."

"Well, now you can."

"I was thinking about moving to Denver. Would that upset you and Mom?"

Sven Enders turned and leaned against the fence, looking back toward the sprawling farmhouse. They could hear Iris and her mother singing as they washed the dinner dishes.

"We'll miss you," Sven said quietly. It was an understatement of mammoth proportions and Ivy knew it. "But I reckon there isn't much heel-kicking to be done in Limon. And I guess it's time."

Excitement mixed with anxiety lit Ivy's eyes. Yes, it was time. She was edging perilously close to spinsterhood, by small-town standards. Most of the men she knew were either married, or they were men she'd rejected years ago as unsuitable for one reason or another. If she stayed in Limon, it was likely she'd end up an old maid. Maybe that wasn't such a bad thing; maybe she wasn't destined to marry. But she didn't have to be a *dull* old maid. The sweepstakes money meant she could go and do and see and experience.

"I'm going to give Mom a check for twenty thousand dollars," she said. "I've made up my mind, so don't try to talk me out of it. She's been wanting a new kitchen for years. And I plan to give Iris a check for the same amount. She and Frank can make a down payment on their own place."

Her father was silent for a time, then he sighed and squeezed her hand. "You don't have to do that." He held up a hand to halt her protest. "All right, I'd probably do the same in your place. But don't be too generous, honey. Twenty years will pass before you know it. Take my advice and be selfish for once. Think about Ivy. You have a chance that most people will never have. Enjoy it. Take the first year's check and blow it." When her mouth dropped, he smiled. "Get it out of your system. Buy all the things you ever wanted to buy. Do all the things you ever wanted to do. Then think about the future. Land, maybe."

It was a long speech for Sven Enders. For Ivy it was the first link in a long chain of advice.

"HAVE YOU DECIDED what you'll do, Ivy?" said Mary Enders.

"Pop told you I'm thinking about moving to Denver?"

Her mother dropped her gaze so that Ivy wouldn't see how much the plan disturbed her. "It's a good idea. There's so much to do in Denver. And it isn't like you can't come home every now and then. It's not really too long a drive."

"Oh, Mom," Ivy said, giving her a quick hug.

"What I really think you should do is travel. Remember the mother in that movie—*Breaking Away*? How she had a passport in her purse? Well, I don't have a passport, but I've always wanted to travel." She cupped Ivy's face and laughed. "No, I don't want you to buy me a ticket somewhere. You know how busy we are in the summer. But I think *you* should go. See the world. That's my advice."

Iris was next. She advised her sister to get a new wardrobe immediately. "Store bought, not homemade. And a fur coat. You should have a fur coat," she insisted. "If I were you, I'd buy a mink coat that sweeps the floor. And real jewelry."

Frank thought she should rush right out and trade her old Chevy for something newer and smarter. "One of those foreign jobs. A Porsche, maybe. That's what I'd do. I'd get one of those foreign cars. Long and sleek and red."

When she went to the office to quit her secretarial job, Mr. Batterson advised her to buy insurance and annuities, preferably from him. The young woman at the desk next to Ivy's advised her to take a vacation at Club Med and meet a lot of rich, single men. The town druggist advised her to invest in an up-and-coming local business like his own. Mrs. Haddock, the hairdresser, thought Ivy should buy stocks and bonds, and she suggested a cousin who was a broker in Denver.

Ivy's head swam with advice. But she decided not to do anything until after the meeting Jo Jo had told her about.

Next week a seminar was being held in Denver for people who had won very large amounts in lotteries or sweepstakes or who had suddenly inherited large sums of money. Jo Jo had recommended that Ivy attend.

Meanwhile there was Friday night to get through. Iris invited a few friends; Ivy's mother invited a few friends. The house was packed. They borrowed chairs from the nearest neighbors and placed them in the living room in front of the TV.

Ivy stood at the back of the room near the archway that led into the kitchen. The minute the Celtex commercial came on the screen, she pressed her fingers to her cheeks, feeling her skin heat. Living it again, she watched Bob Barker present checks to the smaller winners, saw the woman in the blue silk run lightly up to the dais, saw the grinning man who'd won the million dollars wave his first check. She was on next.

Her family and friends cheered when Bob Barker announced her name. Thankfully, the TV people had done what they could with her disastrous entrance. But there was only so much that could be done.

"Good heavens, Ivy. You look fat," Iris said. "I always heard TV cameras put on ten pounds. I guess it's true."

"Shhh!"

"Ivy! Where are your glasses? You've got your face all scrunched up like a corkscrew!"

The lens appeared to zoom in on her face, but Ivy knew this was the moment she had almost stumbled into the camera. Watching it now, she wanted to cry. Her eyes were narrowed into little slits. She looked dazed, uncomprehending, and her prim and proper dress made her look like a chubby teenager.

"Look at that. Bob Barker himself is escorting her up to the dais. He didn't do that for any of the others."

"What's he really like, Ivy?"

"Sven! Sven, did you remember to turn on the VCR? Are we getting a tape of this?"

Ivy noticed that the part where she stumbled on the steps and almost fell had been cut. She wished they had cut the part where she had to talk. Her voice was a breathless whisper, scarcely audible.

"You sound scared to death!"

"But the red jacket looks nice. Doesn't it look nice, everyone?"

"It looks like she doesn't have any eyes!"

All Ivy could see was her nose. It was huge. Enormous. It looked as if her nose would sweep Bob Barker off the dais if she turned quickly. She couldn't believe no one was commenting on her nose. It had to be that everyone was used to her nose, or they were just being kind. If it had rained on stage, all the stagehands could have taken shelter under her nostrils, she was sure of it. She knew, of course, that she had inherited the family nose, but she hadn't realized just how awful it was. Lowering her head, Ivy covered her eyes, unable to watch anymore.

Later her mother assured her that no one guessed Ivy had ended the program on her hands and knees groping for the dropped check. The TV people had fixed it so she just disappeared from the frame. One minute a squinty, plump young woman in a frumpy dress was standing there attached to her nose; the next minute, she was gone.

"Did you see the show?" Ivy asked Cass Myers the next day. She held the phone tightly and tried to keep her voice level so that Cass couldn't know how much it hurt that she hadn't come out to the farm for the viewing.

"I was busy," Cass said, her voice a verbal shrug.

"Oh." If Cass had been on TV, there was nothing that would have prevented Ivy from watching. "Cassie, is something wrong?"

"Of course not. Why should anything be wrong?"

"I don't know. It's just that . . . you've been acting funny since all this happened." She heard Cass bristle on the other end of the line.

"I'm not the one who's acting funny!"

"What does that mean?"

"You've changed, Ivy Enders. I heard you gave Iris a check for twenty thousand dollars. And that you gave Mrs. Haddock a couple of thousand and gave Myra Lepko a new car. You're just throwing it around, showing off. I didn't think you were that kind."

"Cass, that's just gossip. I haven't changed. I gave Iris and Frank some money, but the rest is untrue." She paused. "Look, let's spend the day together. Let's go to Denver and do some shopping. It will be fun. We'll have lunch somewhere nice and—"

"Forget it. Maybe *you* have money to throw around in expensive shops, but *I* don't. Most people still have to work for their money!"

The phone went dead in Ivy's hand. She stared at it for a long, long time, then quietly replaced the receiver in the cradle.

Jo Jo was right, Ivy thought. Her life was changing. But not all of the changes were for the better.

Chapter Two

"I'm giving notice," Eric North announced. Knowing this would be the last time he would sit in Ross Sonnier's office, he looked around the room carefully. For the past two years he had coveted this office. Now he saw it from a new perspective. It wasn't as large as he had previously believed; the view of Main Street wasn't as impressive. Nor was Ross's job, which he had also hoped to have one day.

"I expected you would." Ross Sonnier smiled. "Hell, you've got practically as much money as the bank does."

"It isn't paid in a lump sum. The lottery commission pays it out over twenty years."

Ross leaned back and laced his fingers over his stomach. "You're lucky. Two hundred and fifty grand a year—for the next twenty years. How does it feel?"

"Damned good." Eric grinned. "Hard to believe."

"I was watching the night you won. Me and the missus. You spun the wheel and the ball bounced in and out of the slots and I thought it was going to stay in the ten-thousand-dollar slot, then it tipped into the five-million-dollar one." He swore and slapped his thigh. "Couldn't believe it. Knew right then I was going to lose the best loan officer this bank has ever had. So, what are you going to do now that you're rich? You going to stay here in Delta or head for the big-city lights?"

"I don't know yet." Winning the Colorado lottery had stunned him.

One minute Eric had been like everyone else, with a drawer full of bills, a middle-of-the-road job, the usual dreams he was beginning to suspect might never come true. Then he had bought a lottery ticket at the grocery store, scraped off the numbers and discovered he had an entry ticket for the big draw. The entry tickets were put into a bin, spun, and a few lucky tickets drawn out. His had been one of them. This qualified him to spin the big wheel on TV. Wherever the ball dropped, that was the amount won. He had won the big one—five million dollars. The minute the ball dropped, his money worries had ended.

He had been a banker too long to imagine he was rich. Five million sounded like a lot of money, but paid out over twenty years, it really wasn't. Two hundred and fifty thousand tax-free dollars a year was nothing to sneeze at, but it didn't qualify him for the jet set. Not in today's world. But it was a lot better than the thirty thousand he was earning at the Delta Bank. A whole lot.

"If you like," he said to Ross, "I'll stay until you hire a replacement." He wondered what Ross made a year. The president of a small-town bank probably didn't make much more than about fifty thousand. A few weeks ago that sum had sounded enormous.

"No point," Ross said with a wave of his hand. "With the economy as depressed as it has been, we aren't getting all that much business. I'd say you can clean out your desk whenever you want. I'm sorry to lose you, Eric. You've been a friend, as well as a good employee. You'll keep in touch, won't you?"

"Any time you feel like playing hooky and doing a little fishing I'm ready. Give me a call."

Even as he said it, Eric knew it wouldn't happen. The thought saddened him. But since winning the lottery, he had

sensed a subtle shift in his relationship with Ross, one neither of them was entirely comfortable with. In the past, Ross
had been the older man, the more experienced man, the
more successful man. The mentor. Ross Sonnier was one of
the town's leading citizens, past president of the Chamber
of Commerce, a leader in the grange association. Ten years
ago he had even been mayor. Now, because of the lottery,
Eric and Ross were on a more equal footing. But Eric suspected Ross wasn't comfortable with equality; Ross was the
type of man who needed to feel a step above his associates.
Odd that Eric hadn't realized it before.

They shook hands warmly and promised to remain in
touch—neither acknowledged the change in their relationship—then Eric cleaned out his desk and teased Miss Molly,
the bank's ancient head teller, for the last time. He loaded
the carton containing his personal items into the back of his
pickup, then drove down Main Street slowly, past the bar-
bershop, past the café where he drank his morning coffee
while he read the newspaper, past the gas station where he'd
had his first job, past all the small businesses that filled the
immediate needs of Delta's residents and made up the fab-
ric of his life.

Feeling a bit foolish because of his sudden, unexpected
burst of nostalgia, he turned off Main Street and rolled
slowly past the new high school. It wasn't new anymore, but
everyone still called it that. Eric looked at the buildings and
smiled. He'd made something of a name for himself in high
school, playing basketball. His mother still had the newspaper clippings. Otherwise, high school had not been a
particularly memorable experience. His body had shot up
all at once, and he'd been all bones and angles, had felt
awkward and clumsy, except on the basketball court. There
he'd displayed a smooth, fluid grace.

Adding to his high-school troubles, he had been a good
student, which made him the butt of jokes on more occa-

sions than he cared to recall. He had genuinely liked school, a peculiarity most of his friends had not understood. From the beginning, he had enjoyed math and history, and in fact the whole learning process.

His biggest problem in high school had been girls, he remembered, a problem that had overlapped into college. He couldn't talk to the really pretty ones. The instant he tried, he became acutely conscious of his thin, lanky frame, of ears that had earned him the childhood nickname of Dumbo. He had spent his school years enduring a series of bright blushes and embarrassed stammers whenever he approached a popular girl like Mary Ellen Nugent.

Mary Ellen Nugent had been the prettiest girl ever to enter Delta High School. For three years he had worshiped her from afar, never finding the courage to actually speak to her. He had been delighted to discover they were both enrolled at the University of Northern Colorado, but he hadn't been able to speak to her there, either. She had dropped out in her second year and married a med student from Denver.

She was probably matronly now, settled firmly in a suburban community with half a dozen children. But in Eric North's heart, she lived on, perpetually young, preserved in his mind wearing her cheerleader uniform and doing cartwheels along the side of the basketball court.

Eric laughed aloud and stepped on the accelerator. To an extent he had outgrown his shyness around women, but he hadn't outgrown a streak of romanticism.

He turned back onto Main Street and tapped his fingers against the steering wheel. The day stretched before him, strangely empty. After a moment's hesitation, he headed the pickup toward the mesa and his parents' house.

Fields of apple and peach orchards began at the edge of town, bursting with blossoms, spicing each breath with heady fragrance. The scent reminded Eric of growing up, of the orchards behind his parents' house. Heavy blossoms in the early spring, shade through the long summers, then the harvest. In early fall the whole town smelled like apples and peaches, the scent centered at the Skyland plant where the fruit was processed into juice and cider.

As always, he experienced a surge of pride as he drove past the acres of orchards belonging to his parents. Years ago, he had helped plant most of the young trees in the west meadow. For a time he had thought he would raise apples and peaches himself. But college had changed his mind. There he admitted an ongoing romance with numbers, and realized he didn't want a life dependent upon the weather. Figures weren't affected by a late-spring freeze, or too much or too little rain, or by wood borers or worms, or the myriad other things that could destroy profits almost overnight.

"Eric! How nice to see you." His mother wiped her hands across her apron, then hugged him. "What are you doing here in the middle of the day? Is something wrong?"

Lifting a finger he smoothed the frown from between her eyes and smiled. "Nothing's wrong. I quit the bank today and didn't know what to do with myself. Thought I'd stop by to see you and Dad."

He followed her into a large country kitchen and sat down at the table. Immediately a cup of steaming coffee and a plate of apple pie appeared before him. The pie was in a deep dish smothered by heavy cream just the way he liked it.

"It's the last of the apples in the cellar. Thought I'd use them up before they go bad," his mother said, sitting across from him. "What did Ross say when you quit?" After Eric related his morning at the bank, she nodded and refilled their cups. "I suppose you had to do it. And it will free up a job for someone else." Sunlight spilled through the windows and illuminated the gray streaks in her hair. "Have you decided what you'll do next?"

"Not really." He felt at loose ends. There was nothing he had to do, and so many things he could do.

"When is that meeting you told us about? The one for big winners."

"Tomorrow. In Denver. I'll leave this evening and stay over for a few days."

"Ginna called last night. She said you sent her and Rob a check for thirty thousand dollars. She was so happy she was crying. That was nice, Eric. Ginna hasn't had an easy time of it, what with Rob being laid off and everything."

"I just wish you and Dad would let me do something for you."

Ellen North smiled. "Like what? We have everything we need."

"I'd like to buy you a fur coat."

"Me? In a fur coat?" His mother laughed, then squeezed his hand affectionately. "Honey, there was a time, years ago, when I might have liked to own a fur coat. But not now. Where would I wear it? To the church bazaar? And what would my friends think? No. Thanks, honey, but you take your money and do something for yourself. All those things you always wanted to do."

"There must be something you want."

"Well, I could use a new potato peeler," she said, her eyes twinkling.

"You've got it. How much are they? About a dollar and a half?" He grinned at her. "I think I can afford to get you one."

They drank their coffee in companionable silence, then his mother looked toward the windows. "I suppose you'll be moving to Grand Junction or Denver."

"If I stay here, I'm going to disappoint a lot of people."

"Everyone wants you to buy something, don't they?" She sighed and nodded. "We've been getting a lot of phone calls asking for your number. I can imagine how many calls you must be getting. Besides, there are more opportunities in a big town. I always wanted to live in a big town. I love Delta, you understand, but it would be nice to live someplace where they have a symphony and plays and big grocery stores. Yes, you should definitely move." She gave her head an emphatic nod the way she did when her mind was made up.

Later, when he took a thermos of coffee out to his father in the orchards, his father agreed.

"Your mother and I talked it over and we think a move would be good for you." His father sipped the coffee and sighed with pleasure. "I wouldn't worry too much about not knowing what you want to do. That'll come. You need some time to get your feet on the ground."

Eric bent a branch from the tree above his head and held the blossoms to his nose. "I can't imagine not working."

"A man needs work," his father agreed. "I swore I wasn't going to offer any advice," he added with a laugh.

"But?" Eric grinned.

"But I think you should take your time before deciding anything. Travel a little, try some new things...then decide if you want to buy a business or whatever. You're only twenty-eight, you have plenty of time." His father winked at him. "Speaking of time—isn't it about time you started thinking about a wife and family?"

Eric's smile widened. "Maybe I'll find me a big-city girl."

"Nothing would make your mother happier. She's pining for grandchildren. Your little sister doesn't seem in any hurry. She and Rob want to wait until Rob's back on his feet. Did your mother tell you Ginna called last night? That was nice of you to send her and Rob a check."

Embarrassed, Eric kicked at the soft grass growing between the rows of trees. "Looks like you could use new pruning gear."

"I have new pruning gear. I just like the old shears better. When's the last time you did any real work?" Smiling, his father pressed the battered shears into Eric's hands. "Take off that banker's jacket and let's see if you still have the touch."

Laughing, Eric threw aside his jacket and pulled off his tie.

THERE WAS TIME to think during the six-hour drive to Denver, but Eric couldn't get past the idea that all things were suddenly possible. It was as if someone had abruptly removed all the normal limitations, all the comfortable perimeters that defined a man's life. He felt a compelling urge to explore his newly expanded horizons. The problem was where to begin. At that point his mind froze, still reacting to limitations that no longer existed.

There must be things he wanted to do, things that hadn't seemed within his grasp a month ago. But he couldn't recall them. Or perhaps his dreams and desires had been so small they'd faded into insignificance under the glare of his changed circumstances. He had wanted new fishing gear, a rod and tackle box. Now he could buy a hundred new items, but they no longer seemed important. He had wanted Ross Sonnier's seat as president of the Delta Bank, but that ambition had died with the spin of the wheel. He had wanted new tires for his pickup and a better stereo system. Small wants that no longer seemed important.

He was glad, but felt a loss as no new wants had appeared to take the place of the old ones. Sure, he'd like to see Europe, and now he probably would, but it wasn't a burning desire. He might buy a new car while he was in Denver, but he didn't actually need one. The pickup suited him fine.

On the other hand, if he wanted one, he could have a Jaguar. He remembered now that he had always wanted a Jaguar. The thought made him feel better. And it confirmed his intention to move to Denver. A Jaguar would be embarrassing in Delta, but probably wouldn't attract much attention in a big city.

Eric was still thinking about a Jaguar after he checked into a Holiday Inn and ordered a cheeseburger from room service. It wasn't until he was almost asleep that it occurred to him that he could have stayed at the Fairmont or the Hilton and he could have ordered up the biggest steak in the place.

His father was right. It would take some time to get used to his changed circumstances.

THE SEMINAR WAS HELD in the Petroleum Club building in downtown Denver. Eric was late, because he hadn't anticipated the traffic or the bewildering array of one-way streets. People might poke fun at small towns, he thought sourly, but at least you could get around in them.

He finally found the meeting room and relaxed when he discovered the group was running behind schedule, just finishing coffee and doughnuts and sitting down in the rows of metal chairs arranged to face a small podium. It was a small group. There were four men and three women. One of the women looked vaguely familiar. After a moment, he chose a chair on the back row, placing a vacant seat between himself and the woman.

She was pretty, he thought, sliding a look toward her. The type that made him uncomfortable to talk to.

"Hi." He felt a need to say something. Thank God he had passed the point of turning red when he spoke to a woman. But when she looked at him he felt certain she was studying his ears, amazed.

"Hi." Her voice was as soft as the waves of light brown hair that curled under on her shoulders. He noticed large dark eyes and a fringe of dark lashes behind her glasses.

"Did I miss much?" He couldn't place where he'd seen her.

"I don't think so. I just got here myself." She clutched her purse in her lap. "I couldn't find the right building."

"Neither could I. Then when I did find it, I couldn't locate a parking place for my truck. Have we met before?"

If that didn't sound like a line, he didn't know what would. No doubt she was cursing her bad luck that she was seated next to a jerk.

She bit her lip and looked down. "Maybe you saw me on television. Did you watch the Celtex Sweepstakes show?"

"Of course!" He stared at her. "Sure, you were the big winner. I remember because you're from Colorado, too."

"Limon."

"I'm from Delta. West side of the state, near Grand Junction. I won the lottery."

"I know. I recognized you."

"You did?" He felt absurdly flattered that such a pretty woman had remembered him. It was probably his ears, he thought suddenly. People didn't forget ears the size of pie plates. He wished he could think of something else to say to her to keep the conversation going, but every time he looked at her shining hair and perfect complexion, his mind went blank.

He was spared from making a possibly inane comment by the man on the other side of him.

"Hi. I'm Kevin McCallister." The man stuck out his hand and Eric shook it.

"Eric North."

"Lottery winner, right? I'm here because my grandfather finally popped off and left me a few million. I never liked the old bastard and he didn't like me. You're looking at a surprised and grateful man."

If anyone else had made such a statement, Eric would have found it distasteful. But Kevin McCallister's open face and boyish charm negated such feelings. Kevin reminded Eric of nothing so much as a good-natured imp. He was slight of stature, wore his hair in a Prince Valiant cut, and a generous helping of mischief sparkled behind his eyes. He was also wearing an exquisitely tailored suit that suggested he was no stranger to money even before inheriting from his grandfather. It wasn't the cut or the material as much as the way he wore it. McCallister wore a five- or six-hundred dollar suit with the same ease and indifference and comfort that Eric felt when he wore jeans and a sweater.

Kevin grinned at him. "You're probably asking yourself: is ole Kevin part of the McCallister family who owns McCallister Enterprises? The same bunch that runs all those commercials for McCallister products? Well, let's get that out of the way. Yes. Granddaddy started ME, Big Daddy runs it, and ole Kevin hates it. End of story. So, how about you, Eric North? Is winning the lottery more of the same for you, too?"

"Not at all. The world of high finance—at least as applied to my own money—is a new experience."

"Then you need help, old son. Lucky for you that Kevin T. McCallister is on the scene."

The seminar started. Throughout the morning, Eric continued to look at Ivy Enders whenever he could. She was much prettier than she had seemed on television. After a while he realized she hadn't been wearing her glasses on TV. He wondered why, because the glasses suited her. They made her look older, more assured, than she had appeared on the sweepstakes program. They made her look studious, which he had always found sexy.

With some difficulty, and only by ignoring Kevin's irreverent comments, he tried to focus on what the man at the podium was saying.

"Welcome. My name is Jim Brock. Five years ago I won the Publisher's Clearing House Sweepstakes for three million dollars. It almost ruined my life. I lost my friends and my wife." Jim Brock looked at them. "I decided then that winners of large sums need a support group. Today we're going to introduce you to others like yourselves who have suddenly come into a large amount of money, and who are going to face many of the same complications. We hope you'll continue to see each other." Jim Brock asked them each to stand and introduce themselves and tell how much they had won or inherited.

Brock grinned at them. "Anybody been receiving more phone calls recently?" They laughed and nodded. "Your names and pictures have been on television and in the newspapers. Believe me, every salesman in the Rocky Mountain region knows who you are and is eager to get in touch with you.

"Take it from me, folks. The salesmen aren't going to go away. They're a resourceful breed and they'll find you. First suggestion: get an answering service or an answering machine, and screen your calls. There's no rule that says you have to call these people back."

"Elementary, my dear Brock," Kevin muttered.

"You're also going to have fund-raisers from all over the country phoning you or appearing on your doorstep. Charities you never heard of are going to find you and plead for donations." His face sobered. "What you need to understand is that you don't have to give your money away to every Tom, Dick and Harry who asks for it. If you have a favorite charity and want to make a donation, fine. But remember: you don't have to. You have the right to say no."

One of the women in front shifted uncomfortably. "I feel so guilty saying no."

"Let's talk about guilt, because that's the crux of the matter. Eric, let's hear from you. Do you feel guilty about winning five million dollars?"

"I guess I do," he said after a minute. "I know I keep wondering: why me?"

"Ivy? How about you?"

An attractive flush of pink spread across her cheeks. "I have an urge to share my winnings with everyone I know. I don't know, I guess I feel like Eric does. That somehow I don't deserve this good luck."

Eric looked at her. She had articulated exactly what he was feeling.

"Hell, no. I don't feel guilty," Kevin said when it was his turn. He shrugged. "If Granddaddy hadn't wanted me to have the money, he would have left it to someone else."

Jim Brock nodded. He wasn't smiling. "Kevin's situation is different, because he grew up with wealth, but most of you didn't. Right now you're experiencing varying degrees of the same thing. In your hearts, you don't really believe you deserve your good fortune. Like Eric mentioned, you're asking yourself: Why me? What did I do to deserve this kind of luck? It's a little frightening. So you're tempted to give it away." He paused and looked at each of them. "Don't do it."

"How do you say no?" A man named Bill swiveled to look at the group. "I don't know about you guys, but suddenly it seems like everyone I know wants a loan. They want a piece of the winnings. And something in me thinks they deserve to win as much as I do. How can I refuse?"

"You refuse by saying no," Jim said, "or you can give in to it like I did. I loaned—or, more correctly, gave away—about a hundred thousand dollars in six months. I didn't know I was giving it away, not on a conscious level. I wanted to believe I was helping friends who needed the money. But none of them believed they actually had to repay the loan. Why should they? I didn't need the money, did I? After all, I was a millionaire. Out of the hundred thousand I loaned out, I was repaid only two thousand. Is that what you want to happen to you? Believe me, the answer is no, because it will cost you your friends.

"Your friends remember you won five million or six million or ten million. They don't remember that you are receiving that sum over a period of twenty or thirty years. They think you are vastly rich. You aren't. Maybe you've guessed that already, maybe it's something you'll learn soon but, folks, you are not rich enough to give away tens of thousands of dollars. Say no. Say it gently, but say it firmly. If you want to share some of your good fortune with your family, go ahead. But draw the line there."

The discussion continued with the various winners sharing their experiences. Two were having serious difficulties in their marriages that involved vastly differing attitudes toward money. Others understood they needed financial guidance but didn't know where to find it. Some were losing lifelong friends; others had new friends they didn't quite trust. At the end of the discussion, Brock suggested a brief recess.

During the break Eric talked to several of the men, discovering all had quit their jobs after winning and now felt as adrift as he did.

"What nonsense," Kevin said grandly. "Gentlemen, there's more to life than nine to five. There's wine, women and song out there just waiting for gents like us."

While Kevin explained a playboy life-style he appeared to know well, Eric watched Ivy Enders across the room. She was wearing a simple skirt and blouse, a navy jacket and low-heeled shoes. He liked that. She wasn't loaded down with conspicuous jewelry like the woman she was talking to, or wearing a dress more suited for a cocktail party than a business meeting. Every now and then her glance met his and he thought he identified a small smile, but he wasn't sure.

It didn't strike him likely that Ivy Enders might be flirting with him. He wasn't the type women threw themselves at. He decided Ivy was just checking him out, that was all.

"Great looking, isn't she?" Kevin asked.

"Terrific."

"Maybe I'll ask her to lunch when this meeting is over. I've got a weakness for redheads. And blondes. And brunettes."

"Redheads? Oh, you're talking about Marisa Anderson. I was talking about Ivy Enders."

"Ivy? She's got possibilities. Not there yet, but great potential. Needs to deep six the glasses and learn to dress. But great potential. The type you could take home to mother, and mother wouldn't choke on her pearls." He laughed.

Kevin's comments were surprising. Eric took another look at Ivy. He liked her glasses and he liked the way she was dressed. Whatever imperfections Kevin noticed, Eric couldn't see them.

After the break Jim Brock discussed various financial vehicles and gave them each a list of counseling services. After five years in a bank Eric could have given the speech himself. He was free to sneak peeks at Ivy Enders and think about inviting her to lunch.

There were dozens of women he could have asked out without giving it a second thought. But when they were as pretty as Ivy, his tongue tied itself in knots.

All right, what was the worst that could happen? She could stare at his Dumbo ears and say no. He'd feel foolish for a minute or two and that would be the end of it.

Throughout the next hour he planned how to do it, what he would say. And he felt a bit foolish that he could be so nervous over a little thing like asking a woman to lunch. But suave he was not. He was no Burt Reynolds, no lady killer. He wasn't glib like Kevin McCallister. He was just a small-town guy with big ears and a battered pickup, nobody special. Not like the men he imagined a girl like Ivy Enders usually went out with. They would be more like Kevin.

On the other hand, it wasn't as if he was asking her to jump into bed with him. She was one sexy woman, but what he liked best was her wholesome, direct look. She looked like a person who would be a good friend. Someone he could talk to. Someone he could genuinely like.

All right, he thought, having worked it through and made the usual assumptions. He'd settle for friendship. Maybe he wasn't the kind of guy girls fell in love with at first sight, but he was the kind of guy girls could talk to. He smiled at her and hoped she was in the market for a friend, hoped she had heard Brock's suggestion that members of the group stay in touch.

Ivy Enders was definitely someone he wanted to touch.

Chapter Three

Ivy noticed Eric North looking at her. As she was sitting with her profile to him, she guessed he was examining her nose, probably wondering if it came off with her glasses like one of those gag items.

Once again, she had worn the wrong thing. The other two women were dressed to the nines, but not her. Before she drove back to Limon she planned to do some serious shopping. She'd find the biggest Cloth World in Denver and buy a dozen bolts of the most expensive material and an armful of Vogue patterns. Then she would hole up in her mother's sewing room and not come out until she had a decent wardrobe.

She studied Eric from the corner of her eyes and suppressed a sigh. A guy that handsome was bound to have women panting after him wherever he went. He probably had a dozen gorgeous girlfriends. And the same description applied to Kevin McCallister. They were the two best-looking men Ivy had seen outside a movie theater. Kevin especially was absolutely dazzling, she thought. It was obvious that he lived in a world Ivy had only read about.

Throughout the meeting, Kevin continually interrupted with the ease of one accustomed to being listened to. His comments were funny and outrageous and definitely opinionated, though he didn't seem to care if the group agreed with his opinions. Ivy envied his unshakable confidence.

Eric, on the other hand, was, almost as quiet as Ivy, though she didn't have a sense that his silence was connected to shyness. Rather, he impressed her as a watchful type, one who observed, considered, then drew his own conclusions. It wasn't an exciting quality, but it was one she had always admired.

She dared another peek at Eric. Strong jaw. Nice warm eyes. Sandy-colored hair that caught the light. She liked his hair; it wasn't too short or too long. He looked like an outdoor type and she liked that, too. Though it was early spring, he already had a tan.

So did Kevin. On Kevin the tan seemed darker because of his blue, blue eyes and light-colored spring suit. Ivy smiled when Kevin McCallister waved a hand and rolled his eyes at something Jim Brock said. His gesture was casually elegant, a product of his upbringing. Ivy wondered what it was like to live in Kevin's world. She recalled everything she had read about the jet set and gazed at him with something akin to awe.

Eric North and Kevin McCallister were definitely out of her league. Men like that didn't look twice at girls like her. Suddenly Ivy knew what she wanted to do as soon as her life was more settled. She wanted to do something about Ivy Enders. She would lose fifteen pounds and sew some terrific clothes and learn about makeup and maybe—probably—she would have a nose job. She would buy a neat little Brooke Shields nose.

When the meeting ended, she jumped to her feet, thanked Jim Brock, accepted a packet of handouts and headed for the door. She wouldn't look for material and patterns today after all. She'd wait until she had lost weight and had her new nose. Finally she had a plan, and it felt good.

To her surprise, Eric North fell into step beside her on the pavement outside the Petroleum Club building. "Are you returning to Limon immediately?"

She stopped and looked up at him, shielding her eyes against the sun. "I was planning to do some shopping, but I changed my mind." She cursed the sudden rise of heat in her cheeks. Why couldn't she talk to a man without blushing?

"I was thinking...I mean, it's about lunchtime and there's a restaurant at the end of the block and I thought, if you're hungry, we could have lunch."

He had his hands in his pockets and was looking away from her, watching the rush of big-city traffic. She couldn't believe he was asking her to lunch.

"I thought we could discuss some of the things we heard this morning," he added when she didn't immediately respond.

She swallowed, wishing Cassie were here to see this. Before she could worry about making conversation or what she would do with her hands, Kevin McCallister appeared.

He dropped an arm over Eric's shoulders, another over Ivy's, glanced up at Eric then down at Ivy. "Looks like we three are the only singles in the bunch. So what's it going to be? Lunch?" Instead of waiting for a reply, he linked arms with them and resumed walking toward the restaurant on the corner. "God, what a bore that was. I didn't want to go, but Daddy's attorneys insisted. This place has wonderful Cajun food—abominable stuff but so in right now. Have you tried it? Attorneys are such a pain, aren't they?" He smiled at them.

Ivy laughed. He was so overwhelming. Kevin McCallister was unique in her experience.

Eric leaned past Kevin and smiled at her. "I hope you intended to accept."

"What's this?" Kevin asked, his impish eyebrows soaring. "You were going to have lunch without me? No, no, no, that won't do at all. We're a support group, didn't you hear? All for one and one for all. You're a cute little thing, did you know that?" he said, hugging Ivy's arm close to his body. "But of course you know that. Pretty women always do. It's their weapon against us men. Am I right, Eric? Of course I'm right. I wonder, do we need reservations? Probably not. It's early yet."

They proceeded like the Three Musketeers, linked by Kevin's flow of conversation and verbal asides. The women they passed on the street stared at Eric and Kevin, then cast Ivy quick, envious glances. Slowly her stiffness evaporated, and she began to feel a warm glow of companionship. This was a dream come true, and she intended to enjoy it.

Okay, she wasn't gorgeous. She didn't have long terrific legs or a bosom that stuck out half a mile. She wasn't exciting and she wasn't particularly interesting. But dammit, she had lots of good qualities. Everyone said she made a great friend. She was a terrific listener, she cared about people, she was kind to her parents and she liked little kids. She stood for Mom, the flag and apple pie. That had to count for something. Oh yes, and she had three hundred thousand dollars. And before she was through spending it, Ivy Enders was going to be interesting and maybe even fascinating. That was the new confidence-building plan.

In the meantime...well, in the meantime, she'd settle for support and networking. And if her personal support system was comprised of two great-looking men, so much the better. For once, she was not going to spoil it by turning shy and timid. Determined not to be a wimp, Ivy swung down the street with Eric and Kevin.

They paused outside the restaurant and examined the menu posted inside a brass frame.

"It's very expensive," Ivy blurted, shocked.

"I think we can afford it," Eric murmured, smiling.

They looked at each other and laughed. Then Kevin opened the door and ushered them inside.

"There aren't too many places in Limon with real linen tablecloths," Ivy observed when they had been seated.

"Not in Delta, either."

"I'm dealing with two provincials," Kevin groaned. From anyone else the comment would have seemed like a put-down, but Kevin spoke with such evident good nature that Ivy didn't feel he was criticizing. "Clearly, I shall have to take you two in hand," he announced. "Introduce you to the good life. Imagine, Kevin T. McCallister the third in the role of teacher. I think I may enjoy it." He beamed at them. "Cajun dishes are hideous, and I predict you'll hate everything, but you should try them. New experiences broaden the soul. Then we'll have to talk about getting you out of Limon and Delta. So sayeth the city mouse to his country-mouse cousins."

"This country mouse wants a steak," Eric said, putting aside the menu. He smiled at Ivy. "I don't think I'm ready yet for something called gumbo."

"Me neither. I'll just have a salad." There was no time like the present to begin working on those fifteen pounds.

Kevin clapped a hand over his heart. "What? Didn't you hear me explain that Cajun is in? Ordering a steak or a salad at this restaurant is like flying to Rome and ordering Chinese. You must try the Cajun. Come, come. If I'm to be your local guru, you must at least pretend to follow my advice." He smiled engagingly. "After all, what's the point of winning all that money if you're not going to enjoy it by trying new things?"

Ivy looked at Eric uncertainly. She wanted to please, but she felt caught in the middle. Then the waiter arrived and there wasn't time for further conversation.

"I...I'll have the gumbo," Ivy said. Kevin was right. She had to broaden her horizons and try new things. Kevin gave her a heart-stopping smile and a nod of approval. They looked at Eric.

"I'll have the New York, medium rare, with a side order of gumbo."

"Well done." Kevin laughed. "A tidy compromise." He handed his menu to the waiter. "I'll have the crab Louis." When Ivy and Eric stared at him, his smile widened. "This city mouse has tried Cajun and loathes it. If I should ever visit Limon or Delta—God forbid—I promise to try the local dishes. You, who already know how loathsome they are, may abstain. Fair enough?" He lifted his wineglass. "A toast. To being rich and carefree. May we support one another through good times and bad. This is an excellent little wine, by the way. Don't you agree?"

There was no point pretending to be something she was not. Ivy tasted the wine and didn't know if it was excellent or mediocre. "I don't know much about wines."

After Kevin told her more than she'd ever wanted to know about wine, Eric smiled and asked, "How big is Limon?"

"Well," Ivy said, her eyes twinkling behind her glasses. The second glass of wine made her feel more relaxed than she had in a week. "On a clear night you can see the city light for miles around."

Eric laughed. "You have city lights? I'm impressed. All we've got is a 20-watt neon over the Chevron."

"Oh, my God," Kevin groaned, covering his eyes.

They grinned at him, then Ivy narrowed her gaze in mock seriousness. "Here's the real test," she said to Eric. "How large was your high-school graduating class?"

"Mine was one of the big ones. Sixty-eight that year." His smile told her he was enjoying Kevin's groans as much as she was.

"My class had nearly a hundred the year I graduated," Ivy volunteered, smiling.

"I'm awestruck."

"I'm appalled," Kevin said, propping his chin in his hand. "I had no idea. You could say you graduated sixty-eighth in your class and it would sound good," he said to Eric. "Amazing." He leaned back as the waiter approached. "Thank heaven. I don't think I can stand any more small-town stories just now. Too, too depressing. We really must get you both moved."

As Kevin had predicted, Ivy didn't care for the gumbo. Neither did Eric. He tasted it, then pushed it aside and concentrated on his steak. They both laughed at the faces Ivy made as she gamely worked through the gumbo.

"You don't have to finish it, you know," Kevin said, taking pity on her efforts. "It's truly nasty stuff. Now, about moving. I assume you've both thought about it."

Eric nodded. "I'm planning to stay here a few days and look for an apartment. I think Brock's advice about not buying until we know for certain what we want to do is a good suggestion."

"Ivy?"

"I've decided to move to Denver, too. But I'm a little uneasy about it. I don't know anyone here, don't know the area."

"Nonsense," Kevin said briskly. "You know me. And I know all the best areas. In fact, Daddy owns Twin Towers, a new luxury complex with a wonderful view of downtown to the east and the mountains to the west. The building I'm in is fully leased, but the other still has units available. I don't have any plans for this afternoon." He smiled. "I never make plans, don't believe in them. Flexibility, that's the key. I'll take you by the Towers, Eric."

Eric was silent a moment, then he nodded. "Thank you. It's a starting place."

"Good. If you like Twin Towers, you can call Ivy and she can have a look. That's settled then. If you'll excuse me a minute, I'll just run back and phone the manager."

When Kevin had gone, Eric smiled. "Kevin's an interesting sort, isn't he?"

"He's wonderful," Ivy said simply. "He knows about everything."

"Yes." He looked out over the restaurant. "Ivy, I think Kevin has the best intentions in the world, but . . ."

"But he's a little overwhelming, isn't he?"

"If you feel like you're being pushed into something, or if you've already made other plans, just say so."

Was he telling her that he wasn't wild about the idea of the three of them living in close proximity? That he didn't want to include her in a threesome?

Ivy's shyness returned full force and she felt the hateful spread of pink rising in her cheeks. "I don't want either Kevin or you to feel responsible for me," she said stiffly. "You don't have to call me about Twin Towers. I can find a place on my own."

"I'm sure you can. I just don't want you to feel that Kevin and I are railroading you into something you might not want to do. I'd like the opportunity to know you better and I'd like having our support system within shouting distance. I guess I'm trying to find out if that's what you'd like, too, or if you feel as if you're just being swept along."

She studied him, feeling the pink recede from her cheeks, appreciating his thoughtfulness. "Actually I feel a little relieved by Kevin's suggestion. This is going to sound silly, but I've always lived at home. Moving is a big step for me. The truth is I don't know where to start."

"Really?" It was his turn to look surprised. "I assumed . . . actually, living at home doesn't sound silly at all. My sister, Ginna, lived at home until she married."

From what Eric said, Ivy had the impression he saw her as something better than she was. She hated to demolish whatever he was thinking, but if they were going to live practically next door to each other, he would find out anyway.

She sighed and pulled at her napkin. "I really am a country mouse, Eric. In every sense of the phrase. I don't know the first thing about living in a big city. Or living by myself. It's exciting, and I'm looking forward to it. But it's also intimidating." She looked up at him. "I hate to ask a favor of a stranger, but I really would appreciate knowing your opinion of Twin Towers."

"I'm flattered." To her surprise, he seemed to mean it. "But I should tell you that I'm a country mouse, too." He smiled at the metaphor. "My opinion should be taken with a grain of salt. Frankly it isn't going to take much to impress me. If the Towers has the requisite rooms and appliances, I'll probably think it's terrific."

Ivy wasn't sure if he was being kind or if he really didn't mind doing the apartment hunting for both of them. Next to Kevin, Eric seemed reserved, a little old-fashioned. It wasn't difficult to imagine him assuming a traditional role and taking her under his wing.

"You're very easy to talk to," he said suddenly. A faint trace of color appeared beneath his tan. "When I asked you to lunch, I worried we wouldn't have anything to talk about."

"*You* were worried?" It seemed inconceivable. Ivy stared at him, trying to reconcile what he was saying with the image she had of him.

His color deepened along with Ivy's astonishment. "Girls like you have always intimidated me somewhat."

"Girls like me?" Her mouth dropped.

"You know—pretty girls. Career girls. Self-sufficient, assured..."

She couldn't believe what she was hearing. Eric North thought she was pretty. Pretty enough to be intimidating. Maybe it was the wine, but suddenly Ivy felt giddy.

"Working in an insurance office isn't really a career," she said. "As for being assured, I wish it were true. But all my life I've been shy. I'm afraid timidity doesn't promote confidence." Before he could comment, she nodded toward the plate of gumbo. "I hated that. But I didn't have the confidence to refuse it. I hope having money is going to boost my self-confidence."

Eric leaned forward, but Kevin returned then, sliding into his seat and taking over the conversation.

"We're all set. The manager will meet us at two o'clock. I told him we need two of the best apartments. Dessert, anyone? The fried ice cream is good here, if you like that sort of thing. Now, how soon can you get moved?"

Ivy exchanged a look with Eric and they both smiled. "No dessert for me," Ivy said, glancing at her watch. "In fact, I think I should be going. It's a long drive." Uncertain how she should handle this, she opened her purse and fumbled for her wallet. "How much do I owe?"

Kevin waved a hand. "Lunch is on me. I insist."

Ivy hesitated. A month ago, she would have closed her purse and accepted the offer with gratitude. But she was no longer making six dollars an hour. She was a rich woman. And she had just been telling Eric how she wanted to be more assertive. She drew a deep breath and felt her face flame.

"Thank you, but I'd rather pay my own way," she said lightly. She could feel the heat pulsing in her face, but she was pleased. "If we're going to be support buddies and friends, I think we should each carry our own weight."

"The new equality," Kevin commented, rolling his eyes.

But Eric looked at her with an expression that suggested he understood and approved. Maybe his attitudes weren't as old-fashioned as she had supposed. Both men stood as she rose from the table.

"I'll call you," Eric said, "after I've looked at Twin Towers."

"Thank you, I'd appreciate that."

Outside the restaurant Ivy drew a deep breath and smiled happily. The day had gone much, much better than she had dared to imagine. She couldn't wait to tell Cassie about lunch. It was something out of a movie script.

She paid the parking-lot attendant, then consulted her map and managed to point herself toward Limon. She made the drive in a dreamlike state.

The truth was, she was simply dazzled by Kevin McCallister. Awed, impressed—dazzled. She liked Eric North, liked him a lot, but as ashamed as she was to admit it, when she had discovered his background was similar to hers, her interest had abated somewhat. He was just a small-town person like she was. Not nearly as polished and sophisticated—and exciting—as Kevin.

Who would have believed that Ivy Enders would ever meet one of the McCallisters?

CASS LISTENED IN SILENCE as Ivy bubbled on about the meeting in Denver and the lunch with Eric and Kevin. Eventually Ivy noticed Cassie's uncharacteristic lack of interruptions and she let her voice run down. "Anyway," she finished lamely, "it was fun."

"I'll bet it was," Cass said, sounding bored. She glanced at her watch. "Not everyone gets to go to a fancy club and have lunch with movie-star types."

"It wasn't a club. The Petroleum Club is an office building—it isn't . . ." But Cass was wearing a stony expression that said she had made up her mind and nothing Ivy said would change it. "So, what have you been doing?"

"Not having lunch with a pair of hunks, that's for sure. What do you think I've been doing? The same old thing. Worrying myself sick about making the payments on my car, trying to make ends meet. What else?"

Ivy crossed the kitchen and stood in front of the coffee-pot. "I'm sorry, Cassie. I've been running on about the good things that are happening to me, and I forgot how tough it is for you. I've been insensitive." She poured fresh cups of coffee and touched Cass's shoulder. "The wagon is still acting up?"

"Why should you think about me?" A bitter laugh broke from Cass's lips. "You don't have to worry about a car that's falling apart or about not having enough money to buy a new one." Cass raised her head and met Ivy's eyes. "And nowhere to turn for help."

In the silence, Ivy remembered what Jim Brock had said about making loans to friends. But she also remembered that she and Cassie Myers had been friends since grade school. They had been in Girl Scouts together, had smoked and rejected their first cigarette together, had shared a crush on Richie Martin, had laughed together and cried together.

"Cassie, are you asking me for a loan?"

Anger flashed in Cassie's eyes. "I'd hoped you wouldn't make me come right out and say it. I'd hoped you might offer to help a friend without making me beg."

"Good lord, Cassie, is that what you think I'm doing?" Ivy stared at her with horror. "I apologize. I wasn't sure if we were just talking, or if you were leading up to something."

"If you want me to beg, then I'll beg. Can you—"

"Stop!" Ivy felt sick inside. "Of course I don't want you to beg. Cassie, please." But Cass's face was closed, her eyes resentful. Silently Ivy crossed the kitchen and opened the cupboard near the back door. She removed her checkbook from her purse and returned to the table. "How much?" she asked quietly.

"There's no point trying to fix up the wagon. I need a new one."

"How much?"

"I wouldn't ask if I didn't really need the money."

"Cassie, just tell me how much."

"Ten thousand."

In the silence, Ivy could hear the rattle of her father's tractor in the fields, could hear her pen scratch across the check. She tore the check from the book and extended it across the table.

Cassie folded it neatly and dropped it into her purse. Abruptly she rose from the table and stared at Ivy. "It could have been me, you know. I could have won just as easily."

"I know. It was just dumb luck, Cassie, that's all."

"I suppose I should say thank you."

Ivy just looked at her. Then Cass pushed through the screen door, and after a moment, Ivy heard the Ford wagon cough to life then spin toward the road.

She sat at the table and stared at a point in space, feeling the tears hot behind her eyes.

"Honey?" Ivy's mother entered the kitchen carrying a basket of laundry. After looking at Ivy, she set the basket on the counter and pressed a hand to Ivy's shoulder. "What happened?"

"Jim Brock was right. I just lost my best friend."

Now the tears came, quiet tears of loss and regret. Ivy remembered Cassie running across the school playground, remembered how they had helped each other through their Scout badges. Over the years they had traded clothes and confidences, had been there for each other through the good times and the bad. They had sworn their friendship could survive anything.

But it couldn't survive money. Ivy had seen it in Cassie's eyes when she tucked the check into her purse.

Since she was too upset to eat, Ivy passed on supper and took refuge in her room. She sat by the window, looking out at the maize fields, trying to think of some way to put things right with Cass.

When Iris knocked at her door, she didn't respond.

Iris opened the door anyway, as sisters do, and stepped inside. She was carrying two mugs of coffee. After giving one to Ivy, she sat on the bed and tucked her feet under her. "I heard. I'm sorry, Ivy."

"I can't believe it," Ivy said. "After all these years."

"I know. I lost my best friend, too."

"Betty Kellen. I remember."

Iris pushed a wave of thick, chestnut hair off her forehead and gazed toward the ceiling. "Betty couldn't accept that I was in love with Frank. She kept putting him down. Then after Frank and I were married she didn't seem to understand I couldn't go out with the girls as much as I used to. I didn't want to. Betty thought I was being disloyal to an old friend. But it wasn't that. It was the same thing that happened between you and Cassie."

"Jealousy," Ivy said dully.

"It's hard to keep a friendship going when the friends are no longer equal, honey. When one of the friends has a stroke of good fortune—like finding the right man or winning a big sweepstakes—sometimes the comparison makes the other friend feel like she's worse off than before. If both of you are in the same circumstances, then it's okay. But if the circumstances change for one of you, well, sometimes that's not okay."

"It was just luck. Anyone could have won!"

"I know, but it happened to you and not to Cass. You're looking at a wonderful new life where anything is possible, but Cassie's stuck on the same old treadmill, trying to make ends meet in a small town where the most exciting event is a new dish at the church potluck. Ivy, honey, Cass would have to be superhuman not to feel jealous."

Ivy looked out the window. "Are you jealous, Iris?"

"You bet I am. Ivy, look at me." Leaning forward, she took Ivy's hand. "Of course I'm jealous. Hey, I'd love to win six million dollars. Who wouldn't? When I first heard about it, I lay awake nights thinking what I'd do if I had all that money. But you know what?"

"What?"

"After thinking about it, I discovered I wouldn't do things much differently than I'm doing now. I like my life just as it is. About the only thing I really wanted that I didn't have is a place of our own. And you've made that possible. What I'm saying, Ivy, is that, sure, I wish I'd won. But if I can't win, I'm glad you did."

"Do you mean that?" Ivy asked in a small voice.

"You know I do. I like my life. But, Ivy, I don't think you like yours much. I think there are big changes you want to make, things you want to try. I'm glad you're going to have the chance." She smiled and toasted Ivy with her coffee mug. "I can't wait to hear all about it. And I promise to steal your pink sweater if you omit a single detail!"

"Oh, Iris." Ivy hugged her in a fierce embrace. "Thanks."

"Look, it's rough about Cassie," Iris said. She smoothed a strand of hair behind Ivy's ear. "But you'll find new friends. You're changing, Ivy. It has to happen. And you'll find friends to suit the new you." She tilted a shrewd eyebrow. "From what I hear on the grapevine..."

"Mom."

"You've already met a couple of exciting candidates. And they sound very, very interesting."

Ivy laughed in spite of herself. "Stop looking like that. Right now I could use a few friends. And that's all they are." When Iris continued to give her the raised eyebrow she smiled. "Come on, Iris, you swore you fell in love with Frank the first minute you saw him. You said that's how love happens. Bells went off. Stars exploded. Well, I didn't feel any of that when I met Eric or Kevin. They're my new support system. That's all. No ringing bells, no exploding stars."

"We'll see."

"I know you don't believe it, but men and women can be friends. It's been known to happen."

"Uh-huh."

IN A FARMING COMMUNITY lights-out come early. By eleven o'clock, Ivy was in bed, but she couldn't sleep. She kept thinking about Cassie. She was going to miss her a lot.

But if she'd had any lingering doubts about moving to Denver, now those doubts had faded. She had an awful suspicion that if she remained in Limon, she'd end up with no friends at all. She wanted to stretch her ties, but she didn't want to fully unravel them.

Still, now she had no reason not to go. There was nothing holding her in Limon.

Suddenly, gloriously, Ivy could glimpse a future she had only dared to dream. The Celtex Sweepstakes had made everything possible. And she could hardly wait to get on with the rest of her life.

Chapter Four

Eric moved into Twin Towers the first week in May, and on his recommendation, Ivy moved a few days later. He met her father and brother-in-law and liked them, though he was aware they were giving him a thorough once-over.

Sven Enders gripped Eric's hand and stared at him. "You and that Kevin fellow are the only people my Ivy knows here."

"We'll look out for her, sir."

Sven peered into his eyes. Apparently he found what he was looking for, because finally he released Eric's hand and nodded as if he were satisfied. He hugged Ivy tightly, then he and his son-in-law looked around the apartment once, waved, and closed the door behind them.

"You're going to be fine," Eric said, guessing Ivy's apprehension. She was standing on the apartment balcony, looking down toward the street.

"I know. I'm going to miss everyone, but I'll be okay."

She didn't sound certain. Eric remembered the day his sister, Ginna, had left home and a surge of protectiveness swept him. He would have placed his arm around Ivy's shoulders if Kevin hadn't appeared.

"Who was that peculiar man driving the pickup who made me swear on my mother's grave that I'd look after you?" Kevin poked his head in the doorway. He was wearing tennis whites and carrying a pitcher of martinis and three glasses.

"That was my father," Ivy said in a small voice, "and Frank, my sister's husband."

Kevin winked at Eric. "I assume you, too, have been pressed into service?" He bowed before Ivy. "I assure you, fair maiden, we shall not allow you out of our sight. Now to celebrate this auspicious occasion." He handed around the glasses and filled them to the rim. "To us! To Granddaddy McCallister, the Colorado Lottery, and the Celtex Corporation. What a terrible mess this is, dear Ivy. What on earth's in all those boxes?"

"Books," she said, smiling. It was impossible not to smile when Kevin was present. He bounced from subject to subject, irrepressible.

"Ugh. Who has time to read?"

Eric bent to one of the boxes and folded back the flap. "Ludlum? He's one of my favorites. How about Clancy?"

"I love his work. Do you enjoy reading?"

Eric laughed. "I think I belong to every book club in America. You, too?"

"Oh, God," Kevin said, giving them one of his famous groans. "I'm going to take my martinis and run screaming out of here. Wasn't there anything to do in Limon or Delta? Reading is the cardinal sign of a bored mind."

Ivy looked shocked, and Eric liked her for that. "I love to read!"

"You poor, poor girl."

"I'll bet you were one of those kids who read under the covers with a flashlight," Eric said to Ivy. "Right?"

"You, too?" She laughed and her face flushed prettily. "What am I going to do with all these books?"

"Shelves would seem a good idea," Kevin remarked dryly. "And perhaps a chair or two, maybe a settee. You might also want a table and a few lamps."

"And soon," Ivy agreed.

"I'm planning to shop for furniture today. Would you like to come along?" Eric thought she looked a little overwhelmed, standing in the middle of the boxes gazing at the bare apartment.

Ivy straightened her shoulders. "I know my father made you both promise to look after me. But I don't need any baby-sitters, thank you." She paused and reconsidered. "Perhaps I do, but I don't want to. So thanks, Eric, but no thanks. If I run into trouble, I'll holler. But I want to make it on my own."

"One of the best things and one of the worst things that ever happened to this country is women's lib." Kevin refilled his martini glass. "When you want a liberated woman, you can't find one. They go all stiff and traditional on you. But when you want a traditional girl—" he grinned at Ivy "—they bristle and insist on making it alone. Who can figure it? All right, kiddos, run along and buy furniture. I'll be on the tennis court, thinking about you. By the way, Ivy love—" he dropped an arm around her shoulders and turned her toward the balcony "—see the other Tower? Look up toward the penthouse suites. See the balcony with the yellow umbrella table? That's my place. If you're ever being attacked by a mad salesman, just run out on your balcony and wave toward mine."

When Kevin had gone, Eric carried his glass into Ivy's kitchen, rinsed it, then set it on the drainer. "If you're wondering why I didn't suggest penthouse suites—"

"I doubt we could afford them."

"We probably could, but the price seemed exorbitantly high." His banking background affected his perspective. He couldn't accept spending nearly twice the money for essentially the same amenities, only a few floors higher.

"I like this apartment, really. Eric, you do understand why I want to shop for furniture on my own, don't you?"

She looked so anxious that he smiled. "Of course I do. I didn't mean to suggest you couldn't manage on your own. I just thought it would be more fun to have some company." When she didn't change her mind, he moved toward the door. "Well, if you need any help I'm just two doors away."

"Thanks, Eric. I appreciate the offer."

He didn't see much of her during the next ten days. They passed in the hallway, shared the same elevator, managed coffee once or twice. But they were both busy setting up their apartments.

Eric furnished his sparsely; his primary criterion was that the pieces had to be on sale. This meant driving all over town to various stores, but it helped him get a feel for Denver. For the most part he chose modern pieces, feeling drawn to spare lines and uncluttered spaces. Because he liked the look of his books, he bought shelving to line one of the walls in the living room instead of making a library out of the extra bedroom, as he had originally planned.

Ivy didn't look for sale pieces. She bought everything in one store. Her taste leaned toward what the salesman called country modern. Lots of oak and glass, comfortably upholstered plaids. She, too, decided on a wall of bookshelves in her living room.

"You sew?" Eric asked, when she had shown him through her apartment, her face pink with pride.

"Since I was in junior high school. It's relaxing."

"I like what you've done with the apartment."

It was warm and homey. The room that surprised him the most was her bedroom. He'd expected something pink and frilly. Lots of ruffles and feminine things. Instead, her bedroom was done in quiet creams and blues. Almost as if she had done it with a man in mind.

That shouldn't have surprised him. She was attractive and interesting. Probably she had someone in Limon, someone who would be driving to Denver on weekends.

The phone rang. The answering machine picked up the call and played Kevin's voice over the speaker.

"I know you're there. I saw you across the courtyard. Stay put. I'm coming to inspect what you've been up to."

"That machine is a godsend," Ivy said. She stepped into the kitchen and started a pot of coffee. "I didn't really believe Jim Brock when he said the salesmen would find us even if we moved. Someone phoned last night wanting to sell me a burial plot."

"I got one who was trying to sell solar heating. He didn't care that I was renting."

"Do you answer those calls?"

"There's something irresistible about a ringing phone."

Ivy laughed. "I know. If I listen on the speaker, I feel like I'm eavesdropping. I always think I should pick it up, and I usually do. Do you use sugar? I've forgotten."

"Just cream."

Kevin arrived then, sweeping inside with his usual vigor and brisk vitality. Eric noticed when Ivy poured Kevin's coffee, she added sugar without asking. She hadn't forgotten how Kevin preferred his coffee.

The observation struck him as significant.

For an instant he experienced a pang of jealousy. He liked Ivy Enders, liked her a lot. He liked the way she blushed occasionally, liked the way her shyness was slowly beginning to drop away as she became more comfortable with them. He admired her determination to make it on her own, liked it that she read and sewed.

By now he understood that his initial impression of her had been incorrect. She wasn't as self-assured as he had first imagined. Not as confident or as at ease with herself. But he liked her better for not being perfect. He had hoped... Well, never mind what he had hoped.

He didn't blame her for being drawn to Kevin. Kevin had it all. McCallister was a man Hugh Hefner would have applauded. Kevin drove a Porsche, lived in a penthouse, knew how to play. More than once, Eric had seen two or three beautiful women sunbathing on Kevin's balcony. Kevin knew what was "in"—the in spots, the in sports, the in drinks. He was handsome, rich, irreverently charming. Eric imagined Kevin had never been intimidated by a woman in his life.

"Well," Kevin said expectantly. "Do I get the grand tour?"

"Right this way." Shy pride colored Ivy's throat.

Although Eric had already had the tour, he tagged along, waiting to hear what Kevin would say. Uncharacteristically, Kevin remained silent.

"That's it," Ivy said when they had returned to the living room. She bit her lip. "What do you think?"

"I'll reserve comment until I've seen Eric's place."

They walked down the hallway and Eric let them inside. His apartment lacked the homey touches Ivy had added. By comparison, his apartment seemed almost barren. Without his awareness, an expression of defensiveness firmed his chin.

"I suppose it's too late to return your purchases," Kevin said finally. Eric and Ivy glanced at each other, then looked at Kevin.

"You don't like our apartments?" Ivy asked in a worried tone.

"I should have gone with you, I knew I should have. But I thought you could manage on your own. Come along."

Before they could say anything, he was out the door, leading them to his apartment in the matching tower.

Eric's lips thinned. He didn't care what Kevin thought about his furnishings. But he deeply resented the hurt pinching Ivy's expression. Not for the first time, he wondered if he really liked Kevin. He had an uneasy suspicion that he and Ivy were Kevin's latest project, his latest amusement. For himself, he didn't mind. But he minded for Ivy's sake. He was beginning to believe Ivy regarded Kevin with something akin to hero worship. If so, he hoped Kevin understood that heroes have certain responsibilities.

They didn't speak during the elevator ride to the penthouse apartments.

Ivy gasped as Kevin opened his door. "It's lovely!"

Grudgingly Eric had to agree. Kevin's apartment was furnished with magnificent antique pieces that gleamed softly from decades of wax and loving care. The colors were aged and muted, a mellow splendor of maroon and blue and cream. Bowls of fresh flowers adorned tables that dated from the days of kings and queens. An oriental rug covered oak flooring. The entire apartment was tastefully and exquisitely done. It fairly screamed old money.

"It looks like something out of a magazine," Ivy breathed.

"I had an excellent decorator. If I'd thought you didn't have one of your own, I'd have recommended her. It never occurred to me that you didn't." Moving to a sideboard, Kevin opened the overleaf, disclosing a bar, and dropped ice into crystal tumblers. "Drinks?"

"I'd rather have coffee," Eric said.

Ivy hesitated, then gave Kevin an apologetic look. "It's still early. I'd prefer coffee, too, if it isn't any trouble."

"No trouble at all." As if the words were magic, a man appeared at the entrance to a long corridor. "This is Walter," Kevin said. "Walter, my friends will have coffee." Walter nodded and disappeared as silently as he had arrived.

Ivy's eyes widened. "You have a servant?"

Kevin laughed. "You don't have to whisper. This is excellent Scotch, are you sure . . . ? No? Then we must decide what we'll do today." He made no mention of the contrast between his apartment and theirs; it wasn't necessary. "We can now devote ourselves to some serious playing. Ah, Walter. Put the service on the coffee table. Miss Enders will pour. You don't mind, do you, Ivy?"

"No. No, of course not."

She approached the heavy silver tray and service and studied it for a moment. Then she poured coffee into two fragile-looking china cups. Hesitating, she looked up at Eric.

"Cream," he reminded her.

"What will it be? Tennis? Golf? Racquetball?"

Ivy pressed her lips together. "I don't know how to play those sports," she admitted finally.

"Neither do I," Eric said.

"What? A banker who doesn't golf?" Kevin smiled at him. "Seriously, you're kidding, right? Everyone plays golf and tennis."

"My boss and his wife took me to the Limon Country Club once. For golf." Ivy frowned into her cup. "I was awful. I left holes all over the course."

Eric met Kevin's eyes. "Not everyone has enjoyed the same advantages you have, McCallister. When you were sixteen and following a pro around a golf course, I was pumping gas. I didn't have the time or money to learn the rich-kid sports."

Kevin dropped into a velvet-covered chair and crossed his ankles on a cross-stitched stool. "I swear money is wasted on you two! What do you plan to do with it? Buy books?" He made a clucking sound with his tongue. "All work and no play. I see you have a lot to learn."

Ivy leaned forward, her eyes dark and intense. "I want to learn tennis and golf and how to ski and all the rest!"

"You will, my dear. I'll see to it." Kevin arched an eyebrow at Eric.

"I don't know, Kevin. I've managed to survive this long without chasing a ball around the golf course."

"What *do* you do to amuse yourself?"

"I like to fish." The direction of the conversation was making Eric uncomfortable. All right, he'd never had the opportunity to pursue leisure sports before. He'd also never felt defensive about it before. Or realized how dull he sounded. "I like to ride and hunt."

"I like to fish, too," Ivy admitted in the voice of one who made a reluctant confession. She looked at Kevin. "But that isn't what people with money do, is it?"

"Not that I know of! Children, I am stunned. What do you do when you go to a resort?" He held up a hand. "Don't tell me. You haven't been to a resort. We have a lot of work ahead of us. Now, Eric, don't look so resentful or so judgmental. How else did you plan to fill your days?"

It was a question he hadn't examined too closely. Perhaps because he was uneasy about the answer.

"We'll organize lessons right away. We'll—"

"Wait, Kevin," Ivy interrupted. "I want to learn, but I have some other things I want to do first."

"Like what? What could be more important than learning how to play?"

"I want to buy a car."

"That takes five minutes. What else?"

She looked exquisitely uncomfortable. "Well, I...I want to do something about me."

Kevin studied her. "Let's see. Contacts, right?" She nodded, looking at her hands. "And a good haircut—I'll recommend someone. Blond streaks, I think. And, of course, you'll want to get rid of your sewing machine." Her head snapped up. "Ivy, dear, no one but no one sews their own clothing. I'll take you to Cherry Creek." He tilted his head. "You'll want to lose a few pounds, of course."

"I've started jogging in the mornings. Around the park."

"Good, good. Then there's your nose. I suppose you'll want to have surgery."

She blushed bright crimson and nodded vigorously.

Eric couldn't believe what Kevin was saying or that Ivy was agreeing. He liked her exactly as she was. He liked her glasses and her hair, and he didn't think she was overweight. "What's the matter with your nose?" he asked, staring at her. He was genuinely puzzled; her nose looked fine to him.

She blushed an even deeper rose. "My nose is too big. Isn't it obvious?"

"No, it isn't. There's nothing wrong with your nose."

"The size isn't too objectionable," Kevin said, considering, "but a thinner shape would be more in."

Eric was appalled. "For God's sake, surely people don't follow fads in noses!"

"Eric, please. Kevin is right. I really want a new nose. I've thought about it since I won the sweepstakes." Ivy turned her red face toward Kevin. "Can you recommend a plastic surgeon?"

"Of course. I've had my nose done and my chin shaped. I also had my ears pinned."

Eric looked at him. "You had your ears pinned?"

"Sure. There's nothing to it." Kevin smiled, mischief twinkling behind his gaze.

"I might be interested in that." To his irritation, Eric felt his own color rise.

Ivy turned to study him. "Your ears are fine."

"They stick out a mile."

She leaned forward and he felt an uncomfortable heat increasing in his face. "No, they don't."

"Ivy, come on. The kids called me Dumbo when I was little. Don't tell me my ears aren't the first thing you see when you look at me."

"Eric, I'm telling the truth. I can't see anything unattractive about your ears."

"And I can't see anything unattractive about your nose."

"Now, boys and girls, let's not bicker. If Ivy admits you have ears like a spaniel, will you admit she has a nose like Cyrano?"

They both protested until Kevin fell backward, laughing. "This is so ridiculous," he said, grinning. "Look, what does it matter? If you want a new nose, and you want new ears, so what? If it makes you feel better, do it."

Eric and Ivy were silent during the return to their tower. They didn't speak until the elevator opened onto their floor.

"Would you like another cup of coffee?" Eric asked politely. He wasn't in a good mood and almost hoped Ivy would refuse. But she nodded. "Let's go to my place," he suggested. "No offense, but you make lousy coffee."

"Oh?" For the first time, he saw a flash of anger in the dark eyes behind her glasses. Dammit, he liked her glasses. "How is my coffee different from yours?"

"I grind fresh beans for each pot. Plus, you make it too weak."

He showed her his grinder and a sack filled with French-roast beans. "I use five scoops." She didn't seem interested. She sat on a stool in front of the counter looking toward the balcony window.

"Kevin knows about everything, doesn't he?" she said after she had tasted the coffee. She made no comment about the French-roast beans or the strength of the brew.

"Maybe." Eric hadn't made up his mind about Kevin.

"I was so proud of my apartment until I saw his. He was right, you know. Winning the Celtex Sweepstakes is wasted on me. There's so much I don't know."

"Wait a minute, Ivy." He sat on the stool next to hers and touched her wrist. "I like the way you furnished your apartment. It's warm and inviting. It looks like you." He removed his fingers from her skin and poured cream into his coffee. "If you like the pieces you chose, that's all that's important. You're the one who's going to live with them. It doesn't matter what anyone else thinks."

"I didn't even think about hiring a decorator. It didn't enter my mind."

"Listen, I'd rather spend time in your apartment than in Kevin's. The whole time I was there, I was worried I'd bump against something and break it."

She gave him a shy smile. "I felt that way too, but…Eric, do you think we're cut out to be rich?"

"If you mean rich like Kevin McCallister is rich, probably not. You and I didn't grow up with money."

"All the time I was buying new furniture, I kept worrying about how much money I was spending. It seemed like a king's ransom. But it turns out my whole apartment probably didn't cost as much as Kevin's oriental rug."

"Is that bad?"

"Maybe I should have bought one or two really good pieces then added to them as I could. The trouble is, I don't know where you buy pieces like Kevin has, and even if I did, I wouldn't know a good antique from a poor one."

He wasn't sure what to say to her. She looked so miserable. "Ivy," he said finally. "Winning all this money is supposed to be fun. Are you having fun?"

"I thought I was." Eventually she smiled. "I sure had fun at American Furniture. It was wild and crazy. I just kept saying: I'll take that. And that and that." Her smile faded. "But I don't have the background to know what's good and what isn't. But I want to learn." She sighed. "We're lucky to have Kevin's help, aren't we?"

"So why the long face?"

"I don't know." She looked puzzled and a little embarrassed. "If I were home, I'd be at work. Like Kevin said, I don't know how to play." She spread her hands and laughed. "I feel guilty reading in the middle of the day. So, what am I supposed to do?"

"Spend money," he said firmly, taking her coffee cup from her hands. "Let's go buy ourselves a couple of new cars. We'll feel better."

She studied his grin then laughed. "All right, Mr. North. You've got a deal."

"Unless you'd rather do it by yourself," he added hastily, remembering how she had rejected his offer to accompany her on the furniture spree.

"Not this time. I don't know anything about cars, and I'd appreciate a little guidance."

Feeling better now that they had a purpose, they stopped by Ivy's apartment so she could get her purse.

Eric studied her living room while he waited. "I don't care what you say. I like this room. I like your nose, too."

"I don't want to talk about my nose," she said stubbornly. "If we're going to be friends, Eric, then please don't patronize me."

"I'm not. I honestly like your nose." He also liked her sexy little figure and her legs and the way her summer dress curved over her breasts. "Your nose has character."

"Look," she said, staring up at him. "I honestly think you have nice ears. I don't see anything at all wrong with your ears. But do you want me to keep saying so?"

"I wouldn't believe you."

"Right."

"Okay, I get the point. All right, Cyrano, not another word about your awful nose. Let's go see what Jaguars are selling for these days."

She smiled. "Much better. After you, Dumbo."

Laughing, they linked arms and swung toward the elevator.

ERIC TRADED HIS PICKUP for a blue Jaguar. Ivy watched his face pale when the salesman quoted the price.

"We're supposed to have fun with the money," she said out of the corner of her mouth. "Remember? Next year is the year to be sensible."

"I could buy a house for what this car cost!"

He followed her to the Cadillac dealer where Ivy traded her old Chevy for a wine-colored Seville. She poked her head in the door and inhaled the new-car scent.

"Heaven smells like that," Eric commented, grinning.

"Wrong. I have it on good authority that heaven smells like a mink coat."

"That's next."

She clasped her heart. "Not today. If I write another big check, I'll go into cardiac arrest. My hand starts shaking when I write all those zeros."

"Tell you what. Let's go for a drive in the mountains."

"No. Not today." She softened her refusal with a smile. "But we can't just go home, can we? We have to drive somewhere. Have you been in Denver long enough to know the shopping centers? Which one is the farthest from here?"

"Probably the Westland Mall."

"Good. Tell me how to get there." When he raised an eyebrow, she smiled and pointed out the obvious. "We need cassettes for our tape recorders."

They met at the Westland Mall, both swearing they were driving the car of the century. "Can you imagine what the people in Delta would say if you drove down Main Street in that car?"

"They would say I was a fool for throwing my money away. Showing off."

"The same thing would happen to me in Limon. It really was best to move to Denver."

"Did you have any serious doubts?"

Hesitantly she told him about Cassie, as they entered the mall and searched for a music store.

"I'm sorry, Ivy." He touched her shoulder and for a brief moment, she leaned against him. "Give it time. Maybe Cassie will come around. If not, you'll meet other people, make new friends."

"I already have," Ivy said quietly, looking up at him. "You and Kevin have been wonderful. I always wanted a brother, and now I feel like I have two of them."

Ivy was beginning to feel a brotherly affection for Eric, that was true, but she wasn't sure what she felt for Kevin. She suspected it wasn't brotherly. For the most part her shyness faded when she was with Eric, but when she was with Kevin she often felt tongue-tied and self-conscious.

She couldn't recall ever meeting anyone she admired as much as she admired Kevin McCallister. Everything about him seemed perfect. From the top of his shining head to the bottom of his designer shoes, he was exquisitely perfect. He had the perfect background, the perfect manners and perfect charm. He swept into a room as if everyone there had been waiting for him, and he brought with him his unique brand of vitality and humor. What Ivy wanted most was for Kevin to admire her as much as she admired him.

"Do you think Cadillacs are in?" she asked Eric, suddenly anxious. She wished Kevin had come with them.

"Who cares? If you like it, that's in enough."

They found the music store and parted at the door. Ivy headed for the country-and-western racks; Eric moved toward "easy listening." They met again at "oldies but goodies."

"Country and western?" Eric asked, examining her tapes. He made a face. "Who is Richie Martin?"

"You've never heard of Richie Martin?" She stared at him as if he had just confessed to having never heard of indoor plumbing. "Richie Martin is only the hottest singer around. He grew up in Limon. We went to the same high school. Cassie and I both had terrible crushes on him."

"Still carrying the torch, huh?"

"Hardly. Richie Martin didn't give us the time of day. What tapes did you get?"

"Too bad for Richie Martin, his loss. Is there anyone else who's special?" he asked in a voice that was elaborately casual.

"Not at the moment." Pride prevented Ivy from admitting she had never been in love. It seemed like a character defect. Everyone had had at least one affair by the time they were twenty-six. Except her.

It wasn't for lack of trying. She had dated steadily over the years; she had even had one marriage proposal. But no bells had rung. No stars had exploded.

And she would rather have crawled to China than admit she was still a virgin. It was the single most embarrassing event—or nonevent—of her entire life. No one but no one was still a virgin at twenty-six.

"How about you?" Eric was a wonderful man; she hoped he had a girlfriend who appreciated him, someone as nice as he was.

"I was engaged once, but it didn't work out. At the moment there's no one special."

Ivy wanted to ask why it hadn't worked out, but didn't feel comfortable prying. But she couldn't imagine the fault had been Eric's. Any woman would be lucky to get him.

She looked at his tapes and made a face. "Herb Alpert? And Mantovani? Ick!"

"Ick? What do you mean, ick? These are classics." He looked pained. "Let's see what you've got. Ole Richie

Martin the heartbreaker and Willie Nelson? Give me a break."

"You must be older than you look," Ivy teased. "My parents would love your tapes. Music to nod off to."

"Music to read by or drive by or think by."

"Real toe-tappers," she said, laughing.

"You want toe-tappers? Check these." He showed her tapes of Creedence Clearwater and the Mamas and Papas.

"Better. Your taste definitely improves in oldies."

"You know something, Cyrano?" he asked sourly, staring down at her. "I think I liked you better when you were too shy to be smart-mouthed."

"No, you didn't." She took his arm and tugged him toward the counter. "Come along, Dumbo. We have to pay for these."

"Did the big city ruin you or was it the Cadillac? Give a woman a Cadillac and immediately she turns into a smart-mouth. I don't need these insults." He looked at the top of her head. "What's wrong with Herb Alpert? There's something wrong with a woman who doesn't like Herb Alpert."

Ivy laughed and spilled her tapes over the counter. She wished Kevin was as easy to talk to as Eric.

Ivy JOGGED EVERY DAY, jogged until she was panting for breath, until her sides ached. Sometimes Eric joined her, but more often he ran alone; she was too slow. They would meet afterward in Eric's apartment for morning coffee.

Occasionally, like today, Kevin joined her on the jogging path, but he seldom looked happy about it.

"Oh, God. Every step is agony."

"Another hangover?" Ivy asked, panting. She looked at him from the side of her eyes. Kevin never seemed to break a sweat. He was the only man she knew who didn't sweat. It made her feel self-conscious about the wet areas under her arms and down her back.

"You should have come with us last night. It was a party to end all parties. Do you really get up this early every single day? It's barbaric!"

"I told you," she gasped, trying to breathe and run and talk, "I'm not going to any parties until I get my new nose and my new wardrobe."

"Your nose isn't *that* bad. How far away are you?"

"Three more pounds and I'll be at shopping weight." She couldn't believe that Kevin wasn't even breathing hard. "How come," she said, puffing, "you can drink—" puff, pant "—and party all night—" wheeze "—and can still run without dying?"

"I have no idea." He matched her stride for stride, his breath steady and unlabored.

"Why are you up this early?" She was turning red from the effort to talk and run. "Or haven't you been to bed yet?"

"Do I detect a note of criticism, my dear Ivy? I love to sleep in. Sleep is the balm of the gods. Especially when you've been up until three or four in the morning. But it's a fair question. I'm braving the morning rays because I want to talk to you."

"What about?" The end was almost in sight. They rounded a park bench and she could see the Tower entrance. Size seven, she told herself through gritted teeth. Size seven. It was her mantra. Six weeks ago she hadn't known what a mantra was, much less that mantras were in.

"I'll tell you over coffee."

When they reached the entrance to her tower—Tower B— Ivy headed straight for the small patch of lawn and collapsed on her back, her chest heaving. "I'm dying. Give me the last rites. You do everything else—you can probably do that, too."

She was too winded to care if she was making a fool of herself in front of Kevin McCallister.

Kevin studied the rise and fall of her chest. "I think you should consider ending your diet. You don't want to lose too much. How are the new contacts? Any trouble adjusting?"

When she could speak, she pulled herself up and drew a deep breath of air. "I love my contacts." She'd had them for ten days now. This afternoon she was scheduled for a hair styling at a salon Kevin had chosen. He had promised that the salon was outrageously expensive, but she would emerge a new woman. The Ivy Enders program was progressing on schedule.

Kevin pulled her to her feet, and she felt the heat rise in her cheeks when he touched her hands.

"Morning air," he pronounced, "is foul stuff, you know. Fit only for peasants." She smiled at the expression on his face. "Don't know how you can stand it. God, I hope you have some vodka. I pray you do. A little hair of the dog, as the saying goes. How can you be so cheerful in the face of genuine suffering? What a hard-hearted woman you are, Ivy Enders. Hurry up, will you? Elevators and hangovers wait for no man." He guided her inside and pressed the button. "Did you decide on blond streaks? I told Gregory to give you blond streaks, but he wanted to see you first. Pushy sort. Be sure to get streaked. I wonder if Daddy knows the walls in the Towers are green. Do you suppose he painted them this hideous color just to torment me?"

Ivy was never quite sure how to respond to Kevin's flow of questions and comments. Most often, she just smiled and said nothing. He didn't seem to expect a reply.

When he paused in front of her door, she called over her shoulder. "Morning coffee's at Eric's."

"How cozy. Charming man, Eric." Kevin caught up to her and took her arm. "More there than meets the eye. Good morning, Eric. I was about to tell our Ivy how we painted the town red last night. The coffee smells heavenly. Freshly ground?''

Arm and arm, he and Ivy crossed the living room and sat on the stools facing the kitchen counter.

"You're up early," Eric commented, pushing a mug of coffee toward Kevin. Without being asked, he reached beneath the counter, found a bottle of vodka and slid it forward.

"Ah, relief!" Kevin added a generous splash to his coffee. "You want some of this?" Eric shook his head. "You don't have a hangover? There is no justice."

Ivy smiled at them. "That must have been some party."

"Like I said, you should have been there. Eric cut a swath through the ladies." Kevin grinned across the counter and raised his mug in a gesture of salute. "Did you get the redhead's number? She was all over you, son.''

Eric cast an uncomfortable glance at Ivy, then added cream to his coffee. "What's the plan for today?"

"You don't want to talk about the redhead?" Ivy teased. She wondered if any women had been "all over" Kevin.

"Ivy's getting her hair streaked, I'm going to an afternoon charity reception," said Kevin. "So, Eric, looks like you're on your own."

"A charity function?" Ivy asked curiously.

"You're thinking about Jim Brock's cautions about fundraisers, aren't you? That doesn't apply to me. Daddy always says wealth has its obligations, and charity is one of them. I have to put in an appearance."

Such comments always made Ivy aware of the great gap between her background and Kevin's. His was a social world of great wealth and glamour. At times like this, she felt as if she had her nose pressed to a window, looking in at a world as foreign as the interior of a UFO.

"What was it you wanted to talk to me about, Kevin?" Ivy said now, recalling what he'd said while they were jogging.

"What?" For a moment Kevin looked blank. "Oh, yes. First I need to know if you've scheduled your nose job."

"Eric?" Ivy said suddenly. "Why are you staring at me? Is something wrong?"

"I'm sorry, I didn't realize I was staring." He leaned on the counter and smiled. "I just can't get used to your new contacts. I liked your glasses."

Kevin poured more vodka into his cup. "We're talking about nose jobs."

"I'm scheduled for next week."

"Good. How about your ears, Eric?"

"I'm getting pinned while Ivy's having her nose done."

"Excellent. Now here is what I propose. As soon as you two have recovered from being whittled on, I propose we go to Cannes for the film festival." He looked pleased with himself. "What do you think? It's sheer, delicious madness. If you haven't been before, you must go. The reason I'm bringing it up now is that I assume neither of you has a passport, and the application takes several weeks."

"Cannes," Ivy repeated in a dreamy voice. "I always wanted to go to Europe."

"Then it's settled. The three of us will take Cannes by storm. I'll make the arrangements." Kevin pushed off the stool. "Charity functions are such a bore. A pity one can't just send a check and be done with it." At the door he scowled back at Ivy. "You want it streaked. Insist."

Ivy waited until the door closed behind him before she spun off the stool and whirled around Eric's living room. "Eric, just think of it! Me, in Cannes! I can't imagine it!"

She ended by spinning into his arms as he moved to the other side of the counter. Instinctively his arms tightened around her, and she wrapped her hands around his neck and threw back her head and laughed.

"Europe! Oh, Eric, I'm so happy. All the dreams are coming true!" Impulsively she hugged him, then tried to step away, surprised to discover how tightly he was holding her.

Immediately his arms dropped, and he sat abruptly on one of the stools. To Ivy's astonishment a dark flush spread beneath his tan. It was the hug. She had crossed the bounds of friendship by hugging him. A flood of color rushed into her own cheeks, and suddenly she felt acutely self-conscious.

"You're so beautiful when you're happy," Eric said softly.

The pink in her cheeks deepened. "As beautiful as the redhead you met last night?" she teased, trying to reestablish their usual easy banter. For some reason she didn't want to know the answer. After brushing at her jogging suit, she moved toward the door. "Well, it's the showers for me. Then it's off to Mr. Gregory for my transformation. See you later."

It wasn't until she was toweling off after her shower that Ivy realized Eric had not commented about the trip to Cannes. Curious.

It was also curious how her mind kept returning to the moment when she had spun into Eric's arms. As Mr. Gregory labored to add golden streaks to her hair, she kept thinking how hard and solid Eric's body had been against her own. How good it felt to hug him and feel his arms around her waist. She hadn't realized how tall he was until she'd reached up to circle his neck.

Frowning at the salon mirror, Ivy told herself she was being silly. Of course it felt good to hug a friend. She'd be having the same warm thoughts if she had hugged Kevin.

Still, she wondered about the redhead. Had Eric asked for her phone number? And why on earth should it disturb her if he had?

Chapter Five

When Ivy had gone, Eric stepped into the sunshine flooding his balcony. Automatically he looked toward Tower A, finding the yellow umbrella table that identified Kevin's apartment. Two leggy blondes were sunning themselves on the balcony.

Eric tasted his orange juice and wondered how Kevin managed his playboy life-style without succumbing to exhaustion. His own hangover was equally all-conference as Kevin's had appeared. Only pride had prevented him from admitting it. For a brief moment Eric considered following Kevin's example and adding a splash of vodka to his juice. Almost immediately he rejected the idea. Drinking in the morning was a habit he didn't want to start, no matter how compelling it seemed at the moment.

Dropping into one of the patio chairs, he leaned his head back, closed his eyes and crossed his ankles on top of the railing. That had been some party last night.

The address had been posh—the Polo Grounds, he remembered—and the house had been a mansion. Eric didn't recall meeting their host, but he'd met a couple of hundred other people. It seemed that all of Denver's most beautiful women had attended the party. Several had attached themselves to him and, to his astonishment, seemed to think everything he said was profound or witty. He had been enormously pleased to find himself in such demand until it occurred to him to wonder if the beauties clinging to his arm knew he had won five million dollars. Five million dollars would make just about any man seem attractive.

The thought depressed him now as it had last night. How could he hope to establish a relationship with a woman if he continually wondered if she liked him or his bank account?

When he had asked how Kevin coped with such problems, Kevin had raised an eyebrow and winked. "Who cares? So what if some babe hits on you because she likes the cut of your wallet? Enjoy, Eric old son, enjoy." When Kevin realized Eric was genuinely concerned, he shrugged. "When it comes time to get seriously involved—perish the thought—then you look for a woman who is as rich as you are. Like marries like, *comprende?* Rich folks marry rich folks. That's how great fortunes are amassed and how you avoid someone whose primary goal is a hefty chunk of alimony."

Eric thought about the advice. Like marries like. Assuming he wanted to marry someday, where was he going to find someone like himself? Someone with a secured income of six figures but with a solid middle-class upbringing and solid middle-class values?

He suspected he wasn't going to meet such a woman at one of Kevin's parties. Gorgeous as those women were, their values weren't the same as his. At least none whom he had met last night or at the other parties he had attended with Kevin. Before the evening ended, which was about three o'clock in the morning, naked people had been running through the mansion looking for the hot tub. And there were drugs.

He supposed drugs were around in Delta too, but if so, he hadn't been exposed to them. In the past couple of weeks, though, he had observed more than he would have seen in a lifetime if he had remained in Delta. He hadn't yet sorted out how he felt about that. On the one hand, he didn't like being the odd man out, the one who didn't fit into the scene. On the other hand, he had a horror of drug use. He'd bought the warnings about drugs and had a vague, perhaps unrealistic, image of a drug user as crazed and wild-eyed. One thing he did know: the scene wasn't for him.

If that made him square, dull and unsophisticated, so be it. Being square, dull and unsophisticated was nothing new, he thought sourly. He had never been an exciting type. And if glamour meant sniffing powder, he wasn't destined for the glamour crowd. He was comfortable with the thought, but it put him in a dour mood.

The phone rang and he started to rise, then said to hell with it. There was absolutely no one he wanted to talk to right now. After draining his juice, he closed his eyes again and listened to the answering machine speaker. A breathy female voice spoke after the beep.

"Hi, Eric, this is Babs. I'm the redhead you were playing footsy with in the hot tub last night, remember?"

He remembered. Tall, luscious, startling figure, the longest legs he had ever seen.

"I'm having a little get-together at my place tonight and I hope you'll come. Just you, me and a couple of friends. If you want, you can bring some champagne." She gave her address and phone number in a purring voice. "Call me before five if you can make it."

She was beautiful, willing, and it appeared she was interested in him. He couldn't pinpoint why he hoped he would never see her again.

Since there was nowhere he had to go, nothing he had to do until his tennis lesson at two o'clock, Eric remained on the balcony, sipping a pitcher of orange juice, monitoring his phone calls.

Three salesmen called, two charities, one wrong number, three more women he had met at the party, someone who claimed to have known him in high school, the Jaguar dealership inquiring if everything was all right with his new car, the stereo shop wanting to sell him a service agreement on his new stereo equipment. He stopped listening.

After a while, he realized he was bored. The admission impressed him as something he should feel guilty about. Millions of people would give anything to be sitting in the sunshine on a Tuesday morning with nothing to do but amuse themselves. So why was he sitting here, wondering what was going on at the Delta bank? Wondering if Jed Anderson was keeping up his second mortgage payments and whether Stella Jankowski had gotten her loan for the beauty shop?

Standing, he glanced at his watch. Ten o'clock. Four more hours until his tennis lesson. He didn't even particularly like tennis. The only thing good about the lessons was seeing Ivy. But she wouldn't be there today.

Walking into his living room, he stood for a moment, surveying his collection of new toys. He had a huge big-screen TV; the newest VCR; the best, most sophisticated stereo system on the market; a personal computer and top-quality printer. He had a record and cassette collection that would be the envy of everyone he knew in Delta. He had good prints on the walls, furniture he liked, a freezer packed with steaks—not the kind that came wrapped in plastic; but the kind you bought from a butcher, thick and perfectly cut—a top-of-the-line gas grill on his balcony to cook them on. He had a Jaguar in the parking garage below, fully loaded with every option known to man. His closet was packed with new clothes for every occasion.

He had everything his heart desired. So why wasn't he smiling? Why wasn't he deliriously happy?

The phone rang again and he turned off the speaker so he wouldn't hear who it was. Then he wandered into the kitchen and, for something to do, ground fresh beans and put on a pot of coffee. Four more hours until his lesson.

"Forget it," he muttered, turning off the switch under the coffee in midcycle.

He waited until the answering machine fell silent, then he phoned the club and canceled his tennis lesson. After changing into jeans and a light sweater, he rummaged in the back of his hall closet until he found his favorite old fishing pole and battered tackle box. He threw them in the back seat of the Jaguar and headed west, looking for a cold, quiet mountain stream.

He found the perfect spot outside Silverthorne, on the Blue River. Happy, really happy for the first time in weeks, he attached a fly to the end of his line and cast. Even wearing hip waders, the rushing water felt icy against his legs. But it was a good kind of cold.

The air was crisp and clean, the high mountain peaks rising above were capped with snow that never melted. Wildflowers nodded along the river banks. The scent of pine and aspen and clear, cold water filled his nostrils.

He loved it. Tennis couldn't hold a candle to fishing. A man couldn't think while he was swatting a ball around a tennis court. He couldn't relax and let his mind wander. Slowly the tension eased from his shoulders.

Near one o'clock, he stuck his pole in the ground and ate the sandwiches he'd purchased from a fast-food place in Silverthorne. This was the life. The only thing missing was company. Enjoying the magnificent scenery, he wished Ivy was here to see the wild flowers and the mountain peaks. He remembered hearing her say that she liked to fish, too.

The idea made him laugh aloud. Maybe she had enjoyed fishing once, but he doubted she would now. Even in the short time he had known her, Ivy had changed a great deal. He knew what she was doing, of course. She was becoming the type of woman that would appeal to Kevin. There was nothing wrong in that. He wished her luck. He liked her enough to want her to have whatever it was that would make her happy.

He ate his sandwiches and lifted his face to the sunshine. Maybe he liked Ivy too much.

It was certainly true they spent a lot of time together, and when they weren't together he found himself thinking about her. He didn't think he thought of her in a romantic way. Of course he couldn't help noticing how pretty she was and what a dynamite figure she had. But mostly he thought of her as a friend. A very good and valued friend.

Over the years there had been several women with whom he had shared a friendship. But there was something different, something deeper, about his feelings for Ivy Enders. He felt a bond with her that he hadn't felt with other women friends. A commonality. An easy companionship that was becoming more important to him the longer he knew her.

That was probably why he would agree to go to the Cannes Film Festival, an event he had absolutely no interest in attending. He wanted to be part of Ivy's first visit to Europe. He wanted to share her wonder and pleasure. He could almost see her wide eyes now.

And without the glasses, he would certainly see her eyes. She had lovely eyes, as dark and liquid as melting chocolate. Grudgingly, he conceded that contacts had been a good choice for her. She was sexy even without her glasses.

But without glasses, she seemed more vulnerable. A little defenseless. In view of her determination to be self-sufficient, she wouldn't have liked that description, but that was how he felt when she wore her contacts. He felt protective toward her, felt a brotherly concern.

One of his concerns was her crush on Kevin. Rising, Eric waded back into the river and flicked his wrist, casting out into the water.

He couldn't really see Ivy fitting into Kevin's life-style. Into the wild parties, the drug scene, the impulsive decisions. Of course, she hadn't seen that side of Kevin yet. It was also possible that Eric hadn't seen all sides of Ivy. Maybe she would fit into Kevin's life after all. He felt a little uneasy about that.

He fished a while, letting his mind wander, storing images and impressions to share with Ivy when he returned.

Eventually he relaxed enough to permit himself to remember the hug she had given him. Remembering embarrassed him. His response had been instinctive and immediate. He had forgotten this was Ivy, his friend, and had reacted to Ivy the woman. He'd felt her warmth in his arms, her generous curves pressed against his body, and for one quick thoughtless moment he had wanted her.

Had she guessed? He hoped not. He didn't want the man/woman thing to interfere with their friendship. He thought about the calls on his answering machine and knew he could always find a woman. But he couldn't always find a good friend. Ivy was special and he valued her friendship. He hoped she wouldn't hug him again.

He did hope that. Didn't he?

"SMASHING! ABSOLUTELY SMASHING! Turn around." Kevin's hands closed on Ivy's shoulders and he turned her so that he could inspect the back of her hair. "I love it. Love it! The gold streaks make your face glow. Gregory is a born artist!"

A flush of pleasure illuminated her face. "I'm so glad you like it."

"Well, don't you? The cut and style are perfect and the streaking is an inspiration. Mine, need I add?"

They were in Kevin's apartment, sipping wine and catching up with each other. To Ivy's disappointment, Kevin had been gone when she returned from the salon eager to learn his opinion about her new hair. A hasty message on her answering machine informed her that he and some friends had decided to fly down to Acapulco for a few days.

"It was ghastly, actually," he said, tipping more wine into her crystal glass. "Too hot, too humid, too boring."

Ivy laughed. "Why do you pretend to hate everything or be bored by it? If you felt that way, you wouldn't go."

"I go because it seems like a good idea at the time. Because I forget I've been there before and how boring it is. The same places, the same people, the same jokes, the same conversation. Besides, what else is there to do?"

"You could go to work in Daddy's corporation," Ivy teased. She could no more imagine Kevin McCallister behind a desk putting in a day's work than she could imagine him wearing a frayed collar.

Kevin shuddered. "Me? In that chamber of horrors Daddy calls an office? Never! You really are looking wonderful, Ivy. Have I told you often enough? The weight loss did wonders. And the contacts." He opened the door for her and they stepped out onto his balcony. "Your new hair is sensational! And I loved our shopping spree. That day was definitely not boring. Ah, Walter put out caviar. Try some."

"Not right now."

He lifted an eyebrow. "Now that I think of it, I've never seen you eat caviar. Don't you like it? Ivy, darling, it's impossible not to like caviar!"

"I've never tried it."

"Never tasted caviar?" He stared at her, incredulous. "That's a criminal omission. Here, I insist you treat yourself this very minute."

Pink tinted her cheeks. "I'm saving caviar for a special occasion. I—I have it all planned."

"How intriguing. What sort of occasion do you have in mind?"

Her blush deepened to scarlet. "I'd rather not say."

Curiosity intensified his examination of her flaming cheeks. "How fascinating. I didn't take you for a woman with secrets. Very mysterious. You're sure you won't try just a nibble?" When she shook her head, he smiled and shrugged and ate the toast point he had prepared for her. "I admire your self-restraint. But you don't know what you're missing.

Leaning against the railing, Ivy automatically sought out her own apartment across the courtyard in Tower B. When she found it, she noticed the balcony screen was opened. She thought she had closed it.

Wanting to change the subject, she returned to their earlier conversation concerning the three-day shopping spree they had undertaken to buy her a "decent" wardrobe. "I didn't dream people spent that much on clothes," she said now.

"If you tell me one more time how you could sew the dress you're wearing for a fourth the cost, I shall consider you hopeless. Ivy, darling, I don't know anyone except your sweet self who even owns a sewing machine."

"I might as well not own one," she said, tasting the wine. It was very good. She was beginning to know the difference between a good wine and one that was so-so. "I haven't used it in weeks. Not since I moved here."

"I should hope not!"

"Actually it's relaxing to sew. Even when I'm making things that will eventually become dust rags." She smiled. "Not all my efforts are successful."

"For heaven's sake, don't tell anyone what you just told me. They'll think you're hopelessly provincial."

She looked away from him. Some days she felt hopelessly provincial, and this was one of them. Hearing about Kevin's Acapulco trip had given her that nose-pressed-to-the-glass feeling again. It sounded so glamorous. A few friends sitting around talking, then someone says, "Let's go to Mexico." Everyone puts down their drinks, drives to the airport and a couple of hours later they're sipping margaritas in Acapulco. It was a stunning idea. Ivy wondered if the day would come when she, too, could think indulging such an impulse was ordinary and reasonable.

"I do wish you had come with us," Kevin said, looking at her with a smile. "When will this nose thing be over? And have you applied yet for your passport?" He dropped his hand over hers on the railing and Ivy caught her breath. She waited, but he didn't move his fingers. A flush of color warmed her cheeks.

Flustered, she tried to recall his questions. "I go in for the nose job at the end of the week. And, yes, I've applied for my passport."

A movement on Eric's balcony caught her attention. She watched him throw open the screen door and glance around his balcony then look up toward them. He waved both arms.

"That's odd," Ivy said, frowning.

Kevin lifted his hand from hers and waved. Why couldn't Eric have appeared a few minutes later? Suppressing a sigh, Ivy waved back. The distance was too great to be certain, but she thought Eric cupped his hands around his mouth and shouted up at them. Suddenly she felt a little uneasy.

"Kevin, how long have we been gone?"

"Well, let's see. I came by for you about eleven. We had lunch, stopped by the gallery and the bookstore for you. Several hours I guess. Why?"

"I'm not sure. I just have a strange, uneasy feeling. It's three o'clock now. That means we've been gone..."

Eric had disappeared from his balcony. A moment later he reappeared on hers. Now she knew something was wrong. As she started to say so, Kevin's telephone rang.

"That's Eric," Ivy said. She didn't wait to hear Kevin answer the phone. She left her wine on the patio table and hurried through Kevin's apartment.

Eric was waiting outside her door when she rushed out of the elevator and turned into the corridor.

"We've been robbed," he said. "They got into both our apartments. I've phoned the police—they'll be here soon."

Wordlessly, Ivy moved past him and pushed her door open. The lock was broken and the door swung easily. She stepped inside and halted abruptly.

Not only had she been robbed, she had been vandalized. Furniture was overturned and ripped open, spilling stuffing. Someone had spray painted "Rich Bitch" across her living-room wall in large red letters. Stunned, she walked slowly, like a sleepwalker, through the debris.

Both TVs were gone, the one in her living room and the one in her bedroom. Gone also was her new emerald cocktail ring and her pearls. The thieves hadn't wanted her sewing machine, but apparently they hadn't wanted her to have it, either. It lay smashed on the floor. Smashed like her new fine china cups and saucers. Her silver flatware was missing and so were the signed prints she had bought for her walls.

Eric put his arm around her and she turned, pressing her face into his shoulder. "All my nice new things," she whispered, trying not to cry.

"I know." His voice was grim and angry.

"How bad did they get you?" He was wearing tennis whites and she guessed he had just returned from his lesson. He smelled pleasantly of heat and sweat and suntan lotion.

"About the same as you." He hugged her quickly and brushed a strand of hair off her forehead. "Come on, we'll go to my place and make some coffee while we wait for the police. I still have a coffeepot."

"I don't?"

"You don't."

Ivy pressed her fingertips hard against her eyelids, then looked around her ruined living room. Her shoulders slumped. "It's not just salesmen who are interested in us." She stared at the words painted on her wall.

"It appears that way," Eric commented shortly.

His apartment was in the same wrecked condition. All his state-of-the-art stereo equipment was gone. And the VCR and the computer components. The big-screen TV must have been too large and heavy to steal, but the thieves hadn't ignored it. They had thrown a chair through the screen.

"They took my antique gun collection," Eric said, picking up a stool and setting it in front of the counter. He moved behind the counter and started a pot of coffee.

Ivy stared at the word "Loser" written in red paint near the shattered TV. "They knew it was us. This wasn't a random burglary. We were specific targets."

Kevin appeared in the doorway. He gazed at the destruction, then rolled his eyes. "What a nuisance! Well, I can see what we'll be doing tomorrow." He kicked aside a fallen lamp and took the stool next to Ivy. "What a bother. Darling, you look so upset." Leaning, he took Ivy's cold hand between his and stroked it. "Don't worry, they didn't take anything that can't be replaced. A little paint, a little shopping, and everything will be as good as new."

Ivy stared at him. She might have said something she would have regretted if Eric hadn't chosen that moment to clear his throat and push a cup of coffee across the counter. Soon afterward the police arrived. There were questions and fingerprint men and people everywhere—in her apartment and in Eric's. At some point Kevin threw up his hands and left after telling Ivy he would stop by later.

Immediately after the police departed, Walter, Kevin's servant, appeared at Ivy's door. "Mr. McCallister sent me, miss. I'm to install new locks on your door and Mr. North's."

It was a thoughtful gesture, and Ivy appreciated it. She also appreciated Kevin's insistence that she and Eric come to his apartment for dinner.

"Come, come," Kevin said after Walter served the salad. "You two are acting like this is the end of the world. It happens all the time." He shrugged. "It's a nuisance, yes, but nothing that can't be overcome. Your insurance will cover everything."

"It isn't the money. It's the sense of violation. Plus I never had real jewelry before," Ivy murmured, poking at a salad with her fork. "I can replace the ring and the pearls, but it won't be the same. They won't be my first real pieces. Remember when we bought them?" She looked at both men. "Remember how you teased me? And if they didn't want my sewing machine, why didn't they just leave it alone?"

"Darling, you don't need a sewing machine. You told me you haven't sewn anything since you won the sweepstakes, and you probably—let us hope—won't sew again."

"But I always wanted a new Singer," she said, knowing he didn't understand. "And, who knows, maybe I will sew something again."

"Perish the thought!"

Eric leaned away from the table. "This definitely has not been a good day."

"You're telling me," Ivy said glumly. She gave up on the salad, hoping Walter wouldn't be offended.

"First my car breaks down, then we're robbed."

"What happened to your car?"

"Who knows?" He spread his hands and his eyes darkened. "It was fine when I drove to my tennis lesson. When I tried to start it afterward, the engine wouldn't turn over. I had to have it towed to the dealer's. They're going to call me."

Kevin nodded and smiled. "You'd better take my advice—buy a backup car."

Later, when she was trying to go to sleep, Ivy thought about Kevin's remarks. Her thoughts made her uncomfortable. Kevin appeared to be saying that no matter what the problem was, if you threw enough money at it the problem went away.

If your belongings were stolen or vandalized, you bought new ones. If your car didn't run properly, you bought a new car. If you didn't like your ears or your nose, you bought new ones. If you were bored, you hired a caterer and threw a party. Or hired a decorator and bought all new furnishings. Or flew to Acapulco. Money solved everything.

But did it really?

She had thought so, too. After winning the Celtex Sweepstakes, she had believed that now she had money, she would be happy. And in many ways she was, happier than she had ever been. But money had cost Ivy her friendship with Cassie. Money had separated her from her family. Money had made her a target for thieves. She didn't like to think about Kevin's being wrong, but she didn't entirely agree that money solved all problems.

In the morning she discovered Eric had left a message on her recorder during the night. She hadn't even heard the phone ring.

"It could have been worse. You could have bought the mink coat you've been thinking about, and the thieves would have gotten that, too. They could have gotten my coffeepot and fishing tackle. When you wake up, come on over dressed for fishing. The mess will keep. What we need is a little peace and quiet, a little sanity. I found a spot on the Blue River you're going to love."

The next message was also from Eric.

"We'll have to drive your car."

The next message was from Kevin.

"Fishing? How incredibly boring. I'd rather watch snails crawl. Thanks for inviting me, kiddos, but I'll pass. I can no more imagine myself handling worms than I can imagine your doing it. Have a wonderfully dull time and if you catch anything, for God's sake don't bring it home."

Ivy smiled. Then she looked around her apartment and her smile faded. She would be days cleaning up this mess. The sooner she got started . . .

On the other hand, Eric was right. The mess would wait. She desperately needed some time away from the city. And she loved to fish.

On impulse, she picked up her telephone and called Eric. She got his recorder. "I'm on my way," she said. "Pack some sandwiches and a thermos of coffee."

Fishing wasn't going to solve this problem, it wasn't going to refurnish her apartment or clean up the debris or repaint her walls. But going fishing felt better at the moment than writing checks.

Before she dressed in her jeans and old plaid shirt, she dialed Kevin's number, hoping to convince him to change his mind and come with them. But she hung up before his service picked up the call. Kevin wouldn't change his mind. He wouldn't be caught dead doing something as mundane as fishing. That wasn't his style.

For a moment Ivy reconsidered. How did fishing fit with her image of the new, sophisticated Ivy Enders? It didn't.

She decided she didn't care. Right now she didn't feel sophisticated. She felt like a small-town girl who had been victimized by the big city. Someone who suddenly felt a little shaky being on her own and needed to be with friends. And she didn't have a better friend than Eric North.

Ivy returned to her bedroom and dug out her old clothes. Despite the robbery, despite her anxiety over her upcoming nose job, she suddenly felt happy. It was going to be a wonderful day, exactly the kind of day she needed. She could almost taste the trout she planned to catch. And her faded jeans and old shirt were more comfortable than any of the fancy new clothes hanging in her closet. Of course, she would never have admitted that to Kevin McCallister.

Chapter Six

After watching Ivy a few minutes, Eric decided she was good, very good. There was control in her wrist action, confidence in the way she held the line and stood in her waders braced against the current. When casting, she alternated between dropping the artificial fly on the swift water or placing it along the quieter bank areas.

"Looks like you've done this before," he said, moving near so they could talk.

"You didn't believe me?" Shy pride lit her face as she cast the lure toward the center of the stream, then grinned at him.

They both leaned against the brisk cold current. Rushing water spilled around their waders. Bright sunshine spun gold through Ivy's hair and warmed her cheeks with color. At some point she had tucked a small bouquet of wild daisies in the collar of her faded shirt. It was all Eric could do not to stare at her. She had never seemed more beautiful than she did now dressed in waders and old clothes, the sunlight glowing on her hair and on her face.

"Why are you chuckling?" Ivy asked, smiling over her shoulder.

"I was thinking how wonderful you look, but it occurred to me that you probably wouldn't agree."

"Are you kidding? With no makeup and dressed in waders and one of my dad's old shirts?" She made a face. "Boy, are you easy to impress. Wait until you see my new clothes. Of course the jewelry is gone. The creeps took that."

"I thought we decided not to talk about the burglary."

"Maybe that was unrealistic." Tilting her head back, she gazed above the pines toward the majestic mountain peaks. "Talking about it here isn't as upsetting as talking about it in the middle of the destruction. There's something about all this—" she indicated the magnificent scenery "—that makes everything else seem insignificant. What did we lose after all? Nothing that can't be replaced." A smile curved her lips, which he noticed were pink even without lipstick. "Thanks for thinking of this. It was a good idea."

Moving slowly, discussing the items they had decided to replace from the burglary and the items they wouldn't, they worked their way upstream. The point wasn't to catch fish and both tacitly recognized this. The point was to relax and put the world at a comfortable distance for a while until they could regain a little of their previous perspective.

"Seriously, Ivy, where did you learn to cast like that?"

When she smiled, Eric tried not to stare. But she was dazzling today. As natural and lovely as the wildflowers nodding along the river bank. Trust him to prefer a centerfold from *Field and Stream* to one from *Playboy,* he thought, grinning. But dressed as she was, Ivy was more of a turn-on today than she would have been dressed in a glitzy gown and swathed in fur. Sometimes he thought men and women were hopelessly misaligned in their attitudes. This wasn't a new thought, but one that had long ago convinced him God must have an impish sense of humor.

"My father and I used to fish when I was a kid," Ivy explained. Her wrist and forearm moved in smooth unison and her fly sailed toward the swift current tumbling over the rocks marking the center of the stream. "Each year after the crop was in, Mom and Pop would take Iris and me camping. It was the closest thing we had to family vacation." She smiled. "Mom and Iris don't like to fish, but Dad and I loved it."

"My family camped, too. The part I liked best, aside from the fishing, was sitting around the fire at night."

"Telling stories?"

"I heard all the Edgar Rice Burroughs stories sitting around a camp fire. Remember the John Carter stories? John Carter goes to Mars? And all the others?"

"I read the John Carter books—and loved them—in high school."

"I believed my dad made them up. I didn't discover Burroughs was the author until years later. Ginna and I thought Dad was a born storyteller." He grinned.

Ivy had a bite and gave a shout, but the trout wriggled off the line. "Tell me about Ginna," she said as she reeled in and changed lures.

"You'd like her and she'd like you. In many ways, you're a lot alike. But until we were in high school, I thought she was a pain in the neck. Like most kid sisters."

"Watch it, fella. You're talking to a kid sister."

"She sews, like you, and can bake a peach pie that tastes like heaven. Can you bake a peach pie?"

"Probably not as well as Ginna. But I bake a pecan pie that melts in your mouth. Come Thanksgiving I'll show you."

He liked the thought. "Ginna dropped out of college to marry Rob Weedle. They live in Pittsburgh. Right now they're having a rough time of it. But Rob's bright and ambitious and so is Ginna. They'll land on their feet."

She looked at him. "Do you miss her?"

"A lot." He adjusted his line, glanced behind him to judge the space for casting then dropped his fly near a quiet pool. "Especially lately. Talking to Ginna always helped me sort out what I was thinking."

"That's how it is with Iris and me. Iris has a way of putting things in perspective. When I first moved to Denver, I talked to her once a week on the phone. But lately, well ... she and Frank are busy getting moved to their new place, and I'm busy, too." Ivy focused on the far bank and her voice softened. "I miss her. Iris is probably my best friend."

They fished in silence for a while, following the curves of the stream, enjoying the sunshine and the mountain air. At midday, they left the water and walked along the highway back to where they had left the car. Eric spread a plaid blanket over a grassy spot near the river bank and Ivy laid out sandwiches, cheese and apples.

"Are you too sophisticated now to have a beer?" Shortly after they arrived, he had placed several cans in the river to chill.

"On a day like this I'd rather have a Coors than champagne. But don't tell Kevin I said that." They both laughed. "I can't imagine Kevin fishing, can you?"

"He doesn't know what he's missing." Settling his back against the white trunk of an aspen, Eric bit into a roast-beef sandwich and took a long, icy swallow of beer. "Life doesn't get much better than this."

Ivy shook out her hair and tilted her face upward to the sun. "Right now I'd agree with you. This is heaven."

"Right now?"

"I wouldn't want to go fishing everyday, but it's great right now. Just what the doctor ordered. I'd forgotten air could smell this crisp and clean."

"What would you rather do everyday?" He cut the wheel of yellow cheese into wedges and offered one to her.

"Ah, the big question: how do rich people fill their days?" A furrow appeared between her eyes and she lowered her head to look at the cheese. "I haven't figured that out yet." After a pause she lifted her head. "Have you?"

He had given the question a great deal of thought recently. "I'm not sure what I want to do with the rest of my life, but I'm beginning to recognize things I don't want to do."

"Like what?"

Instead of answering immediately, he collected the sandwich wrappers and opened fresh beers for them both.

Ivy stretched out on her stomach, holding the beer between her hands as she watched him settle back against the tree trunk. "Are you hedging, Dumbo?"

He laughed, enjoying her company, enjoying the day. Most of all he enjoyed their easy companionship. He couldn't remember when they had progressed from the shy care one employed with strangers to the more intimate ease of friendship. It had happened gradually enough that he hadn't taken notice.

"You sound like Ginna, Ms. Cyrano."

"Thanks." She looked pleased. "I think this is where Ginna would say: stop beating around the bush and tell me everything. What do you hate most about being rich?"

He returned her grin, then leaned his head against the tree trunk and let the grin fade. "I don't think I'm cut out to be retired. Sounds crazy, doesn't it? Everyone dreams of retiring young, but I'm discovering I don't like it."

"That doesn't sound crazy, not really." Rolling onto her back, she held the beer against her stomach and closed her eyes against the sunshine. Her hair fell in silky ripples over the plaid blanket. "Want to hear something just as crazy? Every now and then I find myself wondering if Hedley Greene's claim got settled, and who Mr. Batterson hired in my place, and if Doris is watering the plant on my old desk. Sometimes I ask myself why I'm taking tennis lessons and golf lessons, if I'm just filling up the days. I hate golf."

He didn't laugh because he had decided he hated golf, too. "It's uncomfortable waking up without an office to go to, without a sense of purpose. I seem to spend most days looking for new ways to kill time. And some of those ways are more frustrating than pleasurable."

"I suppose we have to give it more time," Ivy said finally. "Kevin was right. You and I don't know how to play. We haven't had the time before, or the money to do it."

"I don't think time is going to change my attitudes, Ivy. I doubt I'm ever going to be fully comfortable having recess every day. I don't know if I'm saying this well, but full-time playing seems a waste to me." He tasted his beer and frowned at the blanket. "For the first time I'm starting to understand my father. For years I've wondered why he didn't sell the orchards and retire to a condominium in Florida. Now I'm beginning to understand that retirement is damned boring."

"Maybe you need a project."

"As a matter of fact, I have something in mind." Immediately he bit his tongue. He hadn't intended to tell anyone. The sunshine and the relaxed companionship had lulled him into a confidence he hadn't intended to make.

As if she sensed the conversation had become important, Ivy sat up, crossed her legs Indian fashion, and studied him. "Well, give. What are you considering?"

For the first time he felt uncomfortable with the conversation. "You'll probably think this is foolish."

"Try me. We're good-enough friends to trust each other, aren't we?"

That's what he'd been telling himself all day. He drew a breath. "Well, I've been thinking about writing a book."

To his relief, she didn't laugh. "That's a great idea. What's your book about?"

"I'm not planning the great American novel or anything like that. I was thinking about a book on fishing in the

Rockies. I thought I'd combine practical tips with a bit of humor, that kind of thing."

Maybe everyone, he thought, who read as much as he did eventually wondered if he could write a book. In the past there hadn't been time to pursue the possibility. But now that he had more leisure than he knew what to do with, attempting a book seemed a better use of his time than knocking a tiny ball around a golf course.

"Have you started yet?"

One of the nicest things about Ivy was the way she listened, really listened. Most people didn't listen well. Instead they seemed only to be waiting for their chance to talk. But Ivy wasn't like that. When Eric spoke, she watched his eyes and his expression, listened to the nuances and the emotion behind the words. She made a connection.

There was nothing secluded about the spot they had chosen for lunch. A few yards away cars whizzed past on the highway, a few hikers went by, another fisherman worked the far side of the river. But when Ivy looked at him, focused her entire attention on him as she was doing now, it felt as if they were alone, as if there were no other people in the world.

"I have some notes. At least I did before my computer was stolen. Whoever took the computer also got my notes."

"Tell me what you remember."

Because writing was a new endeavor, he felt awkward and a little vulnerable telling her about his ideas for the book. He should have known better. In a moment she was offering enthusiastic suggestions and in another few minutes they were arguing mildly about how the book should be structured and presented.

"Thanks for the help," he said later, tucking away the notes he had made. Some of her suggestions were excellent. "Are you ready for another try at a trophy trout? We aren't exactly setting records today."

"Actually the sun and the air and the conversation have made me lazy. I'd rather talk about your eventual bestsell-erdom. Is that a word?" Stretching out, she rested her head on his thigh and crossed her feet at the ankles. "This is great. Do you mind?"

"Not at all." He would have submitted to torture before admitting that her head on his thigh made him feel uncom-fortably warm. Odd thoughts intruded on the ease he'd felt earlier with her. He stared at the spill of golden brown hair waving across his lap. Then he leaned his head back against the aspen and closed his eyes.

"Enough about my book. Let's talk about you. How do you feel about being retired? Does being a lady of leisure agree with you? What is Ivy Enders looking for?"

"I'd rather take a nap," she said drowsily.

"No fair."

"What am I looking for?" she said after a minute. "I don't know. The usual things, I guess. Someday a husband and a family. A sewing room. A dog and cat. That sounds dull, doesn't it?" She frowned at the sky. "I also want to travel and be part of the beautiful people. I suppose that's what the nose job and the contacts and the jogging is all about."

"I imagine a few of the beautiful people have husbands and families, cats and dogs. That doesn't seem incompati-ble."

"Thanks, but a settled family life isn't what people usu-ally think of when they think about people like Kevin and his friends. They think of glamour and exciting parties and exotic places and interesting people. I want to be part of that excitement." She adjusted her head against his thigh and studied the sky. "I used to read about that kind of life when I lived in Limon, yearn for it maybe, without ever believing I could actually be part of it."

This was an area where they didn't agree, but Eric didn't tell her that. From what he had seen, he suspected he didn't fit into a glamorous life-style and he was beginning to understand he didn't want to. Some of the people he'd met through Kevin were interesting, true, but most weren't. Most were concerned with subjects Eric privately considered trivial, and many effected a permanent facade of boredom. Boredom wasn't a quality Eric admired. Nor was the seemingly constant search for fresh stimulation, fresh experience.

"It's there if you want it, Ivy," he said at length, trying not to think about her hair flowing across his lap.

"I don't know." She looked up at him then dropped her gaze. "I'm tugged in two directions; I haven't worked my feelings out yet. And I guess I'm a little apprehensive about life in the fast lane. The only fast lane in Limon is a jogging path." He saw her bite her lip as if she was considering whether or not she trusted him enough to say more. "Have you seen those women sunbathing on Kevin's balcony? Sometimes they don't wear anything." Before he could comment, she rushed on, "Things like that make me feel very, very small townish."

"There's nothing wrong with small-town values."

"But how do they fit into the world of the beautiful people?" She stared up at him. "How do I fit into that world? I've never even—" She stopped abruptly and looked away, pressing her lips together.

"Never even what?"

"Never mind. I can't tell you."

It wasn't the words that hurt, it was knowing she didn't trust him. This, after he had confided his intention to attempt a book. Sitting up, she looked at his expression and swore beneath her breath.

All right, he had made a mistake. He had assumed the trust was mutual. Feeling foolish, he made a small production of pushing back his cuff and looking at his watch. "Well," he said, sounding stiff even to himself, "maybe we should think about starting back."

"Look, I'd tell you except . . . it's just that . . ."

Lifting a hand, he waved her to silence as if it was no big deal, but the hurt was in his tone. "Hey, if you don't want to talk about something, it's okay."

"It's not okay. You think I don't trust you or something. But that isn't it."

For a moment he studied her crimson cheeks, then he tossed their empty beer cans into the sack. "You'll do fine in the world of the beautiful people," he said, putting a finish to the topic. If she didn't want to tell him, that was her choice.

"No, I won't, because . . . dammit . . . because I'm a virgin."

She said it in a low mumble and he almost thought he had misunderstood her. Her flaming face told him he hadn't.

Anger and embarrassment deepened the crimson in her cheeks. "There, you made me say it."

"I didn't make—"

"Yes, you did. If I hadn't told you, you'd have thought it was because I didn't trust you, not because it embarrasses me to death!" She closed her eyes. "And it does."

"Ivy . . ." He had no idea what he had expected, but this wasn't it. "Hey, look . . ." But he didn't have the faintest notion of what to say.

She opened her eyes, but didn't look at him. "So how am I going to fit into a sophisticated world where women sunbathe nude without a thought, and casual sex is a given?" When she finally looked at him, her expression was defensive. "It isn't like I planned to be a virgin at my age. I had opportunities, plenty of them—"

"Ivy, for God's sake. You don't have to explain anything." To his irritation, a flush of color spread across his own cheeks. Her embarrassment was catching.

"You know what it's like in a small town. Everyone knows everyone's business. And I lived at home. I didn't want everyone whispering and gossiping about me, embarrassing my parents. So I just . . ." Her voice trailed off and she threw up her hands. "Then after a while, I guess I attached certain standards or maybe fantasies to the whole business." Her face was the color of a cherry. "I didn't want it to happen in a car or anywhere that might seem tacky. I wanted it to be special. Is that so awful?"

"Of course not." He liked the idea that she hadn't been with anyone else. The fact of her virginity was surprising, but not the reasons behind it. Everything she had said about small towns was true. Affairs were common knowledge, discussed with relish over bridge tables and bingo cards. Secrets weren't safe. "I admire you for not wanting to be the target of gossips." The statement was meant to be reassuring because he sensed she needed reassurance. But it was a sad comment on the state of the world that anyone needed to be assured virginity was acceptable.

The defensive look was still in her eyes. "I know I'm being old-fashioned about this, but I want the first time to be something wonderful."

"There's nothing wrong with that."

"I want it to be romantic. Soft music and a fire in a fireplace. Champagne and iced caviar. Most of all, I don't want it to be impulsive or casual. I want it to be with a man I love and a man who loves me."

"Ivy, you don't have to convince me, and you don't have to be defensive. This is me, Eric, remember? Your friend." Reaching, he took her hand and held it, partly because he didn't know what else to do, partly because he felt a need to touch her. But touching her made him want to hold her.

At first her hand remained rigid and unresponsive in his. Then slowly she relaxed and squeezed his fingers.

"I can't believe I told you all that," she said, dropping her head. That was the understatement of the year. She hadn't even told Cass Myers that she was still a virgin. After drawing a deep breath, Ivy managed a wobbly smile. "If you ever tell anyone about this, I promise I'll find you and strangle you. There's no place you can hide—the world isn't big enough."

A relieved smile lifted his expression and she realized this hadn't been a comfortable conversation for Eric, either.

"The Grand Inquisitor himself couldn't drag this out of me," he said. "If anybody should ask, I'll swear you've slept with half the men in Denver."

She stared at him, then burst into laughter. Whatever awkwardness had intruded between them vanished. "You don't have to go quite that far," she said, grinning at him.

"Hey, it's no trouble at all. Anything to help a friend."

They smiled and suddenly Ivy felt very close to him. She'd had male friends before, but none she had trusted enough to speak to as frankly as she had spoken to Eric. None to whom she had confided the secret of her virginity.

"This is what it must feel like to have a brother. Thanks, Eric, for being my friend." She pressed his hand, grateful for the strength she found there. "Thanks for listening and . . . and good luck with your book. I hope it sells a million copies."

"I appreciate that, and I wish you the same. Good luck with your . . . well, you know what I mean."

This time they both laughed. Then, their easy companionship restored, they cleaned up the remains of their picnic and returned the blanket to the trunk of Ivy's car, and packed away the fishing gear.

"When do you get your car back?" Ivy asked, as she guided the Cadillac up the ramp onto the highway and back toward Denver.

"Tomorrow, I hope."

"Should have bought a Cadillac," she said smugly, teasing him. He pulled his cap down over his eyes and settled back, ignoring her and pretending to take a nap.

Smiling, Ivy pushed in a Willie Nelson tape and thought how nice it was that they were comfortable enough with each other that Eric could nap and leave the driving to her. They didn't feel the need to make conversation just to fill a silence. She liked that.

She wished she had that kind of relationship with Kevin. But Kevin wasn't comfortable with silence. He had to fill the gaps with conversation even if the conversation was trivial and led nowhere. As for confiding in Kevin, she would like to have felt that close to him, but she could no more imagine telling him she was still a virgin than she could imagine herself sunbathing nude on his balcony.

The realization troubled her. After thinking it through while she drove, she finally admitted she didn't trust Kevin's reaction. She didn't think he would actually laugh at her, but he would be astonished; consequently she would feel hopelessly out of step with his world. And she was, she knew it. Her attitudes about sex were about as up-to-date as dinosaurs. The part of her that wanted to be admired by Kevin McCallister was worried.

If her relationship with Kevin progressed as she hoped it would, eventually she would have to tell him.

By the time she rounded a curve and spotted the band of smog overhanging Denver, Ivy decided she was being unfair to Kevin. She was assuming an attitude that probably didn't exist. Most likely Kevin would be as understanding and as sensitive as Eric had been. Of course he would be.

Smiling, she parked the car and gently shook Eric's shoulder. "Wake up. We're home."

He opened his eyes and smiled at her, softly, as if she were part of a dream he was still enjoying. "Hi." Then he came fully awake and sat up and rubbed his chin. "I was out like a light. Sorry."

"No problem, I enjoyed the drive."

"Well," he said, as they carried their gear inside the tower, "are you ready to face the mess?"

"More ready than I was." Stopping before her door, she smiled up at him. "Thanks for a terrific day."

He looked down at her and for a moment she thought he might hug her. And she suddenly wanted him to. But their arms were filled with sacks and fishing gear. "Anytime."

"Do you want to go shopping tomorrow? I'd like to have everything in order before my nose job."

"What? And miss a golf lesson? I'd love to!" He managed to free two fingers enough to wave, then he moved down the corridor toward his apartment.

Ivy watched him go, smiling after him. Eric North was a very nice and very special man. She wondered if he was dating the redhead Kevin teased him about. Something akin to jealousy tightened her lips for a moment. How odd. But the feeling persisted and she shook it off with difficulty.

"LORD," KEVIN GROANED, pushing open Ivy's door and staggering inside. "I've seen some shopping sprees in my time, but this was an all-time great! Where shall I put these boxes? I can't even remember what we bought."

"Put the boxes on the counter, please." Inhaling the scent of new paint, Ivy leaned to inspect the living-room wall, then nodded with satisfaction. "The painters are finished. Good. Let's see, we bought two TV sets, a VCR, and stereo equipment." She dropped the parcels she was carrying on the sofa and rubbed her arms. "I remember a couple of pieces of jewelry, a lamp, a few kitchen appliances, china and silver. Did I miss anything?''

''The sewing machine.'' Kevin stuck his head out into the corridor. ''Eric? Mix up a pitcher of martinis. We'll be there in a minute.'' He looked back at Ivy. ''You aren't going to put all this away right now, are you? I need a drink. I cannot believe I was party to the purchase of a sewing machine. It was a horrifying experience. Do you think anyone saw us?''

Ivy laughed. ''I doubt any of your friends frequent such places. Your reputation remains intact.''

''You know you aren't going to sew a stitch ever again, Ivy darling. So why are you so stubborn? You need a sewing machine like you need a vacuum cleaner.''

''I don't need a vacuum cleaner?'' Now that they had replaced the stolen items and were home again, a weariness stole up on her.

''Your cleaning lady needs a vacuum cleaner. You don't. What time is it? I'm taking Mummy to the summer symphony tonight and Mummy hates it when I'm late. Do you suppose Eric has the martinis mixed yet? Come along, Ivy, all this will wait. Are you worried about your nose job?''

Throwing up her hands, Ivy laughed. ''One thing at a time.'' She followed him out the door and down the corridor to Eric's apartment. ''What time do you have to be at your mother's?''

''Thank heavens!'' Lifting the martini Eric had waiting on the counter, Kevin drained it and extended his goblet for another. ''Seven-thirty—shockingly early. Well, look at this. Everything's in order. One would never guess you'd had a burglary.''

''Seven-thirty?'' Eric asked. ''Did I miss something?''

''Mummy and the symphony. Boring. I'd rather be at Cheek's party. Are you going? He said he invited you.''

''No, I thought I'd turn in early tonight.''

"That's right, ears and nose tomorrow, right? And you two want to be rested for the ordeal." Kevin raised his goblet in a toast. "To the new beautiful you, both of you."

"Here's to Cyrano and Dumbo," Ivy echoed, smiling.

Eric grinned at her. "To their timely demise."

"Let's see, you're just in and out, right?" Kevin asked Eric. Eric nodded. "But you're in the hospital for two nights?" he asked Ivy.

"Three nights. I check in the night before surgery then come home two days later."

"You can't drive yourself, of course. I'd be happy to have Walter drive you. I would myself, but I'm not good with sick people. So depressing." He said it so cheerfully that Ivy smiled. "Will your family be here?"

"No, I haven't told them I'm doing this."

"It's best that way. Family is such a bore."

"Actually—"

"Well, kiddos, I have to run. Can't keep Mummy waiting." A quick kiss grazed Ivy's cheek and he waved to Eric. "Good luck tomorrow. I'll be thinking about you both."

When he had gone, Ivy sank into a chair and propped her feet on the coffee table. "I'm so tired, I don't think I can move."

"I'll decorate around you."

She smiled. "Are you concerned about the ear surgery?"

"It's a simple procedure. The worst part is afterward. I understand I'll have to wear bandages wrapped around my head to keep my ears from moving."

"For how long?"

"Only a couple of days. Then I have to wear a stocking cap to bed for a few weeks." He leaned on the counter and looked at her. "How about you? Yours is a more serious procedure. Are you worried or frightened?"

"No," Ivy lied. "Not at all."

She looked so brave and so anxious that he wanted to take her in his arms. He didn't. But it occurred to him that he'd been having a lot of thoughts like that lately.

Chapter Seven

When the hospital attendants came with the gurney to wheel Ivy downstairs, she stared at them with wide eyes and a heart that was pounding like a threshing machine.

"You know," she commented faintly, as they transferred her to the gurney, "this nose really isn't so bad." No one paid her any attention. They wheeled her out into the corridor and toward the elevators.

She squeezed her eyes shut and tried not to remember what her doctor had said when he described the operation. It would be performed through the nostrils so there would be no visible scarring. The procedure sounded awful.

"Hi." Her doctor looked down at her from over his surgical mask. "We're going to put you to sleep now."

She tried to explain that she had changed her mind, that she had conceived a sudden and passionate affection for her old nose. But the words blurred and slurred and trailed into a series of incoherent sounds.

When Ivy opened her eyes, she was in a room with several other gurneys and inert figures. A white-capped face smiled at her, and reassured, she closed her eyes again.

The next time she awoke, she was back in her room in bed. And she felt as if a balloon supported by scaffolding was stuck on her face where her nose should have been. Her eyes crossed as she tried to see the splints and bandages.

Surprisingly she was experiencing very little pain. The packing in her nostrils was acutely uncomfortable, but not really painful.

A nurse brought her a mild sedative, she dozed, and later she sucked on ice chips as breathing through her mouth had dried her throat. And slowly the excitement built. She couldn't wait to see her new nose.

"You can't see anything yet," the nurse explained. "The packing won't come out until tomorrow and the splint stays on for another week."

"How about the swelling?" Her voice sounded thick and nasal.

"The worst of it will disappear in about a week or ten days. So will the bruising. But the swelling won't disappear entirely for at least three months." The nurse held up a hand and smiled at Ivy's stricken expression. "Don't worry, the residual swelling is so minimal only you will be aware of it."

Bruising? What bruising? Ivy waited until evening then she slipped out of bed, careful not to jar anything, and entered the bathroom. What she saw in the mirror shocked her. She looked as if she had been in one hell of a fight.

Both her eyes were blackened and swollen. She was wearing a nose diaper, for want of a better description, that caught the tiny drops of blood oozing from her nostrils. Her nose, what little she could see of it, was grotesquely swollen under the bandages and splint work.

"Oh, my God." Considering how ghastly she looked, she couldn't believe she wasn't suffering terrible pain.

"Ivy?"

Oh, no. She closed her blackened eyes and leaned on the sink.

"Ivy? It's Eric. Are you in there?"

"Eric? What are you doing here?" she called in the thick nasal voice, wishing she were hallucinating. The last thing she wanted was to have him see her like this.

"I came to check on you. I brought you some magazines and books."

After a long pause Ivy drew a breath. "Are we good-enough friends that you would understand if I asked you to just leave the magazines and go? I don't want anyone to see me."

"Not a chance, Cyrano. We're good-enough friends that I don't care what you look like. I care about you. Come on out."

It was what she would have expected from him, and it was a quality she admired. Only not right now. Right now she wished he would just go away. "I'll be out in a minute." She drew another long breath through her dry mouth. "Ah, is Kevin with you?" If he was, nothing on earth was going to get her through the bathroom door.

There was a hesitation. "Kevin had some family business to attend to. It's just me."

Thank heaven for small favors. Gathering her courage and hating this, Ivy placed her hand on the latch. She reminded herself that no one she knew of had ever died of embarrassment, then she wet her lips and opened the door.

"Good God!" Eric stared at her over a bouquet of roses. "You look awful!"

Didn't she know it. After getting back in bed, she clasped her hands on top of the blanket and examined him. "You look pretty weird yourself," she said irritably. A bandage wound over his head and ears. "Shades of the mummy."

"Seriously, Ivy, do you feel as bad as you look?" He continued to stare at her. "Should I call someone for a pain pill or something?"

She would have laughed, except laughter would have jiggled her nose and she already knew how much that hurt. "There isn't much pain. I feel fine."

Plainly he didn't believe her. "Honestly?"

"Honestly. I feel pretty good except my mouth is dry. How do you feel?"

"Terrific. Eager to see what's under the bandages." Slowly, he sat on the chair next to the bed and leaned forward, studying her. "That has got to hurt."

"The packing is uncomfortable and I'm aware of the splint and bandages, but I'm really feeling okay. Honestly, Eric. I'd tell you if I was hurting. I'm the type who thinks a hangnail is a big deal."

His expression indicated he believed she was being very brave. "When do you get to see the results?"

Now that it was over, she was eager to talk about the operation. Getting a new nose wasn't done the way she had imagined. For some reason, she'd had an idea that she would leaf through a book of photos and pick out the nose she wanted. But it wasn't done that way. She and the doctor had identified her problem and he had told her how it could be corrected. Her new nose would be her old nose, only without the imperfections.

Responding to Eric's interest and feeling better about his visit, she explained that she had to remain in bed for two days and keep her head elevated to minimize any bleeding. She could only eat soft foods and liquids. And she wouldn't he able to participate in any physical sports for at least three, maybe four, weeks.

"Lucky you, having a good excuse to miss golf." He looked at her and smiled. "You really do look godawful."

"Thanks a lot." She returned his smile. Carefully. "So tell me about your operation."

"Nothing to tell. It was done in the doctor's office. If I'd known it was this easy and painless, I'd have had my ears done years ago."

"I know you won't believe this, but—"

He raised a hand. "I know, you don't think I needed them done in the first place. But you aren't the one the other kids called Dumbo. And you didn't tape your ears back before you went to bed."

"You did that?"

"When I was a kid. I thought I could train them to lie flat. It didn't work."

"Oh, lord, Eric, stop making those faces every time you look at me. I don't dare laugh. I'm already living in fear of a sneeze."

"Do you want me to leave?"

Now that the embarrassment of having him see her had been faced, Ivy could admit she was glad he had come. She reached for his hand and pressed it. "No. Just stop making those weird faces."

He squeezed her hand. "What do you want first—more ice chips or your phone messages?"

"Ice chips, please. My throat feels like sandpaper."

The phone messages weren't urgent. And she thanked him for watering her plants, which she had forgotten to do. Then the nurse brought Ivy some ice cream and Eric a cup of coffee and they watched TV until visiting hours ended.

"Thanks for coming," she said as he prepared to depart. She looked up at him through her puffy, blackened eyes. "Eric, if you see Kevin will you tell him I'd rather he didn't come by until the splint comes off? I know it sounds vain, but I don't want him to see me like this."

His expression stilled for a moment, then he smiled and released her hand. "Sure. I'll tell him."

ERIC TOLD HIMSELF it didn't matter that Ivy didn't mind if he saw her looking like hell but didn't want Kevin to see her that way. But it bothered him. Just as it bothered him that Kevin didn't override Ivy's protests and make an effort to stop by her apartment when she returned home from the hospital. Kevin filled her apartment with flowers and phoned every day, but he didn't come by in person. Eric thought he should have.

"Eric? Can you reach the volume on the answering machine? It might be Kevin."

They were in Ivy's apartment. She was stretched out on the sofa reading, and he was making notes for his book. Every day her eyes looked better; the puffiness had gone and the color had almost faded. They both believed the swelling had abated beneath the splint and bandages.

Now that she was home, she could have managed on her own, but he liked doing things for her—making the coffee, tidying the apartment, sparing her any motion that might have jiggled her nose. Plus, he enjoyed discussing his book ideas with her as they occurred to him. Once or twice, as they were reading together, or later watching television, it occurred to him that he had never felt this comfortable with a woman.

Somewhere along the line he had accepted the idea that a relationship had to be kept alive with activity—movies, dinners, sports. He hadn't realized how nice it was to do nothing with someone. To spend the hours quietly and relaxed, but knowing she was there if he wanted to comment on something in a book or a favorite TV program. To share a look, or an occasional brush of fingers.

"Eric? You're nearer the machine than I am. Would you mind terribly...?"

"Sorry, I was daydreaming." Reaching, he turned up the volume and Kevin's bright chatter filled the living room.

"Hello to the housebound! You're missing some wonderful parties, both of you. Eric, your favorite redhead is pouting because you've gone into hiding. Ivy darling, all the arrangements for Cannes are in place. We'll launch the new you there. If you haven't bought a daring new swimsuit yet, we'll make that the first item on the agenda when you emerge. When does the splint come off? Not this afternoon, I hope. Daddy insists I be present for the ground breaking of another McCallister building. Poor Daddy. He does keep trying. No, don't pick up the phone, there's nothing more to tell. Ta-ta, kiddos, see you soon."

"Has Kevin seen your ears?" Ivy asked after Eric turned the volume off. "What does he think?"

"I'm more interested in what you think."

She tilted her head and laid a finger against the nose splint. "You know, I really thought you were making a big deal out of nothing, but now that it's done, I think I see what you meant. You're even more handsome than you were. And I like your new haircut. The shorter style looks good on you."

He lifted his head and turned away from the coffeepot to stare at her. He hadn't known she thought he was handsome. Apparently she considered the description self-evident, as she didn't seem to think she had said anything out of the ordinary. She had resettled herself into the corner of the sofa and returned to the book she was reading. He studied her for a moment, running his eyes from her bare toes up her designer jeans to the curve of a summer sweater and then to the splint that dominated her face. Since she couldn't shampoo until the splint came off, she was wearing a scarf around her hair. He wished he had a photo of her like this, relaxed and at ease with herself.

So, she thought he was handsome. After checking to be certain she was engrossed in her book, he bent and tried to see his reflection in the shiny surface of the toaster. For once in his life the first thing he saw was not his ears. Feeling good—feeling great, in fact—he poured the coffee and carried two mugs into the living room. He wished he had the nerve to ask her exactly what it was about him that she considered handsome.

"Thanks," Ivy said, looking up as he placed her mug on the coffee table. Frowning, she closed her book on her stomach and tasted the coffee. "Why do you suppose Kevin fights his father so hard? I'd think he would be interested in McCallister Enterprises. Why do you think he isn't?"

Eric shrugged and crossed his feet on the ottoman. "I don't know." He had considered the question often enough to believe that in Kevin's place he would have done things very differently.

"Do you think it could be because there's no challenge? His grandfather and his father fought the good fight and made the fortune and now there are no challenges left?"

"I would imagine there is a certain amount of challenge in preserving a fortune, keeping it intact." Sensing Ivy's hero worship, he spoke carefully.

"You mean he may be afraid of the challenge?"

"Possibly. I don't know."

After considering that, Ivy chuckled and carefully shook her head. "I don't think so. I can't imagine Kevin being afraid of anything. More likely he's rebelling against his parents, or maybe McCallister Enterprises is simply a business that doesn't appeal to him."

After a while Eric carried his mug out onto the balcony and leaned on the railing, looking up toward Kevin's penthouse. Although Kevin had never mentioned how old he was, Eric guessed they were about the same age, well beyond the years of parental rebellion. As to Ivy's suggestion that McCallister Enterprises didn't appeal, he doubted any business would appeal to Kevin. At least he'd never displayed an inclination in that direction.

Many of Kevin's friends were involved in business. Several were stockbrokers, lawyers, or engaged in family-held businesses. Kevin seemed to prefer the minority that appeared content to drift through life with no discernible purpose.

Perhaps, Eric thought, that explained why Kevin McCallister had taken up with Ivy and himself. Kevin needed someone to keep him amused while his other friends toiled in the market, the courts, or behind a plush office desk. The possibility made him uncomfortable, as if he and Ivy were exotic pets, merely a new diversion.

"Eric!" Ivy appeared in the balcony doorway, her eyes sparkling above the bandages. "The mail just came and look! My passport!" Holding the blue book against her breast, she spun in a circle then stopped and covered her nose. "It's all going to happen. We're really going to Europe! Can you imagine it?"

He grinned at her, enjoying her pleasure.

"You'll take Cannes by storm," he predicted. She was so heartachingly lovely.

"YOU CAN SHAMPOO NOW, but do it carefully, with your head back."

"Can I see it now?"

The doctor smiled. "In a minute. I think you'll be pleased." He adjusted her head this way and that, nodding. "It will take several months for the swelling to disappear entirely, but it's so minute no one will notice but you."

"Dr. Harris, please."

He led her to a three-way mirror and stepped back.

Ivy gasped and tears of happiness sprang into her eyes. "Oh, it's ... I'd hoped it would be like this, but I ... I don't know what to say, I just ..."

"I take it you like what you see?" Dr. Harris asked, laughing.

"I love it! I just ... I *love* it!"

IVY RUBBED HER HANDS nervously and glanced around her apartment. Everything was ready. She looked at her watch, then stared into the mirror near the front door. Every time she looked into the mirror, she felt a burst of wonder and amazement. The woman smiling back at her bore little resemblance to the Ivy Enders of old.

This woman was slimmer and more smartly dressed. Tonight she wore an off-the-shoulder, black shantung dress that curved over her breasts before dropping to a soft skirt that swirled around her legs when she moved. Her golden brown hair was feathered forward on one cheek, swept up behind her ear on the other side. Her eyes were large and dark, and since getting her contacts she'd learned to accent her long lashes with mascara and apply a sweep of smoky eyeshadow to her lids. And her nose, her wonderful new nose.

It wasn't Brooke Shields' nose; it was hers. This nose didn't overwhelm her face; it was the nose she should have been born with. Thin, delicate, unobtrusive.

Ivy stared at the girl in the mirror and thought she might have been examining a cover-girl model. The immodest thought raised a blush to her cheeks and she looked away. But not for long. The mirror drew her eyes like a magnet. Eventually she would become accustomed to this new image, but it hadn't happened yet. Each time she felt a little thrill of surprise when she glimpsed herself. Feeling wonderful, she laughed out loud.

Then she heard them in the corridor outside. Leaving the door opened a crack, she ran to her bedroom and stood in the darkness awaiting her grand entrance, smiling at nothing, smiling for the joy of smiling.

"We're here," Kevin called. "Let the celebration begin."

"Come out of hiding, Cyrano. Give us a look."

Drawing a breath, Ivy held her head high and strolled down the hallway to her living room. Good evening, gentlemen. May I offer you a drink?" She imagined this was the way Joan Collins would enter a room. And both Eric and Kevin looked as she imagined Joan Collins's suitors would look. Both were dressed in dark dinner jackets and silk cummerbunds for the occasion.

Kevin stepped back and whistled, his eyes wide. Behind him, Eric stared.

"Ivy darling, you're absolutely smashing! Beautiful! Good lord, girl, turn around—slowly—so we can see all of you. Are those the pearls we bought a few weeks ago? Look at that profile! You used to be a pastel type, but no longer. The black is wonderful on you. And textured stockings? My, we are stepping up and out, aren't we?"

Catching her around the waist, Kevin swung her into a waltz and danced her around the room. She felt her skirt flare around her legs and she threw back her head and laughed with happiness. Kevin thought she was beautiful and tonight, for the first time in her life, she felt beautiful.

When Kevin ended the dance, she looked up at Eric, her eyes bright and her cheeks flushed. "Well? What do you think?"

"Lovely," he said softly, looking down into her eyes.

For a long moment their gaze held and the color deepened in Ivy's cheeks. For some reason, Eric's one word meant more to her than Kevin's gushing. Perhaps it was because she believed Kevin would have been kind enough to gush even if she had emerged still looking like Cyrano. But Eric was forthright enough to tell her the truth.

"Thank you," she whispered.

"Will you two stop staring into each other's eyes? I'm getting jealous at being excluded. Come see what I brought for our celebration." Kevin opened a wicker hamper sitting on the counter. "First, Dom Perignon, perfectly chilled, of course. And caviar. Russian beluga." He dropped an arm around Ivy's waist and hugged her. "You said you were saving caviar for a special occasion, and this impresses me as being a very special occasion. Our Ivy emerges from her cocoon as a beautiful butterfly."

Ivy regarded the black caviar nestled in a silver ice dish then glanced quickly at Eric, remembering she had confided her special plans for her first taste of caviar. A fresh wave of heat colored her cheeks.

"Thank you, Kevin, but not tonight." At least she knew Eric had kept his promise; he hadn't told Kevin about her virginity and her fantasies.

"Tonight isn't special enough?" Kevin clapped a hand over his heart and stared at her in astonishment. "What could possibly be more special than the moment of your unveiling?"

Blushing furiously, Ivy glanced at Eric who was studying a point on the ceiling, a half smile playing about his lips.

Kevin noticed. "Is this a private joke or something?"

"No, no, nothing like that." Ivy touched his arm. "I'm just not ready for caviar yet. This isn't the right moment." She steadfastly refused to look at Eric again, knowing her blush would deepen to scarlet if she did. "But I would love some champagne. It's definitely a champagne occasion."

Kevin threw up his hands. "Women. Will we ever understand them? Remember when we first met her, Eric?" After peeling back the foil, he worked off the wire. "She seemed like such a compliant little thing. Who would have suspected this streak of stubbornness?"

"Somehow I sense the stubbornness is nothing new," Eric said, smiling. There was something in his eyes that caught Ivy and made her feel a little breathless. Perhaps it was the occasion, or perhaps it was the cut of his tuxedo, perfectly fitted over his wide shoulders. Off balance, she continued to return his steady gaze until the champagne cork flew off with a loud pop and bubbles foamed from the mouth of the bottle. Kevin filled the fluted glasses.

"To Ivy," Kevin said, raising his glass, "Denver's newest reigning beauty! And to Cannes and to great fun! To caviar and champagne and the good things in life!"

Eric touched his glass to hers and smiled into her eyes, the moment oddly private. "To Ivy."

Afterward they went to Mr. Blues, the hottest new club in town, the newest "in" spot. This time when people looked at them, Ivy felt they weren't looking only at Kevin and Eric. They were looking at her, too.

They ended the evening at three in the morning, four blocks from the Towers. Eric's Jaguar coughed, sputtered, then glided to the curb. He hit the wheel with his fist and swore while Kevin and Ivy laughed.

"This damned car spends more time in the shop than on the road." He climbed out and opened the door for Ivy.

"I think you got a lemon," Kevin agreed.

"We should have taken my car." Ivy grinned when Eric made a face at her.

Then they hooked arms and danced down the middle of the street, singing and laughing in the warm summer night.

"Didn't I see this scene in an old Gene Kelly movie?" Kevin asked.

"You're out of step, McCallister. Follow Ivy's lead. And try to sing on key."

"I'm doing harmony, old son. You must be tone-deaf."

Laughing, Ivy hugged their arms close to her and loved them both. It was the best night of her life. The very best.

Finally her life had begun. And it was as wonderful as she had dreamed it would be.

BECAUSE ERIC WAS BUSY organizing his book, she spent the next few weeks with Kevin, shopping for the clothes she would take to Cannes. Not daring to buy something without his approval, she pulled him from shop to shop, trying on this gown and that beach outfit, then stepping out of the dressing room to get his opinion.

"I'm exhausted," Ivy groaned when they stopped for lunch. Leaning her head back against the upholstered banquette, she closed her eyes. "Honestly, Kevin, we've been to six shops looking for just the right scarf. Does it really make that much difference?"

"Of course it does, Ivy darling. Accessories are the key to a put-together look." He glanced up at the waiter. "We'll both have a Scotch and soda."

"I'd rather have white wine," Ivy interrupted. She smiled at the waiter. "The house wine will do."

"My, my. How assertive we've become."

Ivy's brow rose. "Me? Do you think so?"

"I think our country mouse is rapidly becoming a city mouse."

"I'd forgotten about that," she said softly. "I suppose I have changed."

"Changed? That's an understatement, dear Ivy. You simply aren't the same person you were when we met."

"That's what Iris said."

"Ah, yes, I meant to ask about your weekend. How are things in . . . let's see, Limon, isn't it?"

She nodded then lowered her head and fussed with her cocktail napkin. The gesture was one the old Ivy Enders would have used. Smiling without humor, she moved her hands and clasped them in her lap.

"Everything's fine at home. Iris and Frank are settled and happy. Did I tell you Iris is expecting another baby?"

"Hooray." Smiling falsely, he twirled one finger in the air.

"You don't like babies?"

"No offense, darling, but having a passel of babies seems so middle-class, don't you think?"

"Two doesn't qualify as a passel, and Frank and Iris *are* middle-class." She lifted an eyebrow, then smiled. "You're a hopeless snob, did you know that?"

"Of course, darling. I work at it. Go on. What else exciting is happening in Limon?"

"It's going to be a good crop this year." Some of the light faded from her dark eyes. This was the first year she wouldn't be home for the harvest. The first year she wouldn't watch the combines moving through the fields, wouldn't smell the dust and chaff and cut green.

Harvest was the most exciting time of the year. It represented the culmination of months of back-breaking labor, months of hope and uneasy dreams. Farmers didn't refer to years as much as they referred to harvests. Her parents remembered things before or after the eighty-two harvest or the eighty-five harvest. And each year was the same. Each year as the combines lumbered into the fields, her parents would look at each other and they would say: "Maybe this year..."

This year Ivy would be in Cannes.

"Well? What did they think of the new you?"

"They were...surprised."

"Surprised?" Kevin rolled his eyes. "That's all? Surprised?"

She gazed into her wineglass remembering Iris's gasp and sudden silence, the strange shyness that had arisen between her and her sister. If she had needed additional proof that she had changed, Iris's reaction had provided it.

"You look...beautiful," Iris had said finally. "The clothes, your hair. Are you wearing contacts? I don't think I would have recognized you."

For the trip home she had worn a lime-colored linen suit, which Kevin had helped her select, and the pearls she loved so much. But it had been a mistake. She'd known that immediately when she saw Iris wearing jeans and a pink maternity blouse, even though Iris didn't need the maternity blouse yet. Ivy had felt grossly overdressed and uncomfortable. Her intention had been to show off a little for her family, but she had ended by overwhelming them.

"I don't know," she said, lifting her head to look at Kevin. "I made the changes gradually. You know, I lost the weight, got the contacts, then my hair and nose. The new clothes. I guess I had time to get accustomed to each step, but they didn't. I hit them with it all at once."

"Surely they approve. I mean, who wouldn't?"

"I think they approve. It's just that...I think maybe they're worried I'll get lost along the way."

"What nonsense." After glancing at the menu, he gave his order then cast her a pointed look. "I wouldn't dare order for you, darling."

"For which I thank you. I still haven't forgiven you for that Cajun lunch."

"Now then," Kevin said. "What's left on our list? Have we found the right shoes for your silver lamé? And did we remember the fox stole?"

She burst out laughing. "Maybe you can forget a fox stole, but I can't. I slept with it last night."

"How very—"

"Middle-class," she finished for him, laughing. "Do you realize how many suitcases I'll have to have to get all this to Cannes?" Her eyes widened. "Kevin, I don't have nearly enough luggage!" She groaned. "Add luggage to the list."

They continued discussing clothes through lunch then gossiped about people Kevin knew, who was seeing whom, who had worn what to which charity ball. Some of the people Ivy had met; most she hadn't. Many she would meet in Cannes.

"Everyone will be dying to know who you are," Kevin said. "What shall I tell them?"

"Is there a choice?"

"We could tell them you're one of the Bermuda Enders. Then they'll all think they know you and there won't be any awkward questions about your background."

"Oh, I see." In Kevin's world background was everything. A farmer's daughter from podunk didn't fit into the picture.

For one uncertain moment Ivy looked across the table and saw a stranger. Shining Prince Valiant hair, an impish grin, a crisp summer suit ordered from London. A man whose values sometimes surprised and startled her.

But she was beginning to understand them, a bit at a time. She understood enough to realize that, thanks to the Celtex Sweepstakes, she had the money, she had the clothing, and she had acquired the look, but she couldn't buy the background. Her mother wasn't a society belle, and she couldn't trace her ancestry back to the *Mayflower*.

"Tell your friends whatever you like," she said after a hesitation, understanding she had just agreed to become one of the Bermuda Enders. But she didn't feel good about it. Some of the lightness and pleasure faded from the afternoon.

That night, after slipping on her nightgown and creaming her face, Ivy stared into the mirror and surprised herself by trying to recognize vestiges of her old nose, the Enders family nose. But no traces remained. Oddly, that disturbed her.

"You're being silly," she said aloud. She loved her new nose and her new persona.

Changing her nose had changed other things, as well. For the better. Eric had been first to notice. A few days after the splint and bandages came off, he had watched her walking down the corridor to his apartment for their morning coffee and had remarked that she was walking differently. When she asked what he meant, he had said he wasn't certain, but he thought she held her shoulders differently. He thought she walked with an air of confidence that hadn't been present before.

. . . be tempted!

See inside for special
4 FREE BOOKS offer

 Harlequin American Romance®

Discover deliciously different romance with 4 Free Novels from

Harlequin American Romance ®

Sit back and enjoy four exciting romances—yours **FREE** from Harlequin Reader Service! But wait . . . there's *even more* to this great offer!

A Useful, Practical Digital Clock/Calendar—FREE

As a free gift simply to thank you for accepting four free books we'll send you a stylish digital quartz clock/calendar—a handsome addition to any decor! The changeable, month-at-a-glance calendar pops out, and may be replaced with a favorite photograph.

PLUS A FREE MYSTERY GIFT—a surprise bonus that will delight you!

All this just for trying our Reader Service!

MONEY-SAVING HOME DELIVERY

Once you receive 4 FREE books and gifts, you'll be able to preview more great romance reading in the convenience of your own home at less than retail prices. Every month we'll deliver 4 brand-new Harlequin American Romance novels right to your door months before they appear in stores. If you decide to keep them, they'll be yours for only $2.49 each! That's 26¢ less per book than the retail price—with no additional charges for home delivery. And you may cancel at any time, for any reason, and still keep your free books and gifts, just by dropping us a line!

SPECIAL EXTRAS—FREE

You'll also get our newsletter with each shipment, packed with news of your favorite authors and upcoming books—FREE! And as a valued reader, we'll be sending you additional free gifts from time to time—as a token of our appreciation.

BE TEMPTED! COMPLETE, DETACH AND MAIL YOUR POSTPAID ORDER CARD TODAY AND RECEIVE 4 FREE BOOKS, A DIGITAL CLOCK/CALENDAR AND MYSTERY GIFT—PLUS LOTS MORE!

A FREE
Digital Clock/Calendar
and Mystery Gift *await you, too!*

Harlequin American Romance®

Harlequin Reader Service®
901 Fuhrmann Blvd., P.O. Box 1867, Buffalo, NY14240-9952

☐ **YES!** Please rush me my four Harlequin American Romance novels with my FREE Digital Clock/Calendar and Mystery Gift. As explained on the opposite page, I understand that I am under no obligation to purchase any books. The free books and gifts remain mine to keep.

154 CIH NBA8

NAME _____ (please print)

ADDRESS _____ APT. _____

CITY _____ STATE _____ ZIP CODE _____

Offer limited to one per household and not valid to current American Romance subscribers. Prices subject to change.

HARLEQUIN READER SERVICE "NO-RISK" GUARANTEE

- There's no obligation to buy—and the free books and gifts remain yours to keep.
- You pay the lowest price possible and receive books before they appear in stores.
- You may end your subscription anytime—just write and let us know.

NO POSTAGE
NECESSARY
IF MAILED
IN THE
UNITED STATES

BUSINESS REPLY CARD

First Class   Permit No. 717   Buffalo, NY

Postage will be paid by addressee

Harlequin Reader Service
901 Fuhrmann Blvd.
P.O. BOX 1867
BUFFALO, NY 14240-9952

Since then she had tried to notice how she walked, and she had concluded Eric was correct. She did carry herself differently. She held her shoulders back, and when she met someone, she looked them squarely in the eye, no longer worried they might be criticizing her nose. If she walked with confidence it was because she was feeling more confident than she ever had. And she liked the feeling.

Snapping off the bathroom light, she entered her bedroom and opened her closet. The white fox stole shimmered softly in the light from her bedside lamp. Carefully, she laid the fur beside her on the bed where she could touch it and press her cheek against it.

Ivy fell asleep smiling against the fur stole. And she dreamed of Europe and Cannes, surprised even in her dream that she, Ivy Enders from Limon, Colorado, was there, part of a life that had seemed so far out of reach.

Chapter Eight

Throughout most of the fourteen-four flight to Nice, France, Ivy slept with her head pillowed on Kevin's shoulder. Eric sat across the aisle reading through the first three chapters of his book, trying to concentrate on revisions. But the typewritten words wouldn't stay in front of his mind. His thoughts continually drifted toward Ivy.

The trip to Europe was the culmination of a lifelong dream for her. Travel brochures, maps, foreign dictionaries, and historical tracts had covered her coffee table for weeks. And he guessed excitement had prevented her from sleeping recently, because twice he had seen her step onto her balcony at two in the morning.

Excitement wasn't the reason behind his own inability to sleep. He had been sitting on his balcony at two in the morning lost in introspection, attempting to understand why he was flying to Cannes and how he fit into the scheme of things. Giving up on revisions, he closed the binder over his manuscript and turned his face to the window.

Back in the pre-lottery days, he had occasionally thought about traveling to Europe, but the desire hadn't ranked high on his list of wants. On those rare occasions when he daydreamed of traveling, he imagined London, Paris, Rome, and other major capitals. Not once had he considered Cannes.

But he had allowed himself to be swept up in Kevin's plans and enthusiasm. When Kevin had first suggested the idea, Eric had considered himself and Ivy and Kevin a tight threesome, sharing common problems and adjustments, new experiences. He had considered their little group a triad. One for all and all for one. Equality in friendship.

But the friendship wasn't equal; he was beginning to understand that.

He looked across the aisle at Ivy, at her long lashes feathered across her cheeks, at the soft rise and fall of her breasts. Then he leaned backward and signaled the flight attendant for a drink.

He cared enough for Ivy Enders that he wanted her to be happy. But he was beginning to reluctantly, painfully, accept that Ivy believed her happiness depended on Kevin McCallister. She had said often enough that what she wanted most was to be part of Kevin's world. And she had been spending a lot of time with Kevin recently. Plus, it was Kevin she looked to for approval of her hair, her clothing, her attitudes.

And why not? What did Eric know about women's hair and clothing? He knew next to nothing about lines and labels or what made one hairstyle chic and another ordinary. Besides, he had believed Ivy was lovely the day he met her, long before she made herself over.

Holding the Bloody Mary on his tongue, he thought back to the day he and Ivy had fished on the Blue River. That was the day that had sparked his recent period of introspection, because that was the day he had begun to suspect his friendship for her might be something more, something deeper. If he had been a different kind of man, he might have seized the moment and might have bent to kiss her when she'd rested her head on his thigh. He might have told her that what he had called an abiding friendship had deepened. If he were that man, he could have waxed romantic and confessed that her fingertips on his wrist were enough to paralyze him and send his heartbeat into overdrive. He could have told her that occasionally he lost himself in her smile, feeling absurdly happy simply because she was happy. Or that he dreamed of holding her in his arms, that he wished her head was on his shoulder now.

But he was not that kind of man. He was the sort of man who could be glib with strangers, but found himself tongue-tied when he was with a woman who really mattered to him. A man who felt deeply and intensely, but who was too shy or too private to say the words aloud.

So his moment had passed that day on the Blue River, and the words remained unspoken. Upon reflection, he thanked God they did, otherwise he would have been deeply embarrassed, because it was obvious Ivy didn't share his feelings. She had said she thought of him as a brother.

Glancing across the aisle of the plane, he looked at her shining head cushioned on Kevin's shoulder. She didn't think of Kevin as a brother.

Although Eric tried not to feel jealous or judgmental—he believed in live and let live—Ivy's crush on Kevin worried him. While it was true that Kevin's world possessed an aura of glamour, there was a darker side, as well, one Ivy had not yet seen. At least it was dark by Eric's standards, and he believed Ivy shared many of his values.

How would she respond to Kevin's famous parties, which she hadn't yet attended? Would her value system blur and adjust? Would she eventually repress what Eric was certain would be an initial revulsion and turn her distaste back on herself by chastising herself for being provincial? Did she want to share Kevin's world badly enough to make the necessary compromises?

That was what worried him. Attaining one's heart's desire meant losing something else. It meant compromise, large or small. For every gain, there was a loss. Frequently the loss was acceptable as part of the price to gain a greater end, but sometimes whatever was lost became in the end something of greater importance than the original goal.

Ivy had already lost a nose Eric had liked, and a hobby, sewing, that she had enjoyed. She had lost her best friend in Limon and had hinted that a distance was developing between herself and her family. What else would she lose before she became whatever it was she wanted to be?

This thought led to another. What had *he* lost?

In gaining an assured income, he had lost all sense of purpose. He was drifting and he knew it. If his book eventually became successful, that might provide a new direction. But in truth, he couldn't visualize himself as an author. He had lost his Dumbo ears, but he didn't see that as any great disaster. He had lost his place in a community and the sense of belonging that a large city couldn't provide, and that he did consider a disaster. Finally, he had lost the sense of being in control of his life. He was learning to play golf, for God's sake, without fully understanding why he was bothering. He was attending parties he didn't particularly enjoy, spending money on items he didn't really need. He was simply drifting along the line of least resistance. The realization was deeply troubling.

"Why the long face, old son?" Kevin asked across the aisle.

"Tell me something," said Eric. "Do you ever get tired of playing?"

"Good God, no! What else would I do? Install a desk next to Daddy's?" A shudder constricted Kevin's expression. After finishing his drink, he raised a curious eyebrow. "Why do you ask? Do you disapprove of how I live?"

It suddenly occurred to Eric that his only connection to Kevin McCallister was Ivy. If Ivy hadn't linked them, they would have drifted apart.

He answered carefully. "Approval or disapproval isn't the issue. For the past few months Ivy and I have been exploring a life-style alternative that wasn't possible before. The experience has been interesting and instructive."

"But?"

"But not wholly satisfying."

Kevin smiled. "You can take the man out of the bank, but you can't take the banker out of the man. Is that it?"

"Something like that."

"How appalling. And you look so normal, no one would guess you're mired in a nine-to-five mindset. Let's wake Ivy, shall we? The dear girl wanted to see an ocean and we've been over one for hours. Ivy? We'll be in Nice in an hour or so. Wake up, my dear."

Ivy stirred, turned her face into Kevin's shoulder, then straightened, yawning. "How long have I been sleeping?"

"It seems like days. But you'll be glad you did. Cannes is absolutely mad during the film festival. None of us will be sleeping much. Look out the window. That's an ocean beneath us. The next time you look down, it will be the Mediterranean. Would you like a drink? Something to wake you up? You have a smudge of mascara beneath your right eye and your lipstick is gone. Did you know that our friend, Eric, is writing a book? The mysterious project is revealed. But of course he probably told you, didn't he? I hope you remembered to pack the hot pink swimsuit we bought in Cherry Creek. You did, didn't you?"

Smiling, Ivy held up her hands. "Give me a minute to wake up." Leaning across Kevin, she called across the aisle to Eric. "Didn't you talk to this man while I was sleeping? He sounds like a dam that's just burst."

Kevin answered for him. "Eric is a terrible traveling companion." He winked and turned back to Ivy. "He's been contemplating the horrors of being rich, not speaking to anyone, indulging in Puritan guilt, I suspect, because he's no longer burdened with weighty responsibilities."

"Uh-oh," Ivy said, playing along. "We can't have that." She leveled a mock frown. "Not on this trip. Eric North, you are hereby commanded to enjoy yourself and not to think of anything unpleasant until we return home."

"Yes, your majesty," he said, smiling.

But there was an edge of sadness in his tone. This was the last time the three of them would be together. He sensed this as surely as he sensed Ivy's excitement.

Settling back in his seat, he nursed his drink and listened to the light conversation between Ivy and Kevin. Since the operation on her nose, she had lost the shy awkwardness she had once displayed around Kevin. Now she treated him with the same teasing intimacy Eric had once imagined she reserved for him. He watched the way she looked at Kevin, her dark eyes shining, and saw how her fingers lingered on his sleeve, on his hand.

Then he turned toward the window and told himself it didn't hurt. What mattered was that she was happy.

THERE WAS A SLIGHT DELAY while they went through immigration in the Nice airport, then they were whisked outside to the Mercedes Kevin had arranged to have waiting. The Mercedes swept them along the Grand Corniche to Cannes.

"I can't believe it," Ivy whispered. "We're really in Europe!"

Cannes was as crowded as Kevin had predicted. The wide, sweeping boulevards were jammed, as were the small streets leading off them. Ivy had an impression of red rooftops, people, spreading chestnut trees, people, the Mediterranean sparkling beyond the pebble beaches, people, television and film crews, and more people.

"Was that Clint Eastwood?" she asked, leaning out the window. "And over there. Isn't that Robert Redford?"

Their hotel was in the Promenade of the Croisette, which had begun as the province of café society but had since been taken over by the jet set. Taxis and private limos were snarled in a tangle in front of the hotel, but the McCallister name worked magic, and three liveried bellmen appeared almost immediately to collect their luggage and usher them inside an elegant wood-and-crystal lobby.

Awed, Ivy looked about with wide eyes. She would like to have observed the lobby appointments when the hotel was not as thronged with people. What items she could see were period pieces and gleamed softly from centuries of careful care. But it was impossible to admire them properly now, as waves of people passed through her line of vision.

She saw a tall, statuesque blonde stride toward a sweep of curving staircase, pursued by a TV camera crew. The woman was a French actress whose face Ivy recognized but whose name she couldn't remember. When the blonde disappeared up the staircase, the camera crew did an about-face and rushed past Ivy toward the loud music thumping from the curtained archway leading into the lobby bar. A couple emerged and obligingly posed for the cameras. Someone behind Ivy said it was Princess Caroline and one of her friends. Lights flared, cameras rolled, words were spoken, smiles beamed, then the camera crew dashed toward the doors and the newest celebrity arrivals.

One of the cameramen paused before Ivy and wiped the perspiration from his brow. "Are you anybody?" he asked.

"Me?" Flustered, she looked around for Eric or Kevin. "No, I'm not anybody. I'm nobody."

The cameraman gave her a slow once-over, then grinned. "Too bad, honey. You sure look like somebody."

She stared after him, blushing, then looked up as Eric took her arm and led her through the crush toward the front desk. "That man thought I was somebody."

"You are somebody."

"You know what I mean. Why are you looking so grim?"

"Am I? Sorry." He gazed out at the reigning chaos and smiled. "Not exactly your quiet little hideaway, is it?"

"Hardly," she said, laughing. "I can't believe we're actually here. Eric, this is the Cannes Film Festival! And we're part of it! You and me." She wrapped her arms around her body and hugged herself, trying to contain the excitement. "Thank you, Celtex. Thank you, thank you! Where did Kevin disappear to?"

"He's registering us. My sixth-grade French wasn't equal to the task."

She saw Kevin then, leaning against the counter and leafing through a sheaf of messages. It astonished her that she knew someone who had arrived in France two hours ago and already had a stack of messages.

"This is going to be the best vacation of my life!" she said as she and Eric joined Kevin. In fact, it was so far the *only* vacation of her life. But what a way to begin.

"You and Eric are on the fourth floor, and I'm on the fifth. We're invited to all the important parties and to as many showings as we can bear."

"Isn't that the point of all this?" Eric asked. "To see the films?"

"I suppose someone must attend them," Kevin said, laughing. "But the point is to enjoy ourselves." He snapped his fingers and bellmen appeared to gather their luggage.

A deep color rose beneath Eric's tan, and Ivy quickly placed her hand on his sleeve. "I definitely want to see the new Steven Spielberg film," she said loyally. "Everybody is saying it'll win."

"Who is everybody?" Eric asked, looking at her, his mouth as grim as before.

Now it was Ivy's turn to blush. "Everybody." She waved a hand. "I overheard several people discussing it." Turning, she lifted her head and followed the bellmen up the stairs. The elevators were impossibly jammed, and a long line waited in front of the doors.

She scarcely had time to catch her breath and admire the elegance of her room before the telephone rang.

It was Kevin. "Is your room suitable?"

"It's beautiful!" Turning, she let her gaze wander over a silk-clad four-poster and delicately turned side pieces. A bowl of fruit and a bucket of iced wine waited on the table in front of the window. "I feel like a celebrity. I've never seen a more lavish room."

"Did the wine and fruit basket arrive?"

"Yes. Are they from you? Thank you, I—"

"More important, are you jet-lagged?"

"No." Any suggestion of jet lag had vanished the moment she set foot on European soil.

"Good. Marty Hoffman is having a party in one of the penthouse suites. I'm told it's in its second day. Put on the flowered Halston, collect Eric, and we'll meet there."

"Who is Marty Hoffman?"

"A director and sometime producer, currently under contract to McCallister Enterprises. We're making a duty call, an obligatory appearance. But there may be some interesting people. At least the booze will be top row."

Moving as if in a dream, Ivy drifted toward the closet where a hotel maid was hanging her dresses and gowns. Not wanting to make a fool of herself, she resisted the impulse to throw out her arms and dance around the room.

"I wish Iris was here, or Cassie," she said aloud.

The maid turned to her with a polite smile. "*Madame?*"

"Nothing. It's just—" She shook her head and smiled broadly. "It's nothing."

But she wanted to tell someone about being here, about this room and the blond French actress and about being invited to a movie director's party and about the cameraman who had mistaken her for somebody. She wanted to tell someone who would understand. Who would understand how incredible it was that Ivy Enders from Limon, Colorado, was in Europe preparing to attend a party for international celebrities.

There was someone who would understand.

Whirling, she returned to the telephone and dialed Eric's room. "Eric?" She sounded breathless. "I have to tell someone this. Guess what? I'm in Europe. Me. And you wouldn't believe how many celebrities I saw less than an hour ago. I saw that French actress who does the cosmetic commercials and I think I saw Princess Caroline! Can you believe that?" She covered her mouth with her hand and whispered. "And the maid speaks French!"

Eric's laughter rang in her ear. She could imagine him speaking around a grin when he answered, "No kidding? You're in Europe? I don't believe it! What's a nice girl from Limon doing in a wicked place like Cannes? How did such an unimaginable thing happen?"

"Once upon a dream I won a sweepstakes." Her smile was so wide it hurt her mouth. "Now here I am—me—rubbing shoulders with film celebrities and royalty!"

"That is amazing. I want to hear all the details. Don't forget anything."

"I won't, I can promise you that." A rush of affection warmed her skin. She liked him for going along with her foolishness, for understanding. "I love you, Eric. You're a wonderful friend."

"I hope so." Did she imagine it, or did the laughter suddenly fade from his tone? "When will you be dressed? I've been assigned to escort you upstairs. Kevin went on ahead."

"Give me twenty minutes." Had she said something wrong?

THE PARTY WAS UNLIKE any party Ivy could have imagined. First the doors were wide open when she and Eric stepped off the elevator. She saw immediately that an invitation wasn't necessary. Anyone wandering onto the penthouse floor could crash the party and be unnoticed in the crush of people. Apparently Mr. Hoffman didn't care.

A live rock band pounded out song after song from one corner of a cavernous living room, but no one appeared to be listening. People stood shoulder to shoulder shouting to be heard, gesturing with drink glasses, laughing, making deals. The din was overwhelming.

Ivy saw Arab sheikhs talking to women clad in scanty bathing suits, ladies in evening gowns flirting with boys young enough to be their sons, businessmen flashing contracts and pinky rings, film celebrities chatting with punkers. She saw diamonds in the ears of girls with spiked green hair; a woman in a floor-length sable coat; a man with a Goodyear tire around his neck; a gorgeous black woman wearing nothing but three strategically placed silk roses; and a couple who were kissing and casually undressing each other as if they were alone instead of standing in the midst of several hundred people.

Swallowing, Ivy gripped Eric's arm and moved closer to him. "We'll never find Kevin."

"What?" Eric shouted. "I can't hear you."

But Kevin found them. "Mad, isn't it?" Catching a waiter's arm, he snared drinks. "And things are just getting started."

"You said this party has been going on for two days?" She couldn't believe it. His answer was lost in the noise, but she thought he said the party would continue for several more days, until the awards were announced.

"Would you like to meet Bob Redford and Joan Collins?"

Ivy's mouth dropped and she looked at him with unabashed awe. "You know them?"

"Come along."

In the next few hours reality blurred. Ivy had stepped into a dreamworld where names and faces she had only read about smiled at her, shook her hand, asked if she was enjoying herself. Film stars of giant reputation kissed her cheek as if they knew her—maybe they thought they did—and once she found herself tangled in the trailing boa of a Spanish princess, to be rescued by an Arabian financier....

"Ivy darling, we have to rush. We're having dinner on Kobashi's yacht. You just have time to change. The cream silk slacks and jacket, I think, with the cherry camisole."

She twisted her head, searching for Eric. "We've lost Eric." She was starting to worry. She hadn't seen him for several hours.

"I'll leave a message. Don't forget, the cream silk dinner suit."

She insisted they knock on Eric's door before they departed for Kobashi's yacht, but when they did there was no answer. "I wonder what happened to him?" she asked, frowning.

"Darling, Eric is quite old enough to take care of himself." Kevin took her arms and stepped back to look at her. "Smashing. You look sensational!"

"I feel sensational," she said, laughing because his appraisal made her feel suddenly shy, and laughing was better than blushing, although she suspected she did that, too.

They looked at each other, then his arms went around her and for a moment Ivy's senses reeled with the richly spiced scent of an expensive aftershave. Not knowing if this was an embrace prompted by approval and friendship or if it signaled something more, she looked at him with uncertainty. For a moment she felt like the old Ivy Enders, filled with timid yearning, vulnerable and awkward.

His mouth moved toward hers, then the corridor suddenly filled with noise and people.

"'Scuse me, buddy. Where's the party?" A man, obviously and happily drunk, waved a noisemaker and leaned toward them. "Jim said the fourth floor. Do you know Jim? Big guy, has an accent. Makes those Italian spaghetti flicks?"

A flow of people surged around them, knocking on room doors, laughing, scattering a trail of confetti.

Kevin grinned at Ivy, then kissed her forehead and pulled her out of the crowd and toward the elevators, squeezing inside before the doors shut. They stood pressed together in the elevator crush, then spilled into the lobby.

Kobashi's limo was waiting. Inside were two other couples whom Kevin introduced, but Ivy didn't catch their names. She clasped her hands tightly against her slacks and tried to follow the conversation inside the car, but all she could think about was that moment in the corridor and the feel of Kevin's body pressed against hers in the elevator.

Did her confusion mean something or nothing? And if it meant something, what did it mean and how did she feel about it? For so long she had repressed any romantic feelings. In the beginning she had done so because she didn't see herself as the type of woman Kevin or Eric would be interested in romantically. Then she had carefully suppressed any romantic inclinations because Kevin and Eric were her friends, her buddy system, her personal network.

But she admitted to a few unguarded moments when she had wondered how it would feel to kiss one or the other of them. To really kiss, not in friendship or in passing, but a kiss prompted by passion and emotion. She had experienced such uncomfortable moments with both Kevin and Eric, although she didn't think either of them had guessed what she was thinking. She hoped not. It would be too embarrassing, as neither of the men had indicated they considered her as anything but a friend.

But there had been that moment in the corridor when Kevin looked at her and his arms stole around her....

She peeked at him now as he laughed at something one of the women said, and she drew a soft breath when she saw him look at her. There was something new in his eyes, something she hadn't seen there before. Kevin was still guiding her, still acting as mentor, but when he looked at her, she no longer saw amusement in his glance. She no longer felt he considered her a country mouse to be pitied and tolerated. The distance between them had narrowed, and in so doing their friendship had assumed a new dimension. It had shifted into something as yet undefined.

"I beg your pardon?" The people in the car were looking at her with polite expectancy as if awaiting an answer to a question. "I'm sorry," she said. "I didn't hear. Perhaps I'm suffering jet lag after all."

Sympathetic murmurs ensued. One of the men admitted he could hardly hold his eyes open and announced his plan to nap in one of Kobashi's staterooms until his wife, her ladyship, was ready to leave. Her ladyship, it seemed, was indefatigable and didn't know the meaning of jet lag.

The conversation returned to Ivy as they boarded the tender that would take them out to Kobashi's yacht, and she gradually understood Kevin's friends were probing to discover who she was. Mild panic widened her eyes, and she looked to Kevin for help.

"How wicked you are, Ivy darling," he said, laughing as if Ivy were sophisticated enough to parry polite probes for her own amusement. "Despite her efforts to appear mysterious, our Ivy is really quite ordinary. One of the Bermuda Enders, you know. Dabbles in fashion on occasion."

Ivy stared at him, then understood and smiled. He referred to her sewing, of course.

Her ladyship nodded. "Ah, yes, I see the family resemblance now. I believe I co-chaired the Biafra Ball with your mother a few years ago. Lady Marsha Enders, isn't it?"

"My mother's name is Mary." It slipped out.

"Oh, dear. I could have sworn it was Marsha. How silly of me not to remember."

When Kevin helped her board the yacht, he spoke near her ear. "Careful, darling." Then he was introducing her to Lord and Lady this and Prince and Princess that. Ivy was beginning to feel the effects of the long plane ride and a surfeit of impressions; the names sped past her, forgotten as soon as they were spoken.

Tired, but dreamily happy, she drifted through cocktails and dinner, then danced with a variety of partners as a Mediterranean moon sailed across the sky. It was a scene out of a movie or a glitzy book, an experience she promised herself to remember forever. Later, she vaguely recalled returning to Cannes and driving into the hills to someone's villa for a champagne breakfast as the pink tints of dawn spread across the horizon. Then she was standing in the hotel corridor leaning against her door, a tired but happy smile on her lips.

"Good night, darling Ivy, or should I say good morning?" Kevin's lips grazed her temple, then he inserted her key in her door and pushed it open. "You're half-asleep."

"Mmm." She stumbled inside and held on to the door. "Thank you for the most wonderful night of my life. It was fabulous. Dreams do come true."

Bending, he picked a folded message off the floor. "It seems you have an admirer."

She glanced at the note and yawned. "Afraid not. It's just Eric. Says he'll meet us for breakfast." Blinking, she tried to see her wristwatch. Oh, dear. We're supposed to meet him in an hour."

"Don't worry. I'll leave a message and suggest dinner instead. For dinner, I think the—"

"Emerald silk pajamas."

"Very good," he said, smiling. "Exactly what I had in mind. And you tried to resist buying them." He touched her cheek. "You were terrific tonight. I was the envy of every man."

Ivy opened one eye. "I'd love to hear more, but I'm about to fall asleep standing up."

After calling a good-night down the corridor, Ivy staggered toward the four-poster, certain she had never been this tired in her life. She would be asleep before her head hit the pillow. Dropping to the side of the bed, she kicked off her heels and was about to fall backward when the message from Eric fluttered from her fingers.

She rubbed her eyes and thought she should phone him. Kevin wasn't always reliable about messages. For an instant, she gazed longingly at the pillows, then she pushed herself up. It would only take a moment, then she could sleep.

"Did I wake you?" she asked, hearing the sleep in his voice. "I'm sorry. We just got in."

"What time is it?"

"We lost you at the penthouse party. What happened?"

"I was shanghaied by a scriptwriter. I kept telling her I wasn't a producer, but she didn't believe me."

"Was she pretty?" It was a stupid question and one that just popped out of her mouth.

"Who?"

"The scriptwriter. Oh, never mind."

"So, where did you and Kevin go?"

"Oh, Eric, we had dinner on a yacht! The bathroom fixtures were made of real gold—I wish you could have seen them. And there was a Manet hanging on the dining-room wall, not a copy, the real thing. And I danced with a member of the British parliament and a singer who sang for the royal family last week. Then we went to someone's villa for breakfast and watched the sun come up over the water. It was the most fabulous night of my whole life!"

"It sounds wonderful." He paused then asked casually. "Is Kevin there? I'd like to talk to him a minute."

"No, he's gone and I'm about to go to bed. I'm absolutely dead on my feet. But I wanted to tell you to meet us for dinner instead of breakfast, is that all right?"

"No problem. Get some rest and I'll see you later."

"Eric?" she said quickly, catching him before he hung up. "I really wish you had been with us." She couldn't rave about the yacht's gold fixtures to Kevin who had seen gold fixtures before. But Eric would have been as awed and amused as she was, and he would have said something funny to put everything in perspective. "I missed you." A dozen times she had turned to tell him something but he wasn't there.

"I missed you too," he said softly.

Ivy was right. She was asleep before her head hit the pillow, still wearing her silk dinner slacks.

She dreamed about the party on the yacht, but oddly, it was Eric whom she danced with in her dream. Eric who glided her across the deck in the moonlight and held her in his arms. Eric whose hard, athletic shoulders and thighs set her body on fire.

When she awoke she remembered the dream and blushed. Dreams were peculiar things, a strange mix of near reality and misty fantasy.

But dreams were meaningless, even dreams that seemed very real. Even when she could still almost feel Eric's lips against her temple, his body pressed to hers.

It had seemed so real.

Chapter Nine

"Kevin? It's Eric." Eric adjusted the telephone in his hand and wondered if he was doing the right thing. "Could you spare a few minutes before dinner? I'd like to talk to you."

"It will be a bit of a push, but . . . the lobby bar in, say, twenty minutes?"

"Fine."

Two of Kevin's friends were preparing to leave as Eric entered the bar. Kevin grabbed the stools and waved to him. The dimly lit room was jammed with people trying to find a table or standing in groups wherever space permitted. The noise had reached ear-splitting levels.

Kevin ordered a Scotch-and-water for each of them, cupping his hands around his mouth and shouting to the barman. Rolling his eyes and smiling, he leaned toward Eric. "Mad, isn't it? Are you having a good time?"

"It's interesting."

"Indeed it is," Kevin agreed, laughing. "Anything goes." Casually he withdrew a pouch filled with white powder from his jacket pocket. Tapping some of the stuff out onto the surface of the bar, he invited Eric to partake.

"Thank you, no."

The man seated to their right watched with mild interest as Kevin inhaled some of the powder; otherwise, no one appeared to care or notice. The sight was common enough not to attract much attention.''

"Suit yourself." Shrugging, Kevin returned the pouch to his jacket. "But it's the only way to keep up the pace."

Plain, old-fashioned sleep was another way, Eric thought, but he didn't comment. Drugs were as common in Cannes as suntan lotion; that's how it appeared to him. It wasn't entirely comfortable being the square peg in a town crammed with round holes.

"Kevin, we need to talk about Ivy." Not certain how best to proceed, he tasted his Scotch then moved the glass in damp circles in front of him. "Are you aware she has a crush on you?" Immediately he regretted the phrasing for sounding old-fashioned and adolescent.

"Really? Do you think so? Then I'm flattered. She's made herself into a beautiful woman."

Eric lifted his head and met Kevin's eyes. "She's changed recently, but she's still Ivy inside."

"What does that mean?"

"It means she isn't sophisticated. She's innocent. In many ways, she's younger than her years." Dammit, he wasn't saying this well. "She hasn't been exposed to a lot of things you take for granted. Drugs, casual sex, parties on the wild side. I'm not sure she's ready for those things."

"Let's see if I understand this. You think Ivy has a crush on me, as you so charmingly put it, and further, that I may take advantage of her feelings by corrupting her moral standards? Is that what you're suggesting, Eric?"

He didn't back down. "It's a possibility."

Kevin smiled. "Assuming you're correct, assuming our Ivy does have certain feelings toward me, I don't need your advice on how to conduct a romance, old son."

"Is it a romance, Kevin? I guess that's what I want to know. How do you feel about her?"

Kevin's eyelids dropped. "We're getting a bit personal here, aren't we?"

"I apologize for that. But I don't want Ivy to get hurt. Come on, Kevin, she isn't the type you're usually drawn to." Kevin laughed and agreed. "She's special. The kind you take home to mother, not the type you play with, then drop."

Kevin clapped him on the back. "Relax, friend. Surprising as it may seem, I'm not entirely without sensitivity. I know Ivy's fragile right now, trying her new wings. If it will set your mind at ease, I can promise I don't intend to run roughshod over her."

Frustration furrowed Eric's brow. It wasn't that Ivy was fragile right now; all people were fragile when it came to entanglements of the heart. And he didn't appreciate Kevin's half-humorous approach.

"Look, McCallister, all I'm asking is that you be aware Ivy looks up to you. I don't think she's ready for many of the parties going on around here. There are lots of ways people can get hurt—"

"I don't think I like the turn this conversation has taken. I don't need advice on how to conduct myself. I think I can decide which parties Ivy will enjoy and which would be shocking or offensive to her." Shifting on the stool, Kevin stared. "You're talking as if you don't think I care about her."

"Do you?" Eric challenged.

Kevin looked at him, then swallowed his Scotch. "Maybe you won't believe this, Eric, but I care a lot about Ivy. And you, too. I value both of you as good friends." A look resembling embarrassment crossed his face. "This is going to sound odd, but . . . I really don't have a lot of friends." A wave of his hand discouraged comment. "Oh, I know a lot of people, have a lot of acquaintances, but damned few of them are people I actually consider friends. A handful, maybe. You and Ivy are among them.''

The admission hadn't emerged easily and Eric understood that. He nodded. ''Then you'll take it slow with her. You won't hurt her.''

''Of course not.''

They sat in silence, drinking, observing the people thronging the bar. The conversation had been awkward, but Eric felt better for having made the effort.

As they slid from the stools to meet Ivy, Kevin placed a hand on Eric's shoulder and raised a curious eyebrow.

''How do you feel about her?''

''Ivy is one of my best friends.''

''That's all? You're sure there isn't any jealousy underlying this little chat?''

''Look, Kevin, I care enough for Ivy that I want her to be happy. That's important to me. If you're what it takes for her to be happy, then that's what I want for her. I just want you to be aware of the situation so you don't lead her on or end up hurting her. That's all. If you're ready for something serious, you can't do better than Ivy. But if you're not in the market for a serious relationship, then think about it, okay?''

They stood beside the bar, studying each other, forming an island amid the flow of raucous laughter.

''The truth is,'' Kevin said finally, ''I don't know how I feel about her. Naturally I've thought about taking her to bed—she's become a beautiful woman. But I haven't done anything about it yet because—'' he shrugged ''—she's a friend. You and I can always find a woman for a night, you know that, but friends are harder to come by.''

''If you take her to bed, Kevin, you'd better be prepared to take her home to mother.''

Kevin laughed. ''You're kidding. This is the eighties. Even Ivy isn't that old-fashioned.''

He wanted to tell Kevin that Ivy was a virgin, but he had given his promise. "I think she is."

"Is what?" Ivy asked, smiling up at them. "I figured you two might be in the bar. Were you talking about me?" She kissed them both on the cheek.

"Every man in Cannes is talking about you," Kevin said smoothly, dropping his arm around her waist. "But we have you. And we are treating you to a dinner you won't forget. Right, Eric?"

Eric looked at them standing together and reluctantly conceded they made a strikingly handsome couple. They were a picture out of the society pages: Ivy, beautiful in her emerald silk pajamas, and Kevin, elegant in white jacket and black tie. For the first time he saw Ivy as others must see her: lovely, polished and elegant. The woman she had created would fit easily into Kevin's world. He could visualize her gracing the pages of the society columns, could imagine her pouring tea at a benefit luncheon or standing in the receiving line at a charity ball. Suddenly that day on the Blue River seemed very far away. For a moment he couldn't remember her without makeup or dressed in faded jeans.

Midway through dinner, Ivy slowly lowered her fork and regarded them with a quizzical expression. "You two are behaving very strangely tonight. All this ultra-politeness like we were strangers. Is something wrong?"

"Not at all," Kevin said quickly. "If we seem unusually quiet, it's because we're struck dumb by your beauty."

"And by sheer weariness," Eric added, following Kevin's lead. "Doesn't anyone sleep around here?"

Ivy laughed. "Eric, you just ruined a perfectly good compliment. No, don't apologize, I wouldn't believe you anyway. So, what's on the agenda tonight?"

"Several of the major film companies are having parties to promote their entries. You can take your pick, but the French company's bash will probably be the best." Kevin looked across the table at Eric before he continued. "Then Lady Cleeves is hosting a reception at the Bonaparte Villa. It should be very posh, very elegant. Or there's a street dance in costume, and we've also been invited to a revival of *Grease* at the Palais des Festivals if you're in the mood for that sort of thing."

Candlelight glowed in Ivy's dark eyes and Eric stared at her, trying to engrave her image in his mind. He thought she was easily the most beautiful woman in the dining room, perhaps in Cannes. Only the excitement in her eyes suggested she wasn't accustomed to the rich ambiance and patrician surrounds. Anyone seeing her for the first time would have assumed this was her natural milieu.

"I can't decide," she said finally, her face glowing with the pleasure of the choices. "I want to do everything. What do you think, Eric? Which party shall we go to?"

"Actually I've made plans for this evening," he lied.

"Oh." Surprise lifted her brows, then she looked flustered. "Oh, well, I didn't think of that. I'm sorry, I just assumed... What are you going to do? Are you meeting the scriptwriter?"

"I thought I'd see some of the films."

Kevin grinned and winked at Ivy. "We're left to wonder about the scriptwriter. Well, old son, can you tear yourself away from your scriptwriter long enough to join us for tennis in the morning?"

"Tennis?" Ivy asked, groaning. "In the morning? Where do you find the energy?"

"Have to sweat out this booze somehow. In the afternoon Prince Gerald is taking a party to Monaco on his yacht—your lemon deck outfit will do nicely. We'll have lunch on the yacht, swim a little and spend the evening at the casino in Monte Carlo. If you're not up to a day on the water, we can stay in Cannes, do some shopping, drop in on a few parties and go to the Palm Beach Casino later. It's equally as impressive as the casino in Monte Carlo.''

"Oh, Kevin!" Eyes shining, Ivy turned to Eric. "Can you imagine it? The three of us at the casino in Monte Carlo?"

"Well," Eric said. He touched his tie. "I'm afraid I have plans for tomorrow night, too. You and Kevin will have to break the bank without me.''

Disappointment shadowed Ivy's eyes. "I thought the three of us... No, that isn't fair." She looked at her plate and bit her lip. "Each of us has to do what he wants to do. I guess I had just expected... Well, have either of you inspected the topless beaches?''

"I haven't had time. How about you, Eric?"

"It's true. They're topless, all right."

They all laughed, then ordered white chocolate mousse for dessert.

After dinner Eric walked them through the lobby and saw them off to the French film company's bash. He didn't regret declining as he imagined the party would be much like the one they had attended the night before. But he did regret declining the trip to Monaco. He would have liked to be there when Ivy first saw the casino and tried her hand at twenty-one or roulette.

There was something magical about firsts. The first experience of Europe, the first casino, the first anything. He would have liked to share more of the firsts Ivy was experiencing on this trip, but the decent thing was to absent himself and let Ivy and Kevin be alone together.

A member of the TV camera crew working the lobby rushed up to him. "Are you somebody?" the cameraman asked, sounding harried.

Eric feigned a look of astonishment. "You don't know who I am?" He looked down his nose and gave the cameraman a haughty stare. "You didn't do your homework, did you?"

Then, laughing at the madness of it all, he pushed through the lobby doors. He really did want to see some of the films. Later, he would work on his book, and tomorrow he planned to rent a car and do some sightseeing.

IVY DROPPED HER HEAD in her hand, looked at her brioche and marmalade and sighed. "I have never been this tired in my life." She closed her eyes. Dark circles lay beneath her lashes like faint bruises. "I didn't know a person could be this tired and still be alive."

When Kevin laughed, she opened her eyes and looked at him. His eyes were bright and he looked as fresh as he had before playing tennis. She didn't know how he did it.

Ivy didn't think either of them had slept more than three, possibly four hours at a stretch since the first day. The past five days had begun to blur and run together in her memory, which was dismaying because she wanted to remember everything. But it was impossible; there was just too much and the pace was too frenzied.

Concentrating, she made herself recall the Côte d'Azur racecourse at Haut-de-Cagnes and a glimpse of one of the Grimaldi chateaus, which someone had told her was now a museum. She would have liked to visit the museum, but there wasn't time. Everyone was going to—where was it— oh, yes, a luau on a private beach belonging to a Brazilian tin baron. She remembered a night of casino hopping, the elegant Palm Beach in Cannes, the luxurious Casino Ruhl in Nice, casinos in Antibes and Juan-les-Pins. Then breakfast at a villa perched high on the rocky coast overlooking the Mediterranean. Watching the sun come up for the fifth day in a row, then back to the hotel for a few hours sleep before high tea with a friend of Kevin's mother, dinner on someone's yacht, then the party where a starlet had herself carried into the room naked on a huge silver platter.

"I have a treat for you today."

"What?" She contemplated the brioche and the energy it would take to chew. "A nap, I hope?"

"The rue d'Antibes. You haven't shopped until you've shopped the rue d'Antibes. Everything your heart desires can be found there, plus delights you didn't even know you craved. Designer shops, boutiques, Italian shoes, French silk. Brazilian gems... Are you salivating, dear Ivy?"

"It sounds expensive, and I'm thinking about the money I lost at the roulette wheel." At least she had discovered one thing from the experience: she didn't like to gamble. She had lived without money too long to enjoy risking it on the spin of a wheel. When she had witnessed a man dressed in Arab robes lose fifty thousand dollars in one spin, she had gasped and felt like fainting. The man had shrugged and moved to another table.

"Good things are always expensive."

"I'd argue the point, but I'm too pooped." Fishing on the Blue River wasn't expensive. Sewing a dress for Iris's baby wasn't expensive. Or standing in a field of fresh-cut maize and smelling the richness of the earth. Or reading a great book on a snowy night. Or watching the Broncos beat the Raiders on a Sunday afternoon with a group of friends and lots of popcorn. These were some of the things she loved best—good things that weren't expensive.

"You know, Ivy darling, I could give you something that would wake you up immediately and have you raring to go."

At first she didn't understand. When she did, she cast a hasty glance over her shoulder, then leaned forward and spoke in a low tone. "Don't say that, not even as a joke. Someone might think you're serious." She lowered her tone further. "I don't know if you've noticed, but there are lots of drugs around here."

"Have you ever tried anything?" he asked lightly.

"Me?" Shock widened her eyes. "Of course not. Have you?"

He shrugged. "Everyone tries it."

"Not anyone I know. Don't tell me there's an 'in' drug. Is there?"

"That reminds me of a Robin Williams line: 'Cocaine addiction is God's way of saying you're making too much money.'"

She laughed. "Did you see the video where he imitated a perking coffeepot?" The conversation shifted to comedians and which of them might be in Cannes, and then to various celebrities they had encountered, and then to the incident where two of Kobashi's film-star guests had fallen off the yacht and when they were rescued it was discovered they were married lovers but not married to each other. The media had loved it.

Kevin signaled for their check. "Well, my dear. Let's change, then we'll meet in the lobby and indulge ourselves in a shopping spree to end all shopping sprees. We're having dinner with the Whitneys—you met them at Lady Cleeves's—then we'll decide where to go from there."

"Kevin, have you seen Eric lately?" She'd found a couple of messages from him pushed under her door and she had spoken to him on the phone once, but it was as if he had vanished.

"Eric? I think he's sightseeing, if you can imagine that." A wrinkle of distaste drew Kevin's brow.

"As a matter of fact, I can." She looked at him, crisp and handsome in tennis whites, his Prince Valiant hair shining in the terrace sun. "You know, we've seen casinos and penthouses, bars and restaurants, villas and yachts, but we haven't seen any museums or art galleries and I have no idea what the countryside looks like. I always imagined I'd see the historical things first if I visited Europe."

"How touristy."

"I know, but I'd hate to go home without having seen anything but the interiors of a lot of noisy, smoke-filled rooms. I'm not saying I haven't enjoyed the parties, Kevin. I have. This whole trip is like an episode from *Lifestyles of the Rich and Famous*. But couldn't we tour a little of the countryside?''

His reluctance was polite but obvious.

"This isn't fair of me, is it?" she said after a moment. "You've probably already toured the museums and the churches. You'd rather be here with your friends and the social events."

"Well..."

Talking to herself, she thought out loud. "What I should do is track down Eric and ask if he'd mind some company. Unless he's tied up with the scriptwriter."

"Are you serious? You'd really rather tramp through some dreary museum than shop the rue d'Antibes?"

"Do you want the truth? What I'd really like to do is go upstairs and fall into bed. I'd like to sleep all afternoon and all night, then get up early and see a little of Europe. At something less than a killer pace."

"And here I thought I had a sturdy farmer's daughter," Kevin said, pulling back the chair for her. "And it turns out I've got a weakling who thinks she needs more than a couple of hours' sleep a night."

"This farmer's daughter needs a solid eight hours to function," Ivy said, smiling. In the lobby at the foot of the stairs, she placed her arm on his sleeve. "Seriously, Kevin, do you mind?"

"Of course I mind," he said, smoothing a strand of hair off her forehead. "I've just been deprived of the most beautiful woman in Cannes. And Eric, that lucky dog, got her." Smiling, he lifted her hand to his lips.

"Very continental," she murmured.

"Sleep well. Try not to dream about what you're missing."

Laughing, she turned on the stairs to look back at him. He was so handsome, so perfectly at ease with himself and his surroundings that her heart constricted with yearning and for a moment she wondered if she should reconsider. Then he waved, and a German starlet Ivy vaguely recognized grabbed his arm and he was pulled into a group and whirled away.

The first thing she did was treat herself to a long bubble bath, leaning back and letting the fragrant water coax her muscles to relax. It was delicious knowing that for the first time since their arrival, she didn't have to rush. There was no place she had to be, no one was waiting. She could think about something besides what she was going to wear and whom she was going to meet and if she would remember their names.

What she thought about was Kevin. There had been no repetition of that intimate moment in the corridor outside her room. And that puzzled her. Occasionally during the past few frantic days, she had caught him looking at her with a peculiar intensity, and a burst of heat had fired her cheeks. Perhaps it was the romance of being in Europe or perhaps it was the highly charged atmosphere, but Ivy found herself in a bewildering, nearly constant state of heightened awareness.

Even now, as she tried to relax in the tub, she was acutely aware of the scented water caressing her skin, aware in a sensual manner, as if her body had awakened to touch and texture. Recently she had begun noticing, and responding to, things that had previously escaped her, things that caused a strange tightening in her stomach and made her feel vaguely on edge. Things like the thin film of perspiration on Kevin's upper lip and at his temples when they played tennis. Things like the strong line of Eric's jaw. Or the way Kevin's long, elegant fingers held his wineglass. Or the contrasting snowiness of Eric's shirt collar against his tanned skin. Or the feel of silk lying against her own skin.

Each of these things by itself was insignificant, but her surprising response was not. She could look at the sunshine on Kevin's hair or the warmth in Eric's eyes and suddenly she felt as if a giant eggbeater were churning in her stomach, sending her nerves spinning outward to the surface of her skin.

Her virginal body was waking and stirring—that was it. Of course. Now that she'd identified the cause of her reactions, she almost laughed aloud. She'd felt unworthy of a man's desire for so long that she had put her physical needs in cold storage. She was at last receiving attention for her looks, and her mirror gave further evidence of her attractiveness; her body was no longer content to be placed in suspension.

Sinking back into the rose-scented water and feeling the tiny bubbles on her breasts and shoulders, Ivy thought about her insight and what it might mean. First, it meant she had to be careful. With her body alive to every accidental touch, and her mind melting over every long look, it would be easy to make a mistake she might regret.

Aside from hormones that had awakened and leaped into overdrive, her values hadn't changed. It appeared she had missed the sexual revolution because she wanted love with commitment, love that was more than a scratch for a momentary itch. Her newly awakened body was saying: go for it. But the bedrock values of the old Ivy Enders were saying: you've waited this long, you can wait a little longer; you can wait for commitment and love.

This thought returned her to Kevin and that moment in the corridor outside her door. But aside from his lavish compliments and a few casual pats and touches, he had given no further indication that anything in their relationship had changed.

Part of her was disappointed, she admitted it. But part of her was relieved. If their relationship was changing, she realized that she didn't want it to happen here, in a frantic artificial atmosphere. She wasn't entirely sure she wanted it to happen at all.

There was much about Kevin McCallister that she greatly admired: his unerring taste in clothing and furnishings, his confidence and ease of manner, his charm and irreverent humor. But he also possessed qualities she didn't understand or that secretly made her uneasy. She didn't like his snobbery, for one thing. Even though he joked about it, still it was at his insistence that she was pretending to be a Bermuda Ender instead of a Limon Ender. And, like Eric, she didn't understand Kevin's total lack of ambition and his disinterest in business.

When she thought about it, really thought about it, she didn't have much in common with Kevin McCallister. He bought all the bestselling novels, but for display only; he didn't read them. A quiet evening reading or watching television would have bored him to distraction. He liked crowds; she didn't. She enjoyed fishing, walking, anything that put her in touch with nature; he didn't. The list was endless.

Frowning, she slowly ran the bar of rose-scented soap over her skin, enjoying the silky feel. So where did this leave them? She didn't think two people had to be carbons of each other to have a relationship, but there had to be some common ground to build on. She wondered what Eric thought about this.

That reminded her. If she planned to share his sightseeing, she should let him know and ask if she could tag along.

"I'd be delighted," he said, when she telephoned him. His deep voice, intimate on the phone, caused the peculiar tightening in her stomach, and she made a face at the wall. Coping with her new sexuality or whatever it was both amused and irritated her. "What happened? Did you and Kevin have a falling out?"

"Not a falling out—a falling down. I'm so tired I'm about to drop. I need a break from all this party, party, party. And I really would like to see something of the countryside before we go home." She wound her finger in the telephone cord and closed her eyes, thinking how good it was to hear Eric's voice, regardless of what it was doing to her run-amuck body. "Besides, I feel like I haven't seen you in weeks. I want to catch up on what you've been doing. Unless you have something going with the scriptwriter," she added hastily. "I don't want to butt in."

"It turned out the scriptwriter was more interested in girls than in boys."

"*Really?*"

He laughed at her shocked tone. "How does this sound? Tomorrow, I'll have the hotel pack us a picnic lunch and we'll drive up the Corniche to Eze outside of Monte Carlo. There's a ruin of a medieval castle there. We'll take our time, stop at a couple of museums along the way. Unless you have something else in mind . . ."

"I'd love to see some castle ruins!" Excitement broke past her weariness. "It sounds wonderful!"

"Good. You get some rest and we'll plan an early start. So, tell me about you. Are you meeting a lot of interesting people? Seeing new places, trying new things? Have you sampled caviar yet?"

His voice was so deceptively casual that she almost missed the implication. "Eric North, what are you really asking? Whatever it is, the answer is no! I haven't tried caviar yet. What did you think? That I'd meet some European charmer and get swept off my feet?" Her stomach wound a notch tighter and her cheeks flamed.

"You never can tell. The minute you farm girls get out of town, you go a little crazy."

"Is that so?" she asked, glad he couldn't see how the topic affected her. "Well, how about you bankers and apple pickers? You boys wouldn't know how to have a good time if you had a map."

His laugh was wonderful. "See you tomorrow morning, Cyrano. Wear something comfortable. Leave the silk and slink in your closet."

His teasing put things in perspective. This was Eric, her friend. Ivy groaned. "Would you believe it? I didn't bring anything casual enough for picnicking or climbing around castle ruins. You'll have to take me on the silky side."

In the morning, when the waiter delivered her coffee, there was a bulky package on the room-service table.

"What's this?"

"A gentleman left it at the desk for you, *mademoiselle*. He requested that it be delivered this morning."

After the waiter left, she pulled off the wrappings and laughed out loud. Inside was a pair of Gucci jeans, an oversized Calvin Klein shirt, and a pair of blue tennies bearing an Italian label.

Throwing off her silk slacks and jacket, Ivy put on the jeans and tennies and sighed with pleasure, feeling more comfortable than she had since arriving in Europe. Eric wasn't glib with compliments and she couldn't imagine him kissing a woman's hand, but you had to love a man who sent a pair of jeans when you really needed them. Love him like a friend, that is, one of the best friends she had ever had.

Smiling, eyes bright with anticipation, she ran down the stairs to meet him. She spotted him immediately. Eric North was the only person in the lobby not looking around to see or be seen. He was watching the staircase, waiting for her. And when he smiled, it was like a burst of sunlight.

Chapter Ten

They stopped in Nice to tour the Chagall Museum and the Matisse Museum, then, arguing mildly about the paintings, tapestries and sculptures they saw, they negotiated the road along the cliffs of the Grand Corniche, awestruck by the rocky beauty and the Mediterranean waters sparkling below.

"It's breathtaking," Ivy said. "Fantastic. I can't tell you how much I needed a day like this."

"And here I thought you'd turned into a party animal."

"The parties have been terrific, like something out of *Dynasty*. You know, yachts, villas, tin barons, financial magnates, all of it. I'll remember this week for the rest of my life."

"But?"

He knew her well enough to sense the reservations. "But there's been too much all at once. I can't take it all in. There hasn't been time to savor, to think about each event and enjoy remembering." She laughed. "I never thought I'd hear myself say anything like this, but after a few days you start to take it all for granted. Yes, I've met a few dozen celebrities. Yes, I've dined on a yacht. I've actually yawned in a world-famous casino, and danced with a real prince."

He took his eyes briefly from the narrow, winding road and lifted a curious eyebrow. "Is the trip what you expected? Has it been everything you wanted it to be?"

"And more! Kevin told us a little of what we'd experience, but until I was actually here, actually part of it, I couldn't really imagine Cannes and the festival." She turned her face toward the sea and gradually the enthusiasm faded from her eyes. "But you know something? This is going to sound a little nutty, but I think I'm ready to go home." She cast a wry smile toward Eric's profile. "I'm worn out with feeling frantic over what to wear next and knowing I'm running late again. I've eaten too much rich food. I think I need a little peace and quiet to assimilate the places I've been and the people I've met. This is going to sound even crazier, but I keep thinking the aspens are changing color at home, and I'm not there to see them."

Eric smiled. "You make it sound like we've been gone for months."

"It feels like that. Home seems very far away."

"It is."

They lapsed into an easy silence. Eric concentrated on driving; Ivy leaned her head back and thought how pleasant it was to be so comfortable that they didn't have to fill the quiet spaces with chatter. Enjoying the warm breeze from the open window, feeling relaxed, she shifted slightly so she could see him.

He drove fast but well, his square, tanned hands confident on the wheel. Examining his profile, Ivy was struck by how handsome Eric was. His features were not as classically patrician as Kevin's, but his strength of character was evident in a firm jawline, in the broad sweep of his brow. She hadn't noticed before how long his lashes were or how his lips curved upward in a half smile even in repose. Nor had she realized how broad his shoulders were. The weave of the light sweater he wore widened over his biceps. Pressing her lips together, she dropped her gaze only to notice he drove with his legs comfortably spread, his thigh nearly touching hers in the confined space of the small car.

Suddenly, she could think of nothing but the heat radiating from Eric's leg to hers. The sensation was uncomfortably pleasant, almost arousing. The peculiar sense of unease and awareness that had troubled her throughout this vacation returned in full force, and Ivy found herself staring at his thigh then at his lips. She decided the scriptwriter who preferred women was a fool.

"Is something wrong?" he asked, glancing from the road to smile at her.

Pink flooded her cheeks. "No, I was just . . . wondering when we'd reach Eze."

"You must be getting hungry."

That she was, but not for anything to be found in the picnic basket waiting in the rear seat. Irritated with herself, Ivy faced resolutely forward, pretending to admire the scenery while she tried to sort through her feelings and reactions.

It was embarrassing to be having these strange, heated thoughts about Eric. Kevin, she could understand. From the first she had been drawn to Kevin in much the same way people were drawn to all things new and exciting. But this was Eric whose mouth and body were doing strange things to her nervous system, Eric who was her confidant and friend, her surrogate brother.

A long sigh came up through her entire body. She had not only awakened, but she had done so with a vengeance. The thought raised a secret smile to her lips. No man was safe from the new Ivy Enders, not even her friends. Thank God Eric couldn't read her mind. She had an idea he would have been very surprised.

They parked the rented Mercedes in a lot outside the village of Eze, then began the long walk up a winding road leading to the ruins at the top of a rocky promontory. Long ago the village of Eze had recognized the tourist value of ruins from the Middle Ages and how that value could translate into francs. Carts were spaced along the road selling souvenirs and cold drinks and Italian ices.

"Cherry, please," Ivy said, when Eric asked if she wanted an ice. "Look over there—we didn't escape the TV crews after all."

A camera and sound crew had cornered a French starlet and her fiancé who had also stopped for an ice. Clinging to her fiancé, the starlet obligingly extended her left hand to display a huge diamond.

"We're so much in love," she gushed, gazing adoringly up at her fiancé. "This time it's the real thing. I knew it the moment we met." The fiancé nodded and returned her adoring gaze. They leaned against each other. "It was love at first sight. I knew it instantly."

"Do you believe in love at first sight?" Ivy asked, nibbling at the cherry ice and watching the starlet.

"I think everyone would like to believe in it," Eric answered. Turning, they resumed the climb upward. "I think people often like to believe there is only one person in the world who is meant for them. If they believe that, then they feel almost obligated to believe they should recognize that person instantly. When these two great forces of destiny come together, there should be some signal, some chemistry, some flash of sudden insight that says, yes, this is the one person in the world for me. If it doesn't happen that way, I suspect such people sometimes rearrange their memories a bit."

"Then you don't believe in soul mates? In the idea of one special person being destined just for you?"

"I sure hope that isn't true." He grinned down at her. "What if my soul mate lives in Siberia? Our chances of getting together are slim. We'd both be doomed to a life alone or we'd have to settle for second best.''

"Surely you don't believe you can have a successful relationship with just anyone.''

"No, but I think if two people come from similar backgrounds, share common values, and have a certain amount of chemistry between them, they have a good chance of creating a successful relationship. I don't think love is like lightning, something that strikes instantly and without warning. I think love is something that grows if the other elements are present, and it requires nurturing. Love is hard work.''

"Ever the banker,'' Ivy said, smiling. "Reducing love to practicality. Since when does love have to be practical?''

"I think love that's enduring has to be grounded in practical considerations.'' He laughed when Ivy rolled her eyes. "Okay, that doesn't sound romantic, but it's realistic. If love is going to last it has to be based on more than a person's physical appearance, and that's about all anyone has to go on when they first meet.''

"And what is love, in your esteemed opinion?'' Concentrating on the climb, Ivy didn't look at him.

He didn't answer immediately, not until they had paid the fee at the gate and entered the ruins. Part of the area had been restored and contained shops and restaurants; other parts remained in scenic ruin.

"I think love is a combination of a lot of things,'' Eric said finally, looking down at her. "It's knowing someone well enough to appreciate their good qualities and to recognize but accept their flaws and limitations. It's a heightened appreciation. A good feeling within oneself. It's trusting another person enough to be totally yourself, flaws and all, without pretense. It's wanting to share time together, maybe a lifetime. It's stepping outside yourself and being willing to put another person's happiness before your own.''

Ivy listened with interest. "I would have said love is excitement and passion; it's a state of renewed or heightened awareness. A feeling of exhilaration and new possibilities.''

"That's part of it, too. But for most people I think the period of exhilaration eventually passes. It has to, or no one could concentrate on anything else. The true test comes when the initial excitement and passion mellows. To me, what's left is real love. The passion and excitement are still there, but at more acceptable levels. They aren't the whole thing, just a nice part. But the appreciation and enjoyment of each other—that's the core of loving. I guess I see love as a quieter thing than you do.''

"I'm not sure how I see it." They paused before a shop window and leaned to inspect the display. "Did you love the woman you were engaged to?" Ivy managed to ask the question in an offhand manner without revealing how interested she was in his answer.

"I thought I did. But we were together long enough for the initial passion to mellow. What remained wasn't love. At least not the kind of love strong enough to weather the storms of a lifetime. For that, people need to be friends as well as lovers. Sharon and I were lovers, but I don't think we were really friends.''

Unexpectedly Ivy felt a blush heating her cheeks. Would she ever be sophisticated enough not to blush when love or lovers were mentioned?

An elbow jostled her and she pitched forward against Eric. A paralyzing tingle shot through her where their bodies touched at thighs and arms. For a long moment their eyes held and she felt her blush intensify, then Eric drew a breath and lifted his head. A smile curved his mouth, and he turned her to see who had jostled them.

It was the starlet, only she wasn't dewy eyed now; she was angry. "You jerk!" she hissed at the fiancé, who followed her, gazing uncomfortably at the audience they were attracting.

"*Cara,* baby," he said, wooing her with his deep, Italian-accented voice.

"Don't you *cara* baby me!" The starlet rounded on him, her mascara-coated eyes flashing. "You stood there like a lump of stone. You didn't say a damned thing!"

"But I was adoring you!"

"So why didn't you tell them?" The starlet swore. "You made me look like a fool! Gushing about some idiot who can't open his mouth! You were supposed to tell them how you're wild about me, how you can't live without me, how beautiful I am and how much you love me!"

"You know all that."

"What good is it if the world doesn't know? God, you're boring! Don't you know anything?"

The very public fight moved around a stone wall and out of sight, drawing a considerable following in its wake.

"Do you suppose she'll keep the ring?" Eric asked, grinning.

"Cynic." But she laughed. "Maybe they'll get it worked out."

"Right. Love staged according to a script, just what everyone wants."

Without discussing it, they walked toward a place away from the crowds for their picnic, selecting an elevated rise beside a crumbling stone wall that overlooked the sparkling Mediterranean below.

"Did I say I was ready to go home?" Ivy asked as Eric opened a bottle of red wine. "I must have been suffering a moment of temporary insanity. This is spectacular. What do you suppose it was like to live here in the Middle Ages?"

"I don't imagine it was much different than it is now."

"You're kidding!"

"Well, the external trappings were different, of course. But human nature hasn't changed much. The people who lived here probably worried about the same things you and I do. They probably jockeyed for jobs and position, worried about a place to live and what to wear to their mother-in-law's for Sunday dinner." He grinned when Ivy laughed. "They fell in love, had babies, worked and played. They laughed and cried and hurt and rejoiced."

"You're very philosophical today. Except you make everything, including life, sound so simple."

Leaning back on the grass, he lifted his face to the sunshine. "When you break it down to basics, life is simple, isn't it? What does a man need after all? Shelter, food, a sense of purpose and someone to share it with." He opened one eye and smiled. "And a good fishing hole no one else knows about."

Smiling, Ivy unwrapped the delicacies the hotel had packed in the wicker basket. "And a sewing room, a place where you can leave your patterns and material without having to pick it all up and put it away when you're interrupted. A person certainly needs that."

"And a TV set for the Bronco games. We're missing the opening game, by the way."

"Don't remind me, I can't bear to think about it. We also need a car in this perfect life we're describing. Everyone needs a car."

"A good pickup."

"Not a Jaguar?" she teased, passing him a hard-boiled egg pickled in champagne. Their fingers brushed and for a startling moment, Ivy felt electrified. From a single touch. Thankfully Eric had bent forward and didn't notice her peculiar expression.

"Definitely not a Jaguar. But a good dog. A man needs a good dog. Preferably of uncertain parentage."

"I didn't know you wanted a dog." Amazingly, her voice sounded normal. Yet when she looked at him, her throat dried.

"Not in the city. A city is no place for a dog. But I miss having an animal."

They discussed pets they'd had over the years, and Ivy somehow managed to hold up her end of the conversation. Actually her thoughts were centered on bringing her rebellious body under control. Eric talked about Duke, an Irish setter he'd loved as a child; Ivy remembered Wheatie, a cat that had slept on her bed throughout her childhood.

Suddenly she laughed. "Can you imagine what Kevin would say if he were here to overhear this conversation?" When Eric didn't respond, she answered the question herself. "He'd say we were boring."

"Would you rather talk about jewels or investments? Or we could gossip about Lord and Lady whoever. I'm afraid I'm not very knowledgeable about fashion."

"You did all right with this," Ivy said, indicating her shirt and jeans. "I can't tell you how much I appreciated it. But you spent too much." She was suddenly aware that she had drawn his attention to jeans that were a bit too tight. The strange flashes of heat she had been experiencing all day returned in force.

"Money is no object," he said, looking away from her as if aware he had been staring. "I'm rich, remember? Besides, you can't buy clothes in Cannes that don't carry a designer label. At least I couldn't find any."

"Are you falling asleep?"

"Mmm. Just dozing." He rolled onto his stomach and rested his head on folded arms. The lashes against his cheek looked incredibly long and thick.

Ivy turned away and tasted her wine. That was how he would look in the morning—drowsy, his sandy hair tousled. She shook off the image with some difficulty.

Suppressing a sigh, she leaned back on her elbows and watched the people exploring the maze of narrow lanes below her. Were any of them feeling as confused as she was?

She had believed that today would be an escape from the strange unrest she had been feeling, that being with Eric would put her mind at ease and provide a respite from the peculiar thoughts she'd been having lately. But it hadn't worked that way. Her new sexual awareness included Eric.

Each time his lips opened in a smile, her heart rolled over. Each time she brushed against his masculine solidity, her nerves tingled. His voice surrounded her with warmth, his aftershave teased at her senses. She found herself fascinated by the smallest things: the curve of his ear, the way his hair touched his collar, his hands. Especially his hands. She watched his hands and helplessly wondered if they would be rough or gentle on a woman's skin.

"Stop this," Ivy muttered through her teeth.

She had passed the point of chastising herself for thinking such thoughts about a friend. She had moved into a state of confusion that involved feeling attracted to two men at the same time.

Although she didn't like to compare people, she couldn't help thinking how very different Eric and Kevin were. She couldn't have shared a day like this with Kevin. He wouldn't have sat still for a picnic and a cat nap. He would have laughed at any serious discussion of love, and it wouldn't have occurred to him to wonder about the people who had once lived in these ruins. Like the angry starlet, Kevin was a public person, comfortable among crowds, at ease with holding center stage, glib with strangers. The real Kevin, the one she wanted to reach, remained submerged.

That wasn't the case with Eric. Ivy didn't have a sense that Eric withheld his own preferences in order to conform to fads or other people's opinions. He was what he was. A quiet man, a thoughtful man, a man with simple tastes. And

Ivy was not the only woman to sense Eric's strength. She had noticed dozens of women track him with their eyes as he passed through the hotel lobby or entered a room. She had noticed how women looked at Kevin, but it was Eric they looked at twice. And she didn't blame them. The crowd at Cannes had a peculiar sameness about them: designer clothing, polished exteriors and jaded interiors. In such a group, Eric's rugged individuality stood out like a flashing light.

The strange thing was she was attracted to both men, as different as they were. And her strange new feelings disturbed her. Or had she been unrealistic to suppose men and women could be friends without sexuality interfering at some point?

"A penny for your thoughts, Cyrano."

She jumped. "I thought you were dozing."

"Nope. I was peeking—you look so serious."

"I was just wondering if men and women can really be friends." It occurred to her that he might be hurt by such a statement. "Remember when I told you about Cassie Myers and you said I would make new friends? You were right. I have." Impulsively she took his hand, ignoring the thrill of heat that immediately raced up her arm. "You've become my best friend. But there are things I can't discuss with you that I could with Cassie."

She could see she had hurt him. "The thing is," she went on, "I look at you and..." But she couldn't possibly tell him about her strange yearnings. Trying to cover the lapse, she said quickly, "What I mean is, I can't discuss you with you."

"What?" Then he understood and he laughed. Ivy released his hand and felt herself blushing. "I see what you mean. Well, how big a problem is it? What would you say about me?"

The old hated shyness returned and she found it an effort to speak. "I'm not sure." Then she thought of something to serve as a way out of these dangerous waters. "I might say I don't think winning the lottery has made you particularly happy. That I worry about you."

"No need." Turning aside, he gathered up the remains of the picnic, and she couldn't see his expression. "Sometimes you have to have a lot of money to discover you don't have to have a lot of money. I'm getting it worked out."

"And what have you concluded?" Standing, she folded the linen napkins and placed them in the basket, careful not to touch Eric and send her berserk system off on another tangent.

"Seriously?"

"Of course, seriously. I'm interested."

Taking her arm, he helped her across a pile of rocks then led her toward the maze of narrow lanes. "Do you want to explore some of the shops?"

Her arm tingled. "I'd rather hear your conclusions."

"For one thing," he said, as they walked past the gate and started down the road leading to the parking lot. "I don't think I'm a writer."

"Isn't that for a publisher to decide?"

"I'd be embarrassed for anyone to see the stuff I've done. Frankly it's pretty awful."

"What's the problem? Is it anything I can help with?" They passed the spot where the starlet had confided to the world that she had fallen deeply and passionately in love at first sight.

"I don't think so. For one thing, the book is too short. Most books have more than three chapters, don't they?"

Ivy burst out laughing. "That's all you've got? Three chapters?"

"Well, I have a few more, but how long does it take to say: If you want the best fishing in Colorado, pick a spot along the Blue River and throw in your line?'' He opened the car door for her.

"Maybe you're being too hard on yourself," Ivy suggested. "Why don't you consider sending what you have to a literary agent? If an agent likes the piece, maybe he'll have suggestions on how to expand it."

"That's the next step in the plan, but I'm not too confident about Eric North as an author."

"Which brings us back to my original worry. Winning the lottery hasn't been as wonderful as you expected, has it?"

His hands tightened on the steering wheel. "I've learned more about money since winning the lottery than I learned in several years of banking."

"For instance?" She loved watching him drive. His touch was light but sure, the car an extension of himself.

"For instance, money is only important if you don't have enough. For instance, money isn't the answer. For instance, money creates as many problems as it solves." After expanding on these thoughts, he glanced at her. "Has winning the sweepstakes been as wonderful as you thought it would be?"

"Heavens, yes! That old saw about money not buying happiness isn't true in my case. I'm happier than I've ever been. I have everything I ever wanted. A new nose, new contacts, a new confident me. I have a beautiful apartment, fabulous clothes, a dependable car, and independence. I'm here in Europe on a dream vacation. What more can I ask? I have everything my heart desires."

Eric nodded, not taking his eyes from the sweep of road. "But what next, Ivy?" Now he glanced at her briefly. "Now that you've gotten everything you ever wanted, what do you do or buy next? More of what you already have? Do you rush to buy the next 'in' thing? Chase the latest sensation? Now that you have it all, what do you dream about or hope for?"

The burst of questions surprised and disturbed her. "I don't know," she said finally. "I haven't thought that far ahead. We were so busy preparing for the trip..."

"At some point you'll think about it. You'll wake up one morning and discover your life has become a mini-version of the Cannes Film Festival. A fast-paced round of social events. If that's what you want, then fine. But if it isn't..."

"That isn't what you want, is it, Eric?" she asked quietly.

"I'm not a party animal, Cyrano," he said, injecting a lightness into a conversation that had become serious. "Not like you farm girls."

"We farm girls prefer our parties spread out over several days, not several parties in one day. So maybe I'm not the party girl you think I am. Of course you banker types probably wouldn't recognize a party girl if one dropped in your lap."

"That depends on the size of her balance sheet," he said, grinning.

The rest of the drive passed quickly. They stopped outside Cannes for dinner, choosing an out-of-the-way place with a spectacular view of the Mediterranean.

"Can you remember enough high-school French to translate this menu?" Eric asked, giving her a helpless look across the checkered tablecloth.

"Are you kidding? Without Kevin, we're lost."

But it was fun being lost with Eric. They stumbled through ordering, then gasped and laughed as dish after dish appeared on their table, some of the items recognizable, some not.

"We ordered enough food to feed France!"

"I have no idea what I'm eating, but it's wonderful. Here, try a bite of this." Ivy lifted her fork and watched his lips close around the end. For some reason, Eric eating from her fork struck her as erotic. Heat flooded her face and her mouth turned down in irritation at her crazy thoughts.

Everything struck her as erotic. The sun dropping into the sea, the way their knees occasionally brushed under the table, the strength in Eric's hands as he opened the mussels, the curls of sandy hair peeking from his opened collar, the breeze from the overhead fan on the back of her neck, the taste of new foods, the musky smell of Eric's aftershave...everything. Simply everything.

"There's something seriously wrong with me," she whispered. A small, fierce fire burned in the pit of her stomach. She felt hot one instant, chilled the next. And most of all, she felt a powerful but indefinable yearning for something, but she didn't know precisely what. It wasn't food; she was stuffed. It wasn't clothing; she was dressed appropriately for the restaurant. It wasn't thirst; the table was heavy with water, wine and coffee.

"Are you ill?" Concern intensified Eric's look and the fire in the pit of her stomach burned a little hotter.

"I don't know. I feel...I feel strange."

"Strange? Like how?"

"I can't explain it."

She couldn't tell him about the fire in her stomach, or the chill that accompanied it when he looked at her in a certain way. Nor could she tell him that she was fixated on his mouth, finding his lips as fascinating as his wide shoulders. Or that the candlelight darkened his tan and made his teeth seem snowy white and beautiful. She couldn't tell him that she was sitting there wondering what it would feel like to be in his arms and how she would respond if he kissed her. Certainly she couldn't tell him that her virgin body had awakened with a shout and was now sending strong, urgent signals throughout her nervous system.

"Maybe you're still tired." Eric signaled the waiter and asked for their check. "Come on, party girl, we'll take you back to the hotel and put you to bed."

The thought of Eric putting her to bed paralyzed her for a moment. She looked at his strong, concerned face, handsome in the candlelight, and a series of overwhelmingly erotic images flooded her mind. She imagined him undressing her, slowly, his warm fingers brushing her skin. She visualized him sweeping her naked body into his arms and placing her tenderly upon the bed. And then...

"Ivy, you're starting to worry me. You look as if you have a fever." He stood. "Let's get out of here."

Of course she looked as if she had a fever. She was blushing as bright as a tomato. If someone ever invented a cosmetic operation to excise blushing, she would have been first in line to have it done.

They drove to the hotel in silence. For the first time in Ivy's memory it was not a comfortable silence. Every time she looked at Eric, the blush returned; so did images that made her squirm with embarrassment. And for the first time since unveiling her new nose, she felt as miserably shy and tongue-tied as the old Ivy Enders. She absolutely could not think of a thing to say to him.

Outside the door to her room, Eric clasped her by the shoulders and frowned down at her. "Shall I send for the hotel doctor?"

The heat of his hands on her shoulders made her gasp. And she swayed on her feet, fighting the urge to move forward against his chest and throw her arms around him.

"No, I'm not ill. I'll be fine." She didn't need the hotel doctor, she thought. She needed Dr. Ruth.

"You're sure?"

"Yes. Just leave me alone, will you?" Surprise lifted his eyebrows and she realized she had spoken more sharply than she had intended. "I'm sorry, I just... Oh, Eric, just go away, will you? I'm having some very unfriendly thoughts." Instantly she regretted the last words. She had just told him she was seeing him as something other than a friend, she was seeing him as a man.

His hands dropped from her shoulders and he stiffened. "I was only trying to help."

Her hands were shaking and she couldn't get her room key into the lock. "I know that. And I'm grateful." Thank heaven, it appeared he had misunderstood her. Finally the door opened. "I'm sorry I was snappish, but I really can't be with you right now. Okay? Good night."

She stepped inside and closed the door in his face, leaving him standing in the corridor.

Eric stared at her door, wondering what he had said or done to upset her. He tried to remember exactly when her mood had changed.

The door opened and she scowled at him.

"I forgot to thank you. This was a wonderful day, possibly one of the best days of my life."

He stared at her. "Are you being sarcastic?"

"Of course not." She looked furious. "I mean it. This was a wonderful, wonderful day. Thank you."

Then she slammed the door.

For a moment Eric remained in the corridor, hoping she would open the door again and tell him what this was all about. He had a crazy idea that she was standing just on the other side of the door, listening.

"Ivy?" Silence. "Ivy, if I said something to upset you, I apologize. Talk to me, will you?" Still silence.

He waited a minute more, then after another moment he turned and walked down the corridor to his own room.

The telephone was ringing when he stepped inside, but when he picked it up, no one answered. "Ivy? Is that you?"

He could hear someone breathing, then, after a long pause, there was a click and the phone went dead.

He swore, then poured a splash of brandy into a glass and laid on the bed, staring at the telephone. Should he phone her? Should he wait and hope she phoned him again? If, indeed, the earlier call had been from her. It could have been a wrong number, or it could have been someone he had met in the past few days.

Sipping the brandy, he reviewed his past few hours with Ivy, trying to identify where things had gone wrong. Finally he thought he had it.

She had behaved a little strangely off and on throughout the day, but the moment when things had really changed was when she had said they were lost without Kevin.

Now he understood. He tossed off the brandy and frowned toward the window. She had been missing Kevin. Maybe she had been comparing a day with him to a day with Kevin. Hadn't she said something in Eze about how boring the conversation would have been for Kevin? Maybe it was boring to her, too.

Then when they had dinner and she saw what a fiasco he made of ordering, the comparison had been driven home. Kevin wouldn't have botched dinner by ordering too many items—items he couldn't identify. Sure, Ivy had laughed and had been a good sport about it, but she must have been thinking how different, how much better, it would have been if Kevin had been there.

And of course she had gotten angry with him at the door to her room. There he was, hanging around like he expected her to invite him inside, when she was probably eager to be alone so she could phone Kevin. That business about not feeling very friendly at the moment, not in the mood for company, he supposed, had only been a polite ruse to get rid of him. But he had been too obtuse to see it. Finally, she'd had to come right out and ask him to go away.

Embarrassment tightened his jaw. He had been enjoying the day and her company so much that he had allowed the obvious to flow past him. Well, it wouldn't happen again.

After a shower and another brandy, he propped his pillows against the headboard and reached for the new Michener novel he had started the day before. But he couldn't concentrate.

He was glad they were going home the day after tomorrow. He was ready.

Chapter Eleven

"Are you comfortable?" Kevin asked, fussing with Ivy's seat belt. "That wasn't a good choice for travel," he said, indicating her linen suit. "You'll be a mass of wrinkles before we land. Which reminds me, did you see what the duchess wore last night? The woman's taste has not improved since last year. And didn't you think—"

She looked out the airplane window. "Kevin? I don't want to talk right now."

Turning toward the aisle, she noticed that Eric appeared to be engrossed in a Michener novel. She bit her lower lip. Unless she had imagined it, he had seemed distant when she'd run into him at checkout; polite, as if he had forgotten how rude she had been, but...distant.

Leaning backward, she closed her eyes for takeoff. Maybe she was imagining that Eric seemed distant. Heaven knew, her imagination had been working overtime lately. Most likely she was making a big deal out of nothing.

"Are you glad we're going home?" she asked across the aisle.

"Yes and no," Kevin answered, assuming she had directed the question to him. Eric must have thought so, too, because he didn't glance up from his book. "I'll be glad to escape Panzy Rothschild, won't you? I'm sure he was following us, or does that sound a bit paranoid? Whatever, it seemed wherever we went he turned up, too, and the man is so dreary. He can't talk about anything except his father's business.''

"I thought he was rather charming.''

"My dear Ivy, tell me you're joking! Panzy Rothschild is as charming as a process server. He's not even a Paris Rothschild. He's from somewhere in Ohio.''

"I don't mean to be rude, Kevin, but I can hardly hold my eyes open.'' She pulled the shade down over the window and positioned a pillow between the wall and her seat. "See you in customs.''

"How boring.'' Kevin made a face. "This is shaping up as a repeat of the flight over. You're going to sleep and Eric is reading again. What am I supposed to do?''

"I think I spotted one of the ubiquitous starlets a few rows back. You could talk to her.''

He looked at her for a moment. "I think I will.''

When he had gone, Ivy hesitated, then called across the aisle. "Hey, Dumbo. Would you like to take this vacant seat and lend a lady your shoulder for a pillow?'' She had to call his name twice before he heard her, then repeat the invitation.

"Kevin will return in a few minutes,'' Eric said, as if he guessed she was looking for reassurance.

"I know, but . . . But you want to read, is that it?''

"This one's a page-turner.''

In Ivy's opinion, no Michener book was a page-turner. Once again, she felt a sense of distance between them.

"Eric? We're still friends, aren't we?''

This he heard immediately, and his head snapped up from the book. "How can you ask that? Of course we're friends.''

"You're not angry with me?''

He looked surprised. "Why would I be angry with you?''

"Because I was rude and acted a little weird the other night."

"I'm sure you had your reasons."

"I did." She wondered if the people in the row behind could overhear this across-the-aisle conversation. "I wish I could tell you why I was acting so dumb, but it's a Cassie thing. You know, one of those things I could tell Cassie, but I can't tell you. A girl thing."

"I understand." She knew he didn't.

When he returned to his book, Ivy turned her face into the pillow and closed her eyes, but she didn't fall asleep immediately. She wondered if Kevin was flirting with the starlet, wondered if the starlet was flirting with him. She wished Eric would move across the aisle and sit beside her. She wondered if he had told the truth about the scriptwriter or if that had been a joke and he had been seeing the scriptwriter throughout the trip. Had they exchanged phone numbers and addresses? Kevin might talk about paranoia, but it was she who was exhibiting all the signs, she thought, disgusted with herself.

Well, they would be home soon and everything would return to normal. God knew, she needed some normalcy in her life. She hoped when they got home, everything would return to what it had been. She wouldn't turn to Jell-O whenever Eric or Kevin touched her arm. She wouldn't feel that fluttery upheaval when Eric looked at her. Especially Eric. Her last thought before falling asleep was curiosity about Europe. She wondered if there was something diabolical in France's water that turned people into quivering masses of sexual urgency. Something that turned well-adjusted virgins into maladjusted creatures who erupted into a trembling yearning mass whenever a man looked at them. That day with Eric in Eze had left her devastated.

Finally, she closed her eyes and let the hum of the engines lull her to sleep.

ERIC STRETCHED then swung his feet over the side of the
bed, awakened by the sound of traffic in the street below. It
was good to be home even if home wasn't quite what he
wanted it to be.

While he showered and shaved, he thought about the trip
to Europe—not about the trip itself, but what it represented. The trip had been a goal, then a culmination of
planning and anticipation; now it served as a marker sepa-
rating one period from another.

After pulling on a pair of tan cords and an ivory knit
sweater, he set the coffee to brew, then drank his orange
juice while he read over the résumé he had typed the previous night.

He wouldn't send the résumé out yet, not until he heard
from the agent about his book. That much he had promised himself. But now that the European trip was behind
him, he understood it was time to stop drifting, time to decide the direction of his future.

"You aren't dressed for tennis," Ivy noticed when she
appeared for her morning coffee.

"I'm not going. I've learned all I'm going to learn about
tennis. More lessons would be redundant."

"Your backhand could use some work."

"Agreed. If I planned to play a lot, I'd work on it. But
I'm never going to be more than a Sunday player. So..."

Ivy fidgeted, rearranging items on his countertop. Then
she lifted a serious face and gazed at him intently above the
rim of her coffee cup. "Eric, can we talk straight for a minute?"

"Sure. But first, would you like to have your coffee on the
balcony? Enjoy the good weather while we can?"

The morning was cool but sunny, the smoky gold scent of
late autumn making the air as crisp as a new dollar bill.
Twice in the three weeks since they had returned from Europe, there had been a thin skim of frost on the windshields

in the early mornings. Local forecasters predicted snow before the end of the month.

Ivy stepped to the balcony railing and inhaled deeply. "It smells like an early winter. Cool and slightly damp." Turning, she smiled at him. "At home they say you can predict how deep the snow will get by the height of the skunk cabbage. You haven't seen any skunk cabbage around here, have you?"

"Not lately." Sitting at the table, he crossed his ankles on top of the railing. "So, you want to do some straight talking. What's on your mind, Cyrano?"

"You," Ivy said eventually, taking the seat across from him. "You're on my mind. What's going on with you, Eric? You've seemed... I don't know... different since we returned. Distant."

"Have I? I'm sorry, I've had a lot on my mind."

"First you dropped the golf lessons, now the tennis. I have a feeling you aren't too interested in skiing lessons, either." She was wearing her glasses this morning instead of her contacts. Occasionally he teased her about looking studious when she wore her glasses, but he liked them. This was his favorite part of the day, mainly because he enjoyed seeing her before she put on her makeup, while her face was fresh and rosy and her hair was still pulled back and caught by a rubber band.

"I haven't decided yet about skiing. It depends on several other things."

"The book? Have you sent it to an agent?"

"Last week."

"When will you hear?"

"Three weeks, maybe a month." He shrugged.

She tilted her head and studied him. "You didn't tell me about mailing the manuscript. Eric, I feel like you're cutting me out of your life."

"I'm sorry you think that. That isn't my intention or what I want." He had hoped to clear the way for her romance with Kevin subtly enough that she wouldn't notice. That she had noticed flattered and disturbed him at the same time. "Look, we've both been busy since we got home from Europe. I've had the book, and you've been caught up in the social whirl." That much was true. "Which reminds me, what have you and Kevin been up to lately?"

She gave him a look that indicated she knew he was changing the subject and that they would get back to it later. Then she lifted her head toward Kevin's balcony. "Things are different since the trip. Since my nose job." A pause followed and a sigh. "The pace lately has been almost as frantic as it was in Cannes. We've attended a lot of parties, and I've met most of Kevin's friends. We've been to the symphony, the Central City opera, a designer showing at Montaldos and the opening of a new gallery on Sixteenth Street."

"Sounds interesting."

"Liar." Now she smiled at him. "If you thought these events were interesting, you'd have joined us." The smile faded and she studied him. "Why don't you join us, Eric? It isn't the same without you. Remember the ole one for all and all for one? The ole networking?"

"Things change," he said after a while. "The three of us don't need each other as much as we did in the beginning. We've come a long way, Ivy. Especially you and me. In the beginning we needed each other for support. I think we can stand alone now."

"You're my friend, Eric, and I miss you."

She said it so simply, and her gaze was so open and direct, that his heart constricted. Despite the sophistication she had recently acquired, there was still an innocence about her that he hoped she never lost.

"We see each other every morning," he said, looking away from her. It didn't help. He still saw her face in front of his mind, still wanted to take her into his arms. But the old saying about two being company and three being a crowd held true. Unfortunately he wasn't a member of the two. Ivy wanted someone else.

"I know, but...telling you what I'm doing isn't the same as sharing it with you."

He wasn't sure how to respond. Suddenly he remembered Ivy as she had been when they first met. She couldn't or wouldn't have spoken as frankly then. Nor would he. Both of them had been made cautious and protective by a lifetime of shyness and lack of confidence. Months had been required to reach this point of trust. Genuine friendship had made the difference. Not the money, not the ear pinning or the nose job. But friendship. It required a great deal of friendship and trust for her to speak as openly as she was speaking now. He owed her a careful response.

"Ivy, I don't want you to misunderstand," he said, feeling his way. "I will always be your friend. I will always care about you and be interested in what you're doing and what you're feeling."

"I don't like the sound of this, Eric. It's almost like you're saying goodbye or something." She stared at him.

"It's not goodbye, but I guess we have reached a parting of sorts." At some level, he had known this conversation was coming. But he hadn't expected it this morning. "You and I are moving in different directions. You have stepped into a world that wasn't possible before the sweepstakes, and it's a world you like and enjoy. I've done the same, only I've discovered I don't enjoy most of it. I'm coming to the conclusion that the best of all worlds for me would be something midpoint. What I'm trying to say is not that I'm cutting you out of my life, but that our lives are turning down different paths. But that doesn't mean I care any less about you, or that our friendship has to end. It just has to change.''

Everything he said was the truth, but not the whole truth. What she was sensing was also true: he was trying to establish a distance between them. But he couldn't tell her why. He couldn't tell her that he didn't accompany her and Kevin because it hurt to see them together. Or that he felt jealous every time she mentioned Kevin's name. He couldn't tell her that the only way he could honestly wish for her happiness with another man was if he didn't have to watch the romance developing.

She surprised him by dropping her head. "There are parts of the glamorous life I don't like, either." He didn't press, but waited until she lifted troubled eyes and looked at him across the table. "There are drugs at these parties. Did you know that?" She examined his expression. "Of course you knew. Why didn't you tell me?"

"That's an issue each person has to decide for himself." Even though he had sworn he wouldn't press, he couldn't stop himself from asking, "What have you decided?"

Again she looked toward Kevin's balcony, but this time she frowned. "What did you do when you were going to Kevin's parties?"

"An occasional Scotch-and-water is enough for me."

"It isn't easy being the odd man out. Feeling small-townish. Like a prude." When he said nothing, she bit the inside of her cheek. "No one else seems to have a problem with it. Everyone does it."

"Not everyone."

"I'm worried about Kevin. He drinks too much, does too much of everything. I don't think Kevin has ever heard of moderation. Do you think it would help if I talked to him about his drinking?"

This was an area Eric didn't want to get into. Nor did he wish to play Dear Abby for her. It would be too painful.

Instead of answering, he made an observation. "You care for him a lot, don't you?"

The cool morning had colored her cheeks, and now a blush deepened the pink. "I care a lot for both of you."

"Loyalty is one of your best qualities," he said before she departed for her tennis lesson. Eventually she would have to admit she had chosen Kevin.

"Why do you sound so sad when you say that?"

"No reason. I just hope you won't let loyalty stand in the way of judgment."

IVY STOOD IN FRONT of the mirror, studying her new lace-and-satin lingerie. It was definitely sexy, she thought, feeling her face grow hot. Hastily she dropped a wool-flannel dress over her head, then made a face as she decided the soft flannel was as sensual on her skin as the lingerie, though in a different way.

Sighing, she lifted her brush and pulled it through her hair. If there was something strange in Europe's water, the same peculiar substance was also in Denver's water. Her nervous system hadn't calmed down.

Let Eric or Kevin give her a long, intent look and her heart banged against her ribs, blood surged into her cheeks, and her stomach dropped to her toes. And suddenly she was thinking of a snowy, firelit night with soft music and a large bowl of iced caviar.

The physical yearnings surfaced again during dinner. She watched Kevin talking to Michael and Yvonne and wanted to touch his shining hair, wanted to lean her shoulder against his. As usual he captivated the dinner table, evoking laughter with his anecdotes, murmurs of mock sympathy for his exaggerated troubles. Ivy watched and listened and wished the dinner weren't rushed, wished the group was not going on to a party afterward.

After dessert and liqueurs, Ivy joined Yvonne and Missy in the ladies room. She examined herself in the mirror then applied more concealer under her eyes. The pace was beginning to show. "I don't know how you do it," she said to Yvonne. "These late nights and early mornings are killing me."

"Early mornings?" Yvonne made a face, then leaned to the mirror to apply fresh lipstick. "I haven't seen an early morning in years. And don't plan to." Her eyes met Ivy's in the mirror and she tilted a curious eyebrow. "By the way, congratulations."

"Congratulations? For what?"

"For Kevin, of course. Everyone's talking. We always wondered what type of girl he'd end up with." She flicked a glance at Ivy then returned to her lipstick.

"I think you're a bit premature," Ivy said, smiling. "Kevin and I are just friends. Nothing more."

"Oh, come on," Missy said. "Kevin hasn't dated anyone else since he came home from Europe. This has to be a record. Three weeks with one woman? For Kevin, that's practically an official announcement."

Ivy hadn't thought about it, and now realized she should have. Mentally she swiftly listed the evenings of the previous weeks and realized she had spent nearly all of them with Kevin.

When he took her arm and led her outside to the waiting car, she stared up at him with a thoughtful expression.

"Something wrong, dear Ivy?"

"No, I was just . . . thinking how charming you were at dinner."

"I'm always charming," he said, helping her into the car. He slid in beside her and took her hand as Walter pulled from the curb. "Charm is a McCallister trait. Any McCallister child who does not exhibit charm by the age of three is immediately put out for adoption. It's a survival tactic in our family."

She laughed, but when the laughter faded, her expression turned hesitant, then shy. "Kevin, do we have to go to this party?"

"We said we would."

"Doesn't a quiet evening at home sound good for a change?"

"Darling, it's early. What on earth would we do? Watch TV?"

"Some people do, you know."

"God, how boring." He dropped his arm around her shoulder and his voice settled into a low, gossipy purr. "Now then, what do you think about the outrageous dress Missy is wearing? And did you notice Michael couldn't keep his hands off Yvonne? It's so funny, because Yvonne is Michael's ex-wife's best friend. How do you suppose they're managing that? And I wonder if Alice Ann knows about it?"

The house where the party was being held was enormous, and so lavishly furnished that Ivy was unable to suppress a gasp. Most of the people she recognized by now, but there were always a few newcomers. One caught her eye, a young woman who looked as out of place as Ivy felt.

"Hi," she said, "I'm Ivy Enders."

"I'm Rita Colchek." There was a pause. "I came with Billy Walters."

"Are you having a good time?"

"No," the girl blurted. "I don't belong here." Ivy's surprise showed. "Well, look at me. I'm not dressed right. I'm not beautiful like you and everyone else. And I'm sure not rich." She bit her lip and looked out over the room. "Besides, there're drugs here. I don't want to get messed up with that."

"Not everyone here takes them. No one will push you into something you don't want to do."

Rita Colchek looked at her, then smiled. "You're living in a dreamworld. No one has to push. You push yourself because you want to belong." She swore. "I don't need this. If you see Billy, tell him I went home."

Ivy stared after her. She felt oddly defensive. Rita hadn't given them a chance. No one was rowdy tonight, it was a mellow group. Most of the people here were talking quietly or dancing, just doing what people did at parties.

Then someone shouted, "Snow! It's snowing!"

"Ski season can't be far behind!"

Along with several others, Ivy turned to the bank of French windows along the west wall. Fat wet flakes swirled past the outside spotlights. The ground was too warm for the snow to stick; it would be gone by morning. But it was lovely.

"All right," Yvonne called happily. "Shuck 'em down. It's hot-tub time, everyone!"

To Ivy's embarrassment, a dozen people threw off their clothes, as uninhibited as children, and dashed out the doors through the falling snow, toward a hot tub steaming on the patio.

"Are you coming?" Kevin asked, taking her arm. "It's traditional—hot tubbing on the night of the first snow."

"Naked?" Her mouth felt dry.

He grinned at her. "Unless you brought a swimsuit." His eyes dropped to her breasts and a shiver ran through Ivy's body.

"I—I can't." The idea of group nudity was totally repugnant.

"Suit yourself." He looked into her eyes for a moment, then shrugged. "You don't mind if I join the others? It's a tradition."

"No, of course not. You—you go ahead." She strove mightily to sound indifferent, sophisticated and unconcerned.

Standing not four feet from her, Kevin stripped off his suit and vest and let them fall in a rumpled pile his London tailors would not have approved of. Monogrammed silk jockey shorts followed. Then, showing no signs of embarrassment or discomfort, he filled a wineglass, saluted her and stepped out the French doors.

Ivy swallowed hard.

Fighting a wave of light-headedness and an explosion of revulsion, Ivy watched him stroll through the falling snow then step into the hot tub with the others. She pressed her forehead to the cold glass and struggled to regain some sense of equilibrium. Through the open door, she could hear the people in the hot tub laughing and trading jokes filled with sexual innuendo.

When she turned around to face into the living room, she felt worse. Those who had chosen to remain behind were couples engrossed in each other. Suddenly she felt like Rita Colchek. She didn't belong here.

Almost running, not knowing where she was going until she reached the front door, Ivy asked the man there for her coat and requested a taxi.

"Please tell Mr. McCallister I left. I—I'm not feeling well."

The taxi hadn't traveled ten feet before she regretted her action. What would Kevin think when he found she'd run off? That was something the old Ivy Enders might have done. Would he think she was hopelessly provincial? Beyond redemption? Would he think she was the world's greatest prude?

She stepped off the elevator in Tower B and instinctively hurried toward Eric's apartment. He answered the door dressed in a thick terry robe, his hair standing on end.

"Oh, God," she groaned. "What time is it? I'm sorry, Eric, I didn't think. You were probably in bed..."

"Not yet. I was reading. What's wrong? Did something happen?"

"Yes. I discovered you can take the mouse out of the country, but you can't take the country out of the mouse." She held her hands to the fire he had built in the fireplace and watched the snow tumbling lazily past the balcony doors.

"I think I understand that. Maybe." Smiling, he took her coat. "I have some peach brandy..."

"Sounds wonderful." She wondered if he would put on some clothes, hoped he would. She'd had enough of naked people for one night, and she assumed Eric was naked beneath the robe. Her stomach tightened at the thought and she pressed her lips together.

But he stepped behind the counter and poured two brandies into crystal snifters. Apparently he was so comfortable with their friendship that he didn't feel uneasy wearing his robe. Or he didn't see her as a woman.

"Do you want to talk about it?" he asked gently, watching her pace with the brandy.

"What's to talk about? I'm a small-town prude. As old-fashioned as a sewing machine. My value system is stuck in the Middle Ages." Staring at nothing, she swallowed a third of the brandy.

"I think I'm starting to figure this out."

"If you're thinking hot tubs, you're right." He grinned at her. "Everyone threw off their clothes and ran outside. Just like that. Except me. I turned fourteen shades of red and headed for the nearest taxi." She made a sound of self-disgust. "You know what I kept thinking? I kept wondering what the people in Limon would say if they knew I was naked in a hot tub with a dozen other people. Isn't that stupid?"

Eric settled back in his favorite chair and crossed his ankles on the ottoman. He watched her without comment.

"The problem is me, Eric." She waved her brandy glass then resumed pacing in front of the fire. "Nobody else was embarrassed to show a little skin. Nobody else made a big deal out of it. Just me. I was the only one who couldn't handle it."

"There's nothing wrong with that."

"There's *everything* wrong with that! It looks like I'm standing back with my nose in the air passing judgment!"

"Are you, Ivy?"

She stopped in front of him and stared. "Is that what I'm doing?" Her shoulders dropped. "I don't mean to. I don't want to." Dropping onto the ottoman, she pushed his feet aside and leaned her elbows on her knees and looked into the fire. "There are a lot of ways to live," she said finally. "One way isn't right and another way wrong. They're just different."

They sat in silence, sipping the peach brandy and watching the fire. Finally Ivy sighed and stood. "I'm sorry I barged in here like this." She drew a breath. "For so many years I felt like a kid standing outside the candy store with my nose pressed to the glass. I thought after I won the sweepstakes all that would change. But sometimes I still feel like an outsider."

"That problem doesn't have anything to do with money."

"Maybe. But I wouldn't be in this mess if I hadn't won the sweepstakes."

"Would you rather be filling out claim forms in Limon?"

"No," she said firmly. "I wouldn't have missed this experience for the world. But—but I just don't have everything worked out yet."

At the door, Eric's large hands closed around her shoulders and he smiled down into her eyes. "Trust your instincts, Ivy. You'll do what's best for you."

Trust her instincts? That was a laugh. Right now her instinct was to wind her arms around Eric's neck and press against him and kiss him. For a long moment, she stared at his mouth, then shook herself and ducked out from under his hands.

She mumbled something about being grateful that he'd listened and she thanked him for the peach brandy, then she fled down the hall toward her own apartment.

Once inside, she stood in front of the balcony doors, watching the snowflakes. She was so confused. She had hated it when Kevin shed his clothing so casually. Then, less than an hour later, she had gazed at Eric North's mouth and had wanted to run her hands beneath the collar of his robe and feel his warm skin beneath her palms. It didn't make sense.

She decided she was either very ill or going crazy.

"IVY? IT'S KEVIN. If you're there, pick up the phone."

With reluctance, she switched off the machine and lifted the receiver. "Hi, Kevin."

"Are you feeling better?"

So. They were both going to pretend she had really been ill. "Much better, thank you."

"It's a beautiful day. Too bad the snow didn't stick."

"Yes."

"So. Are you looking forward to the fashion show? I believe this is the first time Valentino has shown a collection in Denver."

"I think I'll beg off."

"Beg off Valentino? Ivy darling, you really are ill. You must go! Everyone will be there."

"I don't think so." A blush fired her cheeks. She stared at the wall, but she kept remembering him naked under circumstances that embarrassed her. She closed her eyes, trying to banish the image.

"What will you do if you miss Valentino?"

"I'm going to sew."

"*Sew?*"

"Yes." Sewing had always calmed her.

He was silent for a long moment. "Ivy, we need to talk."

"This is something you don't understand, Kevin. I like to sew. I have always liked to sew. It's something that helps me relax. It takes my mind off...other things."

"That's not what I meant. Look, let's have dinner. Just the two of us."

"Just the two of us?" She blinked in surprise. It was never Kevin and one other person. He surrounded himself with people. "Are you in trouble or something?"

He laughed. "You might say that. My place? At eight o'clock?"

"All right." What kind of trouble raised a laugh? With Kevin it could be anything.

"Wear your black chiffon, it's my favorite. And your fox coat."

After hanging up the telephone, she stared at it a moment, then turned the machine back on and went into the second bedroom she had set up as a sewing room. Except she hadn't used it until now.

She bent over and searched through her pattern box, looking for patterns for baby dresses, then she spent several minutes deciding which one Iris would like best. Next, she opened the closet and rummaged through her material remnants, choosing a small red-and-blue plaid and a spool of lace.

Finally, almost reverently, Ivy removed the cover from the sewing machine and ran her hand over the cool metal.

Dammit, she liked to sew. Some people liked to golf or to jump into hot tubs, but she liked to sew. And she hadn't sewn since the sweepstakes, much too long ago.

Within minutes, she had the pattern and the material spread over her sewing table, pins in her mouth, and was happily humming to the radio as she cut and pinned.

When she quit to dress for dinner, she felt great. It had been the nicest day she'd spent since she and Eric fished the Blue River. Holding the tiny dress to the light, she inspected the stitches with approval. If she got home early enough tonight, she'd handstitch the lace around the hem. For a moment she considered phoning Kevin and begging off. She hated unfinished projects.

Then she laughed aloud. What was she thinking of? Giving up a one-on-one dinner with Kevin McCallister to stay home and sew? Not a chance. Besides, he had mentioned a problem.

As she showered and dressed, she finally let her mind focus on the meaning of a private dinner with Kevin. And the by now familiar butterflies again fluttered through her stomach. Yvonne's comment returned to memory. First Kevin had stopped seeing other women; now he had invited her to a private dinner.

She wondered if it meant what she thought it did.

Chapter Twelve

"Kevin, do you think it would impose on Eric if I asked his investment advice?" It was something Ivy had been considering for several weeks. "I don't anticipate any more large purchases, my expenses have settled out, and I've been thinking I should do something with my money."

"We have an excellent investment department attached to McCallister Enterprises. I'd be happy to make you an appointment if you'd like."

She looked up from the excellent beef Wellington she was pushing around her plate. "You wouldn't recommend Eric?"

"That isn't the point. As far as I know, Eric's advice is prudent and sound. Judging from the newspapers and trade journals tossed around his apartment, he certainly stays informed. I merely question the wisdom of doing business with a friend. Do you really want a friend knowing everything about your finances?"

Ivy blinked. "I don't keep secrets from Eric. Or you," she added hastily. The last wasn't quite true.

"Maybe you should, darling. One never knows when a friend may become something else."

The arch look he gave her across the array of silver and crystal was ripe with layers of meaning. Ivy bit her lip and suppressed a sigh. Kevin was being very enigmatic tonight.

It seemed nearly everything he said could be interpreted at least two ways. That and being alone with him had placed her in a state of heightened tension.

She smoothed a linen napkin over the lap of her black chiffon. "Kevin, you mentioned you were in some sort of trouble...?"

"That subject will keep until after dinner, Ivy dear. Eat, eat. Walter will be shattered if you don't approve his beef Wellington. And I can promise a bit of heaven for dessert."

He was being so attentive tonight that Ivy's appetite had dwindled and her nerves had drawn tight. "You won't offer a single hint?" she asked, trying to keep her voice as light as his.

"Surely you can guess."

"What?" Now the pressure was on and she shifted in her seat. She didn't have even a remote clue what sort of trouble Kevin was experiencing, but his expression indicated he expected her to know. Lapsing into silence, she frantically tried to recall a word here or a hint there, something to at least lead her in the right direction. Something about his father? "Daddy" was always a sore point, but she couldn't recall anything of recent importance. Mrs. McCallister? She didn't think so. Something involving one of his friends? She bit her lip.

"You're being coy tonight," she commented after Walter had cleared dinner then served peach flambée. Acting coy was one of Kevin's less-attractive traits.

"I'm wounded," he said, falling backward in his chair. His blue, blue eyes twinkled. "You don't know what I'm talking about, do you? I supposed you would guess immediately that I'm referring to you."

"Me?" Her mouth fell open and she stared. "*I'm* your problem?"

Standing, he moved around the table and held her chair. Then he directed Walter to place a tray containing coffee and brandy on the coffee table in the living room. "That will be all for this evening, Walter."

The moment Kevin sat beside her on the sofa, Ivy clasped her hands in her lap and turned to face him. "I feel terrible. I apologize for whatever I've done to cause a problem."

"Darling Ivy," he said softly, smoothing a strand of hair back from her cheek. "You always imagine the worst. You're so quick to assume fault."

"You said you were in trouble. You said—"

"And you managed to create an entire scenario."

His breath smelled pleasantly of the wine they'd had with dinner and now the brandy, which he tasted then replaced on the table.

"The trouble is you, Ivy, because I can't get you out of my mind. Frankly, you're interfering with my backhand and my golf swing. I wonder what you'll be wearing the next time I see you. I wonder how you'll style your wonderful hair. I try to imagine what we'll talk about."

A tiny sound rushed past her lips, and Ivy lifted her fingers to cover her mouth. He was looking at her in a focused way that she didn't associate with Kevin McCallister. Kevin looked at her hair or her nose or her eyes. He didn't look at her total person. But that's what he was doing now. That look combined with the words he was speaking was what she had dreamed of. A tremble appeared in the fingertips she pressed to her lips.

"I think you've had similar thoughts about me. Isn't it time we did something about it?"

"Like what?"

It was the stupidest question she had ever asked, prompted by the nervousness caused by realizing he was about to kiss her.

Leaning forward, so near she could smell the provocative scent of his aftershave and his cologne, he gently removed her hand from her lips, then kissed each trembling finger-tip, watching her as he did so.

"Oh."

Then he cupped her chin in his palm, gazed deeply into her wide eyes, and he brushed his mouth across hers. Once, twice, then he kissed her, really kissed her. His arms went around her and his lips opened over hers.

Ivy closed her eyes and sank against him, giving herself to the kiss she had wanted so long.

And she waited.

She waited for bells to peal and stars to explode behind her eyelids. She waited for the feelings she had been fighting to suppress.

Nothing happened. No pealing, no exploding, no surge of eager hormones suddenly given the go-ahead.

Kevin groaned against her mouth and gently pulled her to her feet. This time, he pressed her against the length of his body as he kissed her, and she felt the stirrings of his erection.

But that was all she felt. Afraid he would notice her lack of response, she wrapped her arms around his neck and returned his kiss, hoping a more active participation would awaken the thrill she had expected to feel.

She didn't know why it didn't. Kevin McCallister was a practiced, expert lover. His kisses began slowly and teasingly, then intensified, sending signals that were unmistakable.

Leaning his forehead against hers, holding her hips tightly to his, he asked in a thick voice, "Do you want me as much as I want you?"

Panic constricted Ivy's throat.

"Kevin..."

He kissed her eyelids, the corner of her mouth. The heels of his hands slid to the sides of her breasts, and he moved his hips against her body, teasing, suggesting.

Then his hands slid up behind her, and she felt his fingers tug the zipper of the black chiffon.

For a moment she froze and her mind refused to function. Then, as the zipper inched downward, she understood something was about to happen that she hadn't anticipated. She wasn't ready for this.

"Please." Reaching behind her, she caught his hand. "Kevin, this is happening too fast."

He smiled against her lips. "Fast? Darling, we've known each other six months."

"But not like this." Placing her hand on his chest, she stepped backward. The last thing she wanted was to offend or embarrass either of them. And she absolutely did not want him to know she had felt nothing when he kissed her. Even if she had understood why herself, she wouldn't have wanted him to know.

"This is rather awkward," he said, his voice stiff. "I thought—"

"You were right," Ivy interrupted. Embarrassment heated her face. If she had been better at dissembling, she might have tried it, but she wasn't. The only way she knew was the truth. The color deepened in her cheeks. "I—I've had something of a crush on you since we met. But I didn't think you . . . I mean, I thought . . ."

"Ah, I think I'm beginning to understand."

At least he didn't sound as wooden. She drew a breath. "One minute I was thinking of you only as a good friend, then you were kissing me, really kissing me, but I couldn't quite make the switch in my mind from friend to . . . something else."

Maybe that was it, the reason she hadn't felt anything when he kissed her. Of course it was. She couldn't suppress an attraction for weeks and months, then in the span of a minute or two sweep away all the months of repressing her feelings.

"From that perspective, I guess it is fast," Kevin said, smiling. Taking her hand, he led her back to the sofa and served them both coffee and more brandy. "I'm still your friend, dearest Ivy, but I'd like to be more. I hope you feel the same."

"I . . . there's something I need to tell you." Now was the moment to confess her virginity.

He placed a finger over her lips. "Later." Then he was kissing her again, kisses calculated to heat her body and stir her passions.

After a while, the panic returned. When she continued to feel nothing more than mild pleasure at being held and kissed, Ivy wondered wildly if there was something wrong with her; maybe she was frigid. These thoughts sped through her mind. Any other woman would be racing toward the bedroom by now. Any other woman would have melted to a puddle under Kevin's skilled kisses and long, teasing caresses.

"You're so tense," Kevin murmured against her mouth. "Relax, darling."

"I'm sorry." Squeezing her eyes shut, she wrapped her arms around his neck and tried to will herself to respond naturally. Nothing happened.

"Look," he said, easing gently away from her. "Let's sit back a minute and relax a little."

"Good heavens! Will you look at the time? I had no idea it was so late." Standing abruptly, she smoothed her hair and pressed down her skirt. She wondered if she had lipstick smeared over her chin.

"Late? It's only ten o'clock."

"I'm going to Limon tomorrow to visit my family." She hadn't known that's what she wanted to do until this instant. "I'd like to get an early start." Right now, she needed some time to herself. Struggling not to run, she walked to the foyer and opened the hall closet.

"Ivy, I'll get your coat."

"No trouble. I've already got it." The air in his apartment was smothering her. "Thank Walter for the wonderful dinner. And I'll see you . . . soon."

"Ivy—"

Too wound up to wait for the elevator, she ran toward the fire stairs, winding down floor after floor until her head spun. When she finally rushed outside, she fell against the brick wall of the building and gulped in great swallows of frosty night air.

When her breath had slowed and her heart resumed a normal beat, she lifted her head and looked up at the opposing tower, her eyes automatically seeking Eric's apartment. His balcony windows were dark.

It was just as well he was out. No one looked their best after a bout of serious necking. Still, it would have been good to talk to Eric and, with his help, try to sort out what had happened and how she felt about it.

It wasn't until Ivy was inside her own apartment relaxing in a tub full of bubbles that she realized she couldn't have discussed Kevin with Eric.

She had believed she could discuss almost anything with Eric, but the thought of telling him about kissing Kevin made her uncomfortable. In fact, when she thought about it, she didn't want Eric to know. She didn't know why she felt that way and she didn't feel comfortable withholding anything from him. But she knew she would.

Finally she let herself think about Kevin. Frustrated, she slapped the bubbles on top of the water. She didn't know why she hadn't responded to him. She should have. She wanted to. And she should have told him she'd never made love to a man before and told him how she had always imagined it. The fire, the soft music—and the caviar.

"MR. NORTH? This is Richard McDonald in New York. Thank you for returning my call."

"I didn't expect to hear from you this soon." Richard McDonald was the agent he had sent his book to.

"My assistant put your manuscript on top of the pile. As I'm a fishing buff, she thought I'd enjoy it. And I did. Very much. The book needs fleshing out and some polish, but I think it's salable. I'd like to represent you on the project."

Eric stood beside the balcony windows, watching snow blow past the glass. "Thank you," he said finally, "but I've decided not to sell it." He heard a sound of surprise over the wire. "I apologize for taking your time."

"May I ask why?" McDonald said finally.

"I doubt the answer will make much sense—but I'm a banker, not a writer."

McDonald laughed. "You're right, that doesn't make much sense. Well, if you change your mind..."

"Thank you, but I don't think I will."

After hanging up, he continued to stand at the window, watching the snow. Until the surprise of Richard McDonald's acceptance, he hadn't realized he had decided not to pursue the fishing book. Now, thinking about it, he understood he had made the decision some time ago. The book was only a delaying mechanism, a reason to put off deciding what he was going to do with the rest of his life.

For weeks he had been discovering what he didn't want to do, but he hadn't put the same thought into what he did want to do.

But he knew. He was a banker, as he had told McDonald. He liked working with figures, enjoyed contact with people who had dreams and the opportunity to help attain those dreams with a bank loan. He enjoyed working with money, investing it, loaning it, the challenge of making it grow. He needed challenge and purpose in his life, something greater than improving his golf score. He needed to be part of a community, needed to know he was making a contribution of time and energy.

Switching on his computer, he printed a half dozen copies of his résumé, turning his thoughts to where he would send them. He wanted a small town like the town he had grown up in, and the town should be situated near great fishing. Somewhere in or near the mountains.

When he had made his choices, he wrote the cover letters, then sealed and stamped the envelopes and leaned back from his desk, sipping coffee that had grown cold.

An ironic smile touched his mouth. Life was strange. After winning the lottery, he had changed everything—his residence, his car, his way of life—thinking that was what he wanted. Now, after seven months of a life-style most people would envy, he was planning to do his damnedest to get back his old life. In the end, the lottery money had proved to be unimportant. Except that it had allowed him to meet Ivy.

A whisper of pain darted across his expression. That would be the hardest part, leaving Ivy.

But, if he were honest, the parting had already begun. He still saw her in the mornings for coffee, but seldom saw her again until the next morning. For a time, she had continued to invite him to join her and Kevin, but when he consistently refused, eventually she had stopped asking.

The distance had widened between them. Once, she would have told him in excited detail everything she and Kevin talked about. She would have described where they went and whom they met and what they did. Now, she covered it in a sentence and turned the conversation to him, or to generalities, or to books or videos or what was happening in the news.

Eric didn't blame her or resent the turn their friendship had taken. There was only space for two in a romance. And it was definitely a romance between Ivy and Kevin. Neither dated anyone else; they spent every moment together.

He leaned backward in his chair and stared at the falling snow. And he wondered if Ivy had sampled caviar yet.

The thought was so painful that he stood immediately and busied himself organizing his files. After a time, he gave it up with a sound of disgust. He couldn't stop thinking about her.

It was a good thing he planned to leave Denver. It would be an act of sheer masochism to stay here.

Pulling on a parka and cap, he stuffed the résumés into his pocket then rode the elevator down to the parking garage. The Jaguar gleamed softly beneath the overhead lights. For a long moment Eric stood beside the elevator doors, his hands thrust in his pockets, staring at the Jaguar.

Then his expression brightened and he grinned. He knew what he was going to do today. He was going to buy himself a Dodge Ram pickup with real sheepskin seat covers and the best stereo system in town.

IVY HAD ALWAYS liked snow, but today the sight of the falling snow depressed her. Mainly because she had to go out when what she really wanted to do was snuggle inside and curl up with a book, or maybe do a little sewing before the game. The Denver Broncos were playing the Miami Dolphins in Miami, and she and Kevin planned to join a group of friends at Lombardi's and watch the game on the big screen. Afterward they planned to drive to Vail for dinner, and if the snow was good, they might stay for a couple of days of midweek skiing.

It sounded wonderful, so why did she feel so low?

Hoping the cold air would clear her thoughts, Ivy opened the balcony doors and stepped outside, lifting her face to the snow.

Most of the group at Lombardi's would be there for the socializing, not for the game. That was one of the problems troubling her. Ivy genuinely liked football; she was a serious fan. It frustrated her to try to watch the ball game while everyone around her was chattering and gossiping and glancing at the screen only when a big play occurred or the Broncos scored. She would have preferred to watch the game from her own living room, settled in with a big bowl of popcorn and one or two friends who were as passionate about football as she was.

The second troubling item was the possible overnight in Vail. Kevin had mentioned it casually, as loathe as ever to commit to an actual plan. The trip to Vail had sounded good the night before; if the impulse lasted through today, they would probably go.

But it was more than dinner and skiing, Ivy sensed. Kevin had been patient, but their relationship was moving steadily toward sexual commitment. She couldn't put him off forever. Maybe that's what he was telling her by suggesting the Vail overnight trip.

Shivering, she stepped back inside and glanced at the clock. Running late, she hurried to her closet and selected an Irish wool pantsuit and a cream-colored turtlenecked sweater.

She had just finished pulling her hair into a French twist when Kevin rang her doorbell. Lifting her mouth for a quick kiss, she told him she'd only be a minute, then she sprayed a little Joy behind her ears and on her wrists.

"You're having a drink?" she asked, surprised, when she returned to the living room. "Do we have time?"

Kevin shrugged. "The world won't end if we miss the kickoff."

"Oh." She tried not to let her disappointment show. "We could watch it here." Her face brightened. "In fact, that's a great idea. Let's forget Lombardi's and stay home. I'll make some popcorn and we'll build a fire—''

"You're kidding. Do you really want to see the game?" His expression indicated this was an amusing idea; it also told her that he hadn't noticed her frustration during the past weeks.

"Kevin, I genuinely love football. But it's so annoying trying to watch at Lombardi's. All the noise and the people moving in front of the screen."

He looked surprised. "I always thought you were joking about being a football fan. If I'd known, Daddy has a private box at the stadium. We'll go next week if it's a home game." Tilting his head, he looked at her. "Meanwhile, if you really like it that much, let's go to today's game."

"What?"

"We'll drive to the airport, get on a plane, and go to Miami." Now his face brightened. "We'll get out of this damned weather, see the game, have a little dinner. There's a great seafood place in Nassau, just a short plane hop away. Yes, I like this. We'll stay in Nassau a couple of days, win some money at the casino, do a little diving. Throw some things into a suitcase, and let's go."

"Wait a minute." Laughing, Ivy raised her hands. "First, by the time we get to Miami, the game will be over. Second, you have a meeting with your father the day after tomorrow. And third...well, third is that I like to plan for things. I enjoy the anticipation as much as the event itself."

The enthusiasm faded from his eyes. "You're saying you don't want to go."

"Not right this minute."

"You never want to do anything on the spur of the moment." He drained his Scotch and moved to the counter to pour another. "You know something, Ivy, you don't know how to enjoy money. You're stuck in some sort of middle-class mind-set that steps back and examines every purchase, every act before you make a move. Frankly it's a little dreary."

The laughter faded from her expression. "I'm sorry you think I'm dreary," she said stiffly. "But I can assure you, I do enjoy my money."

Restless, he paced back toward the balcony windows. "Really? Every dress you bought, you moaned how you could have sewn it cheaper." He waved a hand to indicate the apartment. "You're living in a closet instead of in one of the penthouse apartments. And you don't even like parties!"

"I like parties," she said defensively.

"Really? You've run out on more than you've stayed for. Did you think I hadn't noticed?"

Color flooded her cheeks. "I'm from a small town, Kevin. I'm uncomfortable with people shucking their clothes for any excuse and jumping into hot tubs or chasing each other around the grounds."

"How long are you going to use that small-town bit as an excuse? Are you ever going to grow up and join the real world?"

They stared at each other across the living room.

"What's this really about, Kevin?" Ivy asked eventually, keeping her voice level. She continued to feel the heat in her cheeks. "Is it your father? Are you worrying about the meeting with him?"

"What do you think? I know what that'll be about—the same old thing. 'When are you coming into the business, Kevin? When are you going to stop wasting yourself and do something productive with your life? Do you think McCallister Enterprises runs itself? You have responsibilities, obligations, noblesse oblige.'" He swore.

"Why do you fight it so hard?"

"Because I'm lazy and indifferent. That's what my father would say."

"What do you say?"

He stared at her. "Don't start, Ivy. I don't need this from you." Turning, he faced the snowy windows and tasted his Scotch. "Maybe I'm afraid of failing. Or maybe I'm afraid of succeeding. Who knows? The point is, I'm not interested in business. Never have been, never will be. Who cares?"

"I care."

"Do you?" Swinging around, he faced her. "You have a funny way of showing it." He watched the color deepen in her cheeks. "Let's talk about the real problem, shall we?"

"Kevin—"

"I've been patient, Ivy. I thought about what Eric said, about taking it slow with you, and I realized he was right. So I haven't rushed you. I haven't pushed."

"You and Eric discussed me?" High color flared in her cheeks. "What did he tell you?"

"He said you were special, innocent in a way. The take-home-to-mama type. So, okay. I'll buy that. But you're carrying this innocent bit too far. It's turned into a game and the game is high-school stuff. Adolescent. What the hell do you hope to gain by teasing, then withdrawing? Does it give you some kind of sadistic thrill to keep me dangling? Or is it just a power trip with you?"

Ivy gasped and stepped backward, horrified. "Is that what you think?"

"What else? If there's another explanation, I'm listening."

She turned away and bit her lip, she should have told him long ago. She drew a deep breath. "Kevin, I'm not playing games with you. I . . . I'm a virgin."

"I beg your pardon?"

"I've never made love before."

He stared at her with astonishment. "You're asking me to believe . . ."

"It's the truth." Surely he could see it in her face. She'd blushed before, but not like this. Her face was a scarlet beacon.

"My God." He put his empty glass on the counter. "You're acting like a skittish colt because you are a skittish colt." He stared into space a minute, then a smile curved his mouth. The smile turned into a laugh. "Good Lord, in this day and age! Seriously, are you—Yes, I see it now." Grinning, he dropped to the sofa. "For God's sake, why didn't you tell me sooner?"

The smile and the laugh embarrassed her. Holding her head high, Ivy answered in a whisper. "I wanted to. The right moment just didn't seem to—That isn't true." She drew another breath. "I was embarrassed to tell you. I wasn't sure you'd even believe me. And I guess I was afraid you might laugh."

"Tell me something—does Eric know this?" When she nodded, not looking at him, his voice turned petulant. "You managed to find the right moment with him. Why couldn't you tell me?"

"For the reasons I just told you. And maybe because Eric has been my friend from the beginning, but you—" she bit her lip "—were always something different."

"Ivy, come here." He patted the seat beside him on the sofa.

The anger or the frustration or whatever it was that he'd been feeling when he arrived had disappeared from his expression. His eyes had softened and the gaze he ran over her body was warm and speculative.

Ivy wet her lips. "I told you now to explain why I've been behaving like I have. I don't mean to tease, then withdraw. I haven't been trying to keep you dangling and I haven't been playing games."

"Come here."

"Kevin, you have to know the rest. I . . . this is going to sound silly, but over the years I've built up a fantasy about the first time." It felt as if she had been blushing for an hour. But she'd come this far. Drawing another breath, she finished it. "I want it to be romantic. Music, a crackling fire, snow blowing past the window. Iced champagne and—and caviar."

A broad smile lit his expression. "Finally. The great caviar mystery is solved!"

"I don't want it to be impulsive. It has to mean something."

The register of his voice deepened and he cast a meaningful glance toward the balcony doors. "It's snowing." Standing, he moved to the stereo and found an FM station playing soft romantic instrumentals. "I can have champagne on ice in five minutes and a fire crackling in less than that. I'll call over and ask Walter to bring us caviar." He shook his head and smiled. "It's so simple. Why didn't I see it?"

Again, Ivy had the sensation that events were moving out of control, happening too fast.

"Kevin, wait." Five minutes ago, her thoughts had been centered solely on football. Now Kevin was orchestrating the biggest event of her life and she felt as if she had no part in it.

"I'll phone Walter about the caviar."

Stepping in front of him, she gently took the phone from his hand and replaced it. "Kevin, did you hear the last part? I don't want the first time to be impulsive."

"Planned sex? That's what you want?"

The color returned to her face. "The first time, yes."

"Ivy, for God's sake. This isn't a spur-of-the-moment passion. I've been trying to get you in bed for a month! How long do you expect me to wait?"

"I don't know. Until it's right for both of us."

"What will it take to make it right for you?"

"Kevin, I don't feel comfortable standing here plotting my own seduction. Can you understand that?"

"Not when you've just been telling me that you like to plan things." Stepping forward, he took her into his arms. "Look, darling, I'm trying to be sensitive about this. If you have a fantasy, I'm willing to help make it happen." He kissed her eyelids. "You're trembling."

She leaned against him, drawing comfort from his touch. "There has to be a sense of commitment," she whispered. Her voice was soft, but insistent. "That's the biggest part of it."

"What kind of commitment?" Kisses flowed over her temples, the corners of her mouth.

"What kinds of commitment are there?"

"The best commitment for us, I think, is a commitment to take one step at a time and see where it leads us."

When she looked at him, her eyes were troubled. "I'm not sure that's enough," she said slowly. For a moment she had believed he understood. Now she wasn't as certain.

"Are you talking about love?"

"Would that be so wrong?"

"You know I love you, and I know you love me."

But did she? Ivy wished she felt as confident on that point as he seemed to. Lately she had begun to wonder if possibly she was confusing admiration, hero worship, maybe a mentor/student relationship for something deeper. Maybe she was trying to graft one set of emotions onto another.

"Kevin, do you believe in love at first sight?"

"Sure." He grinned at her. "It's happened to me at least a dozen times."

She thought about falling in and out of love that easily and that often, and the thought saddened her. Gently she disengaged herself. "We've missed the kickoff."

"You won't change your mind about going to Miami?"

"No."

"How about Vail?"

She hesitated, then said, "I don't think so, Kevin. Not yet."

"Well, I can't say I'm not disappointed." He touched her cheek. "I can tell you there's no way I can stay here alone with you and behave myself. So, get your coat, dear Ivy. We're off to Lombardi's." He gave her an exaggerated leer. "You're absolutely positively certain you won't reconsider and share some caviar with me today?"

She smiled. "First I have to work out a couple of things in my mind."

"Don't take too long." He held the door for her. "Meanwhile, from this moment on I'll always have some Beluga iced and waiting."

The snow had stopped when he brought her home about midnight. "It's early yet," Kevin said outside her door, a suggestion dangling.

"I'm really tired," Ivy said, straightening his coat collar. "And I think I need some time alone."

"I have never known anyone who spends as much time alone as you do."

"Not lately. I feel like I haven't had five minutes to myself since my new nose. We've been constantly on the go." Smiling, she turned him toward the elevators. "Speaking of which..."

"Cruel woman."

Laughing, she blew him a kiss, then stepped into her apartment and closed the door and leaned against it. There was so much to think about.

She stood quietly for a moment, then she opened the door and walked down the hall to Eric's apartment. There was no light under the door and she hesitated for a moment. Then she knocked and waited. If he was already in bed, she would apologize. But she needed a dose of Eric's good, hard, common sense.

When there was no answer, she decided maybe he had a date and wasn't home yet. Disappointment tugged her lip downward. She wanted to talk to him, not a surface talk like they'd had lately, but a talk like the talks they used to have. Slowly she turned her steps back to her own apartment.

He wasn't home the next morning, either. Ivy stood outside his door and blinked in surprise. This was the first morning in the months she had known him that she would not share her morning coffee with Eric North.

Where could he be? Immediately a blush heated her face, and she turned abruptly away.

"Okay," she muttered as she hurried back to her own apartment. "So he spent the night with someone. Big deal."

But she felt betrayed.

She had no claim on Eric. She was acting foolish. There was no rule that said they had to have coffee together every single morning. And no rule that said he had to tell her where he was going and when.

But still, she felt peculiar inside. Fair or not, she had expected him to be there for her, and he wasn't.

Where had he gone? And who was he with?

Chapter Thirteen

Because Jackson Hole, Wyoming nestled in the heart of the Teton Mountains, and was a western resort town it had a more polished look and feel than Delta, Colorado. But it was still a small town. People greeted each other by name on the streets, community spirit was strong, and the president of Wyoming National Bank assured Eric there was no better fishing and hunting in the world than in the Jackson Hole area.

"We've got everything. Mountains, lakes, streams, and scenery to take your breath away. And Yellowstone Park is just up the road," Norman Halloran finished. He leaned back from his desk and smiled. "So, Eric, what do you think? You've had a couple of days to look us over. Is Jackson Hole and Wyoming National what you're looking for?"

From where he sat Eric could see out the window into the town square. Although it was early November, a group of men and women were hanging Christmas lights on the massed antlers that formed an archway into the square. One of the local restaurant owners crossed the street carrying a tray of coffee and doughnuts for the workers.

"Jackson Hole is exactly what I'm looking for," Eric said firmly. He had to love a town where the president of the leading bank wore jeans, a corduroy jacket and cowboy boots. One look at Norm Halloran and Eric had known this was his kind of place.

"Actually," Norm said with a smile, "I'm more interested in your opinion of Wyoming National."

"You've been very generous." Norm had offered him a vice-president's position at nearly twice the salary Eric had made in Delta.

Norm grinned. "Who's kidding whom? I've seen your balance sheet. What we're offering must look like a pittance. Hell, Eric, you're going to be one of our largest depositors."

"I've seen your balance sheet, too. I'm small potatoes next to most of the resort owners." He returned Norm's smile, liking him, feeling the beginning of a friendship.

"So, what's it going to be? And how soon can you start?"

Eric laughed. "I accept. But only if you throw in one of those puppies to sweeten the deal." He nodded toward the box of puppies sleeping under Norm's desk. "Is it true what your secretary said? You refuse to approve a loan unless the applicant agrees to take a puppy?"

Norm nodded cheerfully. "No puppy, no loan. I'm shameless about it. If you take one, that's three to go. You can have two if you start next week," he added hopefully.

"Make it the week after and we've got a deal."

"You're a hard negotiator. I'm not sure how we've gotten along without you. What's the holdup?"

"I need to find a house for me and my new dog, tie up a few loose ends in Denver, get moved . . ."

"Are you interested in buying or renting?"

How he answered would indicate his level of commitment. Eric didn't hesitate. "I'm looking to buy." He'd known immediately he could put roots down here. Everything felt right.

Except for one item, one missing person.

"I'll phone Bill over at C-21. I think you might like the Thayer place. The house needs some work, but there's acreage, and a stream runs through the backyard."

Eric liked the Thayer place the instant he saw it. The house was built of dressed logs and featured banks of floor-to-ceiling windows and several balconies overlooking thick stands of pine and aspen. The moment he saw the house, he felt as if he were coming home. As Norm had said, the interior needed some remodeling, but the work would be mostly cosmetic.

"You'll probably want to replace the carpeting," Bill Major said. "And the place could use some fresh paint."

They were standing in the master bedroom admiring a fireplace that was a smaller version of the massive one in the great room.

"I'll take it," Eric said.

"Don't you want the missus to see it first?"

"I'm not married." The house was large for a bachelor: there were five bedrooms and a finished, walk-out basement. But someday, when he got over Ivy, maybe there would be someone else. He stopped in the doorway of a room that had puzzled him earlier. "Why would Thayer put in a table that folds down from the wall? Or install a built-in ironing board in a bedroom?"

Bill Major grinned at him. "If you'd asked that earlier, I would have known you weren't married. This is a sewing room. The skylights give good light all day, the shelves are odd shaped to hold material and patterns. That's a cutting table and I guess the ironing board is to press seams or hems."

"A sewing room," he repeated softly. Ivy's face appeared in front of him so vividly that he felt he could almost touch her cheek. "I have a friend who would love this room." Or would she? As far as he knew, Ivy had never used the Singer she had been so eager to buy. The country mouse had become a city mouse.

"At this price, the house isn't going anywhere. Do you want to take a few days and think it over? Look at some others?"

Usually he wasn't an impulsive type. But standing on the back deck, looking down at the stream gurgling over the rocks, then up at the majestic mountain peaks in the distance, Eric felt as if he was meant to be here. This was his house. It had been waiting for him.

"Let's go back to the office and draw up a contract," he said firmly. Then the banker in him took over. "We'll offer forty thousand below the asking price with ten percent down."

Bill smiled at him. "Norm said you'd drive a hard bargain."

"If the deal is accepted, I'd like to move in immediately. Naturally I'll pay rent until closing."

"Can't see a problem with that." Bill thrust out his hand. "Welcome to Jackson Hole, Eric. Glad to have you with us."

He wore a wide smile during the mile-and-a-half drive back into Jackson Hole. Damn, he loved this place. The clean, brisk air, the friendly people, the sense of community. He liked the casual atmosphere, the smallness of the downtown area. The bank was all he had hoped it would be, and finding a house so perfect this quickly was a joy and an omen.

There was only one thing missing.

"Ivy?" KEVIN OPENED the balcony doors and called to her. "What are you doing out there? It's freezing." Behind him, she heard the sounds of the party, loud music and laughter.

She wrapped her arms around her body and watched her breath emerge like a silver plume against the darkness. "I just needed some fresh air. Is Yvonne still making an ass of herself with Missy's date?''

Frowning, Ivy dropped her head. She was beginning to sound like the others, bored and catty. She had never believed it would happen.

"Come inside and find out for yourself. You're going to catch cold standing out there without a coat."

"Kevin..." Once again she dropped her eyes to Eric's dark apartment. "When was the last time you saw Eric?"

"Eric? I don't know, a couple of weeks ago. Right after he traded the Jag for a pickup, I think. Why?"

Her eyebrows lifted. "Eric bought a pickup?"

"Can you imagine? I couldn't believe it myself. Are you coming inside?"

Why hadn't Eric mentioned the pickup? Because she hadn't seen him, that was why. She had stopped going to his apartment in the mornings. After several incidents of standing in front of his door listening to the silence on the other side, she had quit subjecting herself to the disappointment. It wasn't just that he wasn't there to start the day; it hurt that he didn't leave her a message.

"Obviously you've seen Eric since I have." She told herself she was acting foolishly to feel upset that Eric had remained in contact with Kevin but not her. "Is he...is he seeing someone? Seriously?"

"Who knows? Ivy, it's starting to snow, will you please come inside?"

Before she turned away from the balcony rail, she saw the lights go on in Eric's apartment and she stared at them a moment through the snowflakes. Maybe she would try again tomorrow morning. She missed their morning coffee.

Kevin waited for her in the doorway and caught her around the waist as she approached. A moist kiss brushed the side of her mouth. "It's snowing, my delectable little virgin. And we have a fire going, champagne, and enough caviar to sate Russia. What say we send these silly people home and make wild passionate love until morning?''

"You're high." She saw it in his pupils, heard it in his voice. For weeks she had been fooling herself, trying hard to convince herself he wasn't like the others. Now there seemed to be no denying it.

"And feeling marvelous!"

Stepping past him, Ivy paused beside the fireplace and pulled her lower lip between her teeth. Why did she fight it so hard? Would the earth spin to a halt if she joined them? She was weary of being the odd man out, weary of not quite belonging. Though no one pushed her or made her feel awkward about refusing, she knew they probably talked about her priggishness behind her back. They talked about everything else.

Besides, she wanted to feel marvelous too. Everyone looked like they were having such a wonderful time, laughing at the same tired old jokes, talking to the same old crowd. Maybe that's what made the old jokes new, made the old crowd fascinating again. Maybe if she crossed this last line, she would finally feel as if she belonged, as if it was okay to be an Enders from Limon, as if it was okay to be bored and disappointed with the beautiful people.

It would be so easy to belong. Then suddenly, she heard Rita Colchek's voice in her memory: "No one has to push. You push yourself because you want to belong."

She had not seen Rita since that night, but her words echoed in Ivy's mind. God, what was she thinking of? Spinning on her heel, feeling shaky inside, Ivy fled down the hallway toward the guest bathroom. Yvonne stepped out as she reached the door.

"Well, well, if it isn't our little Ivy." Yvonne's voice was low and bitchy. A nasty smile curved her lips. "So you decided to come in from outside and rejoin the degenerates."

"I just needed some air," Ivy explained quietly. Yvonne was a different person when she had been drinking. She tried to keep that in mind and excuse her sarcastic tone.

"You always seem to need some air just when the party begins to get interesting. Isn't that curious? Hopefully you won't be such a prude after you've had your—" she laughed "—caviar."

Ivy's hand froze on the bathroom door. It could be a coincidence, she told herself. "I beg your pardon?"

"Tell me," Yvonne said, smiling nastily. "Are you *really* a virgin? Mike and Billy are betting you are. Kevin isn't sure. But Missy and I think you're just playing it smart, holding out for a ring. Which is it? You can tell ole Yvonne."

Ivy's face blazed with color, but she felt icy inside. Without responding, she stepped into the bathroom and locked the door behind her, then leaned heavily on the sink. She felt sick.

Kevin had told them. Told them her most intimate secret, and they had discussed it, maybe laughed about it, made wagers on whether or not she had told the truth.

"Oh, God."

She covered her face with shaking fingers, wishing she didn't have to walk back out there and face them all, knowing they were whispering about her, laughing at her.

After dropping the lid of the toilet, she sat on it and let her head fall into her hands. She felt betrayed.

And it was possible the betrayal had just begun. What would happen after she and Kevin made love? Would he give everyone a blow-by-blow account? Would her most private moment be made common knowledge also?

Of course it would. How could she ever have doubted it? Salacious gossip was an antidote for boredom. And Kevin's crowd had made an art of boredom. It wasn't sophisticated to display excitement—that was for provincials like Ivy Enders who hadn't done everything and hadn't been everywhere. And it wasn't sophisticated to treat sex like it was special and important. Sex was just a fact of life, a form of amusement and entertainment—no big thing. Not to the "in" crowd.

But it was to her. She didn't think of sex as sex, she thought of it as lovemaking because that's what she wanted it to be. A statement of commitment, a gesture of love. She didn't want it to be casual, and she for damned sure didn't want it to be a topic for party conversation.

Suddenly Ivy felt bone-tired, weary of trying to belong, weary of trying to be something she was not.

She was tired of pretending not to be impressed by things that impressed her. She'd had it with passing herself off as an Enders from Bermuda. She hated the casual attitudes toward drugs, hated trying to ignore the fact that Kevin partook. She didn't like the frenzied chase from party to party, from event to event. She didn't like the boredom. She was beginning to understand that people who were bored were boring.

Bottom line: she didn't belong.

More important, she didn't want to belong.

The only surprise was that it had taken her so long to recognize it. She had been trying so hard to fit into a life she had always envied that she hadn't stopped long enough to examine that life and ask herself if she really wanted it.

She asked herself now, and the answer was a resounding no.

Her values were different from those of Kevin Mc-Callister and his friends. It had nothing to do with money or background. It had to do with basic character. She wouldn't have fit into this group if she had been born an heiress. She didn't look at the world the way they did; she didn't like the same things they did.

A great weight dropped from her shoulders. It was so simple. If she hadn't been blinded by the glamour and glitter, she would have seen it long ago. Ivy straightened and gazed at herself in the mirror. Beneath the new nose, the new contacts, the new hair and clothing, the old Ivy Enders smiled back at her.

"You know something?" she said aloud. "I like you just as you are." Her mirror image smiled. "You may be a prude, but you're a nice person. It's too bad you were too dumb to know that eight months ago. Too bad you thought you needed money and a nose and all the rest to be worthwhile. You never did."

The truth of what she had just said flowed through her and she straightened her shoulders. She stared at her image another moment, then she laughed. Suddenly she felt marvelous. She was free.

She opened the door and walked down the hallway, through the living room and into the foyer. Behind her, she heard Yvonne talking to someone and heard her name mentioned, but she didn't care. "My coat, please," she said to Walter and let him help her into the silver fox.

"You're leaving, miss?"

"In a moment." First there was something she had to do.

She found Kevin beside the fireplace, talking to Missy and Mike and a crowd of familiar faces. When he saw she was wearing her coat, he groaned. "Not again. What happened, now? Did someone show a flash of skin?" Then he saw the bowl of caviar in her hand and his expression changed. He jumped to his feet and grinned broadly, winking at Mike. "Well, excuse me, folks. I think the lady is inviting me to her apartment." He took her arm and leaned to her ear, his voice low and seductive. "At least that's what I'm hoping. Does that bowl mean what I think it does?"

"I doubt it," she said, staring at him. "But why are you whispering? Is there someone, anyone, here who hasn't heard the story about me?"

Raising the bowl, she upended it over his head then pressed it down. Caviar flooded over his face and shocked eyes, showered down on the shoulders of his cashmere sweater.

"You, my dear Kevin, are an insensitive, tacky bastard. You don't know how to be a friend." He was sputtering and wiping caviar from his eyes. The room had gone absolutely silent. "If I'm very lucky, I'll never see you or talk to you again."

In dead silence, she walked to the foyer then turned and smiled and wiggled her fingers. "*Ciao*, everyone. It's been a real bore."

THE KNOCK SURPRISED HIM. After glancing at the clock, Eric opened the door and smiled with genuine delight. "Ivy! Come in."

"I'm sorry to show up at your door so late, but it's the only time I can catch you. You're never home."

"Let me take your coat." He looked at the fur and went still inside. When he spoke it was an effort to keep his voice light. "Looks like you spilled cav—uh, something," he said, brushing at the fur. Turning so she couldn't see his expression, he hung the fur in the hall closet then relaxed his clenched jaw before he turned back to her. "What can I offer you? Coffee? A drink?"

"You're still drinking coffee at midnight?"

"You've forgotten I'm a confirmed coffeeholic." Stepping behind the counter he busied himself pouring a cup for her, adding a dash of brandy and a dollop of whipped cream. He deliberately forced his mind away from the beads of caviar spilled across her fur coat.

"It's so good to see you!" She had taken a seat at the counter and stared at him across the top. "There's so much I want to tell you, starting with what happened tonight."

Quickly his gaze dropped to her left hand, expecting to see an engagement ring. But she was wearing a simple pearl, the ring she had bought to replace one stolen in the burglary.

"Good news?" he asked, trying to raise a smile for her.

"Yes, I think so." The blush that tinted her cheeks told him nothing, but he could guess. Tonight she and Kevin had made it official; tomorrow they would shop for the ring. "But first," she said, cradling her coffee cup between her hands, "I want to know if it's true that you traded the Jag for a pickup?"

"A Dodge Ram," he said, glad she had changed the subject. "Hasn't been in the shop once, I'm happy to say."

"How does your girlfriend like it?"

"My girlfriend?" He looked at her across the counter. Then he managed a smile that didn't quite reach his eyes. "She hasn't seen the truck yet, but I think she'll like it fine."

Ivy ducked her head and bit her lip. Then she looked up with a bright smile. "Is she anyone I know?"

"No, but I think you'd like her." Now he laughed. "She's about this big, has reddish brown hair and button eyes that grab your heart, does the best cute-dog act I've ever seen. I haven't named her yet."

"You're talking about a dog?"

"A puppy. She's a charmer." Eric looked at her across the counter, thinking she was the loveliest woman he had ever known. God, he had missed her. Keeping busy helped, but she was always with him, just a thought away. He sought to regain some perspective by asking, "So, how's the big romance going?"

"I want to tell you all about it, but first where's this no-name puppy?"

"In Wyoming." He came around the counter to turn down the volume on the stereo. It wasn't until Ivy swiveled on the stool and he heard her gasp that he realized she hadn't noticed the packing boxes until now.

"Eric!" Sliding from the stool, she stood very still and gazed at the empty bookshelves, the vacant desk where his computer had been. The pictures were off the walls and his personal items had been wrapped and packed. Her face turned very pale and when she spoke again her voice was a whisper. "You're moving?"

"I've accepted a position with Wyoming National Bank in Jackson Hole, Wyoming."

Accusation and hurt filled her eyes. "When were you going to tell me?"

"I'm sorry, Ivy. I've been in and out at odd hours, and either you weren't home or it was too late to wake you." He then proceeded to tell her about the different small towns he had visited and the banks he had interviewed and how and why he had decided on Jackson Hole.

She listened in silence, her face expressionless. "What happened to your book?"

Had it been that long since they had really talked? He backed up and explained how he had reached the realization that he didn't want to write, he wanted something more.

"I'm not a city person, Ivy, I like small towns. I grew up in a small town and I want my children to grown up in one. It's a good life; it's what I want. You know how it is in small towns—everyone knows everyone. You can leave your house unlocked and not worry everything you own will be stolen before you return. I like the idea of contributing to a community. And I like the idea of working again at a job I enjoy and do well. This—" he lifted his hands to indicate the apartment and the city beyond "—isn't for me. It isn't what I want."

She nodded her golden brown head, then moved through the boxes like a sleepwalker. Finally she bent and opened a flap, removed a book from the box and looked at it. It seemed she stared at the book for a long time.

"Ivy?"

To his astonishment, she burst into tears.

"No," she said, backing away when he hurried toward her. "I'm all right. I don't know why I'm crying." She brushed at the tears with an embarrassed gesture. "I'm sorry, I—I'm happy for you, Eric, really I am." Wiping her cheeks, she looked up at him. "Dammit, I can't seem to stop crying! It's just that I'll miss you!"

"I'll miss you, too, Ivy. You must know that."

Looking around at the boxes, she lifted her hands and let them fall, then fumbled in her purse for a tissue. "I don't know why this is such a shock. I know it's what you want." She blew her nose and looked at him. "These are tears of happiness. I'm glad for you."

For a happy person, she looked surprisingly miserable. Eric didn't know how to respond because never in his wildest dreams had he imagined she would react to his leaving with tears.

"I'm happy, too," he said lamely, wishing she would let him comfort her.

"We'll still be friends, won't we?"

"Of course. Friends phone and write. We'll keep in touch."

But he knew that wasn't entirely true. Gradually the phone calls would occur less and less frequently, the letters would dwindle to a note at Christmas. She and Kevin would be busy with their lives; he would be busy with his. And eventually, maybe, the hurt would go away and he would find someone else who liked to fish and read and do all the other things he'd shared with Ivy Enders.

"That sounds so final," she said. The tissue she held to her eyes hid her face. "When are you leaving?"

"It depends on how quickly the packing and moving goes. Possibly tomorrow. Maybe the day after."

Her shoulders tightened. "So soon?"

He told her about the house he had bought and how the previous owners had agreed to rent to him until the closing next month. "I hope you and Kevin will visit me someday. I think you'd both like the house." He thought about mentioning the sewing room but decided against it.

Ivy turned on her heel and almost ran to the hall closet where she reached inside and pulled out the fur. "I have to go now," she said abruptly. Frowning, she brushed at the fur then shook the bits of caviar from the coat. "I'm glad for you, Eric, really. I'm happy you've found what you want." Fresh tears sprang to her eyes and she ran out of the door.

Once inside her own apartment, Ivy flung herself across the sofa and surrendered to a storm of weeping. If anyone had asked, she would not have been able to explain why she was sobbing. She certainly wasn't mourning Kevin, and she certainly didn't resent Eric's finding exactly what he wanted. So why wouldn't the stupid tears stop? And why did she feel so utterly miserable?

After a sleepless night, Ivy rose early and dressed in haste. But she took time to put on makeup and fix her hair. Then she hurried down the hall to Eric's apartment. The smell of freshly brewed coffee scented the hallway and her spirits lifted until she remembered this was the last time they would share morning coffee.

Eric's door opened before she knocked and two moving men emerged, carrying the sofa.

"Eric?" After the men moved past her, she entered the apartment, noticing how many items were gone just since last night.

"Hi. I was hoping you'd appear." He pointed to a cup of coffee, poured and waiting.

There were so many things she wanted to say, and Eric looked as if he wanted to say something, too. But the movers were passing in and out of the apartment and privacy was impossible. They talked in generalities. Eventually there seemed nothing more to say.

"Will you need a ride to the airport?" Ivy asked finally.

"I'm driving the pickup. Following the moving van."

"Oh." She'd asked a stupid question. Of course he would drive. The apartment was emptying at an alarming rate, much faster than she would have guessed.

"I'll be leaving today, instead of tomorrow."

He said it quietly, looking at her with an expression she couldn't read.

"Oh, Eric, I don't know what to say." She knew what she wanted to say, but it would have sounded incredibly selfish. She wanted to beg him not to go, wanted to tell him that she needed him, needed his strength and solid friendship. "What time...?"

"This is going faster than I thought it would." He looked away from her the way he sometimes did when he was telling a half truth. "I think we'll have it wrapped up by about three or four o'clock. If we leave immediately instead of waiting until tomorrow, we can make it to Cheyenne for the night. We'll have that much of a head start on tomorrow."

"Yes." The coffee tasted like ashes in her mouth. "Well, I have a few errands to run..." It was a lie, but she knew she had to get out of his apartment. She couldn't bear to watch the dismantling. "You'll stop by before you leave, won't you? To say goodbye?"

"Of course I will."

She looked at him standing behind the counter, tall and handsome, just out of the shower. When would she see him again? The thought disturbed her so greatly that she mumbled, "See you later," and fled to her own apartment.

Ivy couldn't do anything. Couldn't think, couldn't concentrate. She curled into the arm of the sofa, drinking coffee, listening to the moving men passing back and forth in the corridor. The phone rang again and again, but she let the answering machine handle the calls. There was no one she wanted to talk to except the man who was leaving her.

Shortly before three, she went into her bathroom and pressed a cold cloth to her eyes. Then she freshened her makeup and dragged a comb through her hair. For a moment she stared at her lifeless face in the mirror, then she put on a sweater she knew Eric liked and returned to the sofa to wait.

It wasn't until she heard his knock at her door that she realized how much she had been dreading it. Swallowing a fresh onslaught of tears, she slowly approached the door and opened it.

He was dressed to leave. He wore a sheepskin-lined denim jacket and jeans and boots. There was a small overnight bag on the floor beside him.

"Do you have time for a quick cup of coffee?" To her astonishment, her voice sounded almost normal.

"I'd like to, Ivy, but the van is waiting downstairs."

Her muscles were tight and knotted and she wanted to fling herself into his arms. She abandoned the pretense to sound normal. "Oh, Eric," she whispered, "it won't be the same without you. I know how selfish this sounds, how awful, but I don't want you to go."

"Ivy, I have to." Reaching, he caught her cold hand and held it between his. "Right now, we're friends. But if I stay, I'll ruin our friendship."

Looking up, she met his intense gaze and her heart skipped a beat. "What are you talking about? There's nothing you could do to ruin our friendship."

One of the moving men leaned out of the elevator. "We're ready to go when you are, Mr. North."

"I'll be right with you. Give me two minutes." When he looked back at her, his eyes were dark with emotion and he pressed her hand so hard that she winced. "Look, Ivy, I'd have to be a fool not to know that things are serious be-

tween you and Kevin. As your friend, I want to be happy for
you, happy that you and Kevin are…" He drew a breath and
looked away from her mouth. "But if I keep seeing you it
isn't going to happen that way. A better friend would be glad
that you've found Kevin and you're happy. But I'm having
trouble with it. Do you understand?"

"I'm trying to, but—"

"I have to go. Give me a hug, Cyrano."

She threw herself on him and buried her face in the warm
folds of his sheepskin collar. His arms went around her and
he held her for a moment in a tight, fierce embrace. Blindly
Ivy lifted her face and felt the electric shock when his lips
met hers.

The moment his warm mouth touched hers, her body lost
control, as if a puppeteer had assumed control of her limbs.
First she tensed as if an electric current were running hot
from Eric's mouth to every part of her trembling body; then
she went limp and folded against him, because her legs
would no longer support her. Waves of heat raced over her
skin as the kiss deepened and became urgent.

Her hands flew over his face, his hair, pressed against his
broad chest. Beneath his lips, her own parted in breathless
need and she felt his hands on her hips, holding her against
his body. A feeling of faintness swirled like a hot wind
through her mind, and her heart hammered against her ribs.

When he finally released her, Eric stared down at her,
looking as shaken as she felt.

"I will always love you, Ivy, my friend." His breath was
ragged.

Ivy leaned against the wall, staring at him. "I'll always
love you."

Her heart was thundering against her chest, her breath
was coming in gasps. If she hadn't been leaning against the
wall, she thought she would have fallen. Her body felt tingly
and hot.

Lifting a hand, he touched his fingertips to her cheek. Then he was gone.

Ivy stood in the open doorway, watching the floor indicator above the elevator. When the elevator reached the lobby, she whirled and ran to her balcony, leaning over the rail until she could see the moving van and a dark blue pickup.

"Eric!" The wind caught her voice and tumbled it away. She saw him emerge from the tower lobby, stop a moment to stare up at her, then he waved and opened the pickup door. "Eric, wait!"

The van and the pickup moved down the street.

Chapter Fourteen

The telephone rang every few minutes, but Ivy didn't answer. Throughout the day she occasionally played back the answering machine, listening long enough to identify Kevin's voice, then she fast-forwarded the tape to his next message. Finally she erased it without listening anymore. The phone continued to ring.

A half-dozen messengers appeared at her door to deliver flowers and beautifully wrapped packages. She was polite to the messengers, but refused the gifts.

Fortunately she had the presence of mind to look through the peephole in the door before she opened it, so she knew when Kevin himself appeared. She didn't respond to his knock. Instead, knowing he was standing in her hallway, she dialed his apartment and left a succinct message on his machine:

"Kevin, this is Ivy. Don't phone me again. Don't send more flowers or gifts; I won't accept them. You're wasting your time and mine. I meant it when I said I don't want to see you or talk to you."

When she felt certain the coast was clear, she darted out and bought a map of Wyoming, which she spread over her coffee table. She found Jackson Hole and traced Eric's probable route.

And through it all, she cried. She cried when she turned away the flowers and gifts, cried when she bought the map, cried as she pored over it. She cried as she heated a TV dinner for supper, cried as she ate it standing in front of the balcony windows, cried as she ran a bath before bed.

When she creamed her face, she looked at her red and swollen eyes in the mirror and cried some more. She hadn't looked this awful since her nose job. But the tears wouldn't stop.

The next day was a little better. The tears came only intermittently. She cried as she drank her morning coffee and later when she found a book of Eric's she had borrowed and forgotten to return. The rest of the day she was dry-eyed. But she was as depressed as she had ever been.

The depression lingered through the next day and the next. Dressed in sweat pants and a sweat shirt, gray to match her mood, she listlessly played back the answering-machine tape, more from habit than curiosity.

"Ivy darling, it's Martin. I've heard the most delicious gossip about you. Please call back and tell me if it's true."

"Ivy? This is Kevin. For God's sake stop acting like a child, and let's talk. Surely you aren't going to hold this against me forever, one little mistake."

"Hi, we missed you at lunch. Did you forget to check your calendar? This is Alice Ann. Call me."

"How long are you going to sulk? What did you expect me to do anyway? I'm sure you discuss your problems with friends, so why are you so upset that I did?"

"Ivy, this is Yvonne. Kevin asked me to call you. It seems I upset you a few nights ago. Look, you know how I get when I drink... Anyway, I apologize for whatever I said."

"Ivy, this is Missy. Will you for God's sake call Kevin? He's driving all of us crazy."

"Miss Enders? You don't know me, but I read about you in the newspaper. I could sure use a loan. You see, my car broke down about a month ago, and—"

Ivy turned off the machine and erased the tape. The voice she wanted to hear wasn't there.

Before she could press the "on" button, the phone rang beneath her hand. She looked at it a moment, then slowly lifted the receiver.

"Ivy? It's Iris. I can't believe I actually got you instead of that damned machine. How are you?"

"Oh, Iris." Covering her eyes, Ivy sat on the floor and leaned against the wall. "I'm so glad to hear from you."

"What's wrong? You sound funny. Have you been crying?"

"I hate having my morning coffee alone. I hate living in the city with all the noise and the smog and being afraid of another burglary." Opening her eyes, she gazed around her apartment. "I'm living in a beautiful place that I don't give a damn about. Is that crazy? I could walk out the door right now and never miss a single thing in here. And you know something else? I have all these new friends, but there isn't one of them I can really talk to. Oh, Iris, what am I going to do?"

"Whoa. Back up a little. Did you have a fight with Kevin?"

"Eric moved to Wyoming. He's gone."

"Ah, I see." Iris's smile was audible. "And maybe you're beginning to."

"What does that mean?"

"Start from the beginning and tell me everything, every detail. Remember, this is your big sister speaking. Don't leave out a thing."

It poured out of Ivy, a torrent of words and emotion. She spoke steadily for twenty minutes before her voice ran down.

"You did what? You dumped a bowl of caviar on his head?" Iris's shout of delighted laughter burst over the line and Ivy leaned back against the wall and grinned sheepishly.

"Embarrassing, huh?" she asked. "I can't believe I did it."

"Long overdue, I'd say. Then what happened?" Ivy told her about going to Eric's and discovering him packing. She told Iris what she could remember about Eric's goodbye at the door and she also told her sister about the passionate kiss that had rocked her to her socks.

"Most of what Eric said didn't make sense. I wish I could remember it better. Something about how we couldn't continue to be friends if he stayed here so he had to go. That's when he kissed me, and Iris, it was like…like, I don't know. It was like I exploded or something. My knees gave out. It was never like that with Kevin. With Kevin I didn't feel a thing."

Iris laughed. "Dummy. Doesn't that tell you something?"

"Tell me what? I know what I felt, but if that kiss meant anything to Eric, he would have said something."

"Would he? Ivy, think about this a minute. Did you tell Eric that you're through with Kevin?"

"Oh, my God." Ivy sat up straight and blinked. "I meant to, but then I saw all the packing going on and I was so shocked that everything went out of mind except that he was leaving. And…Iris, I didn't tell him what happened! We didn't get to it."

"So Eric thinks you and Kevin are still a hot item."

"Oh, my God!"

"What he was telling you at the door was that he cares about you too much to stay in Denver and watch you with another man. He was telling you that he loves you, Ivy."

"He loves me?" she whispered. Her mind went into overdrive, rearranging memories, trying out different perspectives, recognizing things she had previously overlooked. "He loves me! Iris, Eric loves me!"

"What about you?"

She stared at nothing, then a smile of wonder lit her face. "I love him," she whispered, testing the words on her tongue. "I love Eric North," she said, amazed that she hadn't recognized it before. "I'm not sure when it happened, when we passed from friendship to love, but . . . oh, Iris, I love him. I've been so stupid."

"From what you've told me, you and Eric are two sides of the same coin. I never did understand what you saw in that Kevin person. He sounds so shallow, while Eric sounds so—"

"Iris, I have to hang up. I'm sorry but—tell Mom and Dad— Never mind, I'll work it out and—"

"I'll tell Mom it's time to start planning a wedding," Iris said laughing. "Hang up, little sister. I think you have fences to mend."

Ivy hung up the telephone but she didn't move. She sat with her back against the wall, smiling broadly at nothing, marveling at the emotion swelling her breast.

She loved Eric. She loved the way he looked and smelled, loved the way he laughed and the way his eyes crinkled when he smiled. She loved how his hair stood on end in the mornings and the way his hands curved around the steering wheel of a car. She loved his quiet humor and strength. She loved his commitment to life, his enthusiasm, his sense of purpose. She loved it that he liked to read and fish and she loved it that he hated golf.

Reaching for the phone, her cheeks bright, her eyes damp with unshed tears, Ivy dialed long-distance information. As she couldn't remember the name of the bank where he worked, she asked if he had a private listing.

"Yes, we have a new listing for Eric North," the operator said.

She dialed the number and got his machine. She drew a long, long breath.

"Eric, darling, this is Cyrano. There are two things I want you to know. Three things. First: in case you're wondering, I haven't tasted caviar yet. Second: I love you. I love you, Eric North, with all my heart. I love you! Third: in ten minutes I'm leaving for the airport. I'll be on the next plane to Jackson Hole. Please be there, darling!"

ERIC LEANED BACK from his desk and glanced out the window. The sky was crisp and winter blue, though the local weatherman was predicting snow before tomorrow morning.

Turning back to the papers on his desk, he tried to concentrate, but his mind kept drifting. Finally, frowning, he pushed back his chair and rubbed a hand over his eyes.

He'd been here two days and it wasn't working out. He'd made a mistake. He had believed the perfect small town, the perfect job, the perfect house, the perfect puppy and pickup would make him happy. He was wrong.

None of these things was what he was looking for. Not really. They were the icing on the cake—but he didn't have the cake.

He needed Ivy.

He couldn't sleep, couldn't eat, couldn't concentrate. Instead he kept thinking about her, thinking about kissing her, about her pliant body molded against his, about her lips, softer than he had imagined. He remembered her face in the morning sunshine, the way she nibbled a strand of hair when she was reading. He remembered the way she looked after the nose job, so small and vulnerable, remembered how wholesomely sexy she had looked that day on the Blue River.

And he remembered the flecks of caviar on her silver fox. How many nights now had he tortured himself with images of Ivy and Kevin? Hoping that Kevin had been gentle with her, and considerate, hoping the experience had been wonderful for her. And wishing to God that it had been him instead of Kevin. He could hardly stand to think about it.

Because he loved her. There, he had finally let himself state the truth. He loved her. And dammit, she didn't belong with Kevin, she belonged with him. Here, in a wonderful small town that was a perfect place to raise enough children to fill five bedrooms.

He stared out the window and frowned. He loved her and he believed she was making a mistake with Kevin. So what was he going to do about it? For months, he'd been trying to be her friend, trying to stay out of the way and not complicate her life. Consequently he had lost her, without ever telling her that he loved her beyond the constraints of friendship.

"Hi." Norm Halloran was leaning in Eric's doorway. "How about some lunch? I think the chicken-fried is on special over at Gertrude's."

"Instead of lunch I'd like a couple of days off—starting now."

Norm's brows rose and he grinned. "You need a vacation already?"

"Remember those loose ends I mentioned? There's one that still needs tying."

"Would this have anything to do with that little lady who won the sweepstakes?"

"Did I tell you about Ivy?" He looked surprised.

"Eric, my friend, everyone in town knows about Ivy Enders. When are you going to bring her up here and let us see this paragon?"

"It's . . . complicated."

"Well then, I think you'd better get yourself to Denver and uncomplicate things. There's nothing I'd like better than to see you settled down with a big depositor."

Eric laughed and waved. "Thanks. I'm on my way."

But first he closed his office door and phoned her.

"Ivy? It's Eric. If you're monitoring your calls, please pick up the phone." After a moment of silence, he drew a breath. "Maybe it's easier this way. Ivy, I haven't been truthful with you because I thought if I were truthful I'd complicate your life, embarrass us both, and possibly place an impossible strain on a friendship that's very, very important to me. That's why I didn't tell you that I love you, Ivy. But I do. Remember when I told you in Eze that I didn't believe in love at first sight? That isn't true. I've loved you from the moment I first saw you at that networking meeting.

"Right now you're involved with Kevin, but I don't think he's right for you. I am. You and I are like pieces of a puzzle—we fit together. We like the same things, come from similar backgrounds, share the same values. I think we could be very good together, darling Ivy. So good that I can't imagine a life without you."

He paused, wishing she was here, wishing he could talk to her in person, hold her, love her.

"We have to talk. Please be home tonight, darling. I'm taking the next plane to Denver, and I'm not leaving until you understand how much I love you and need you. Please give us a chance."

She would be surprised, he guessed, maybe dismayed. Maybe she and Kevin had already set a date and he was only going to complicate things and cause a permanent rupture in their friendship.

It didn't matter. What mattered was that he couldn't let her go without a fight.

"Susan?" He paused in front of his secretary and dropped his house keys on her desk. "Jim Henderson is going to stop by for the keys to my house so he can deliver the firewood I ordered. This is the garage key. Please tell him to stack the wood along the north wall."

"Will you be gone long?"

From her expression, he guessed she had overheard his conversation with Norm Halloran. "As long as it takes," he said.

"Good luck." Lifting a hand, she showed him crossed fingers.

"Thanks. I have a feeling I'm going to need it."

IVY'S PLANE LANDED at four o'clock. Eagerly she hurried down the steps and looked for Eric among the small group waiting at the foot of the ramp. He wasn't there.

For a moment, she felt a lump of panic rise in her throat, then reason asserted itself. He hadn't been home yet. He hadn't gotten her message.

After hailing a taxi, she asked the driver to name the banks in Jackson Hole.

"That's it—Wyoming National. Can you get me there before closing time?"

"Sure thing, miss."

Chewing on her lip, she leaned back and tried to quell her nervousness by examining the town. It was a lovely place, and she understood immediately why Eric had chosen it. Jackson Hole managed to blend small-town hospitality with the cosmopolitan ambiance common to a resort area. The result was marvelous. And the scenery breathtaking.

When the taxi stopped, she grabbed her overnight bag and ran inside. Her heart was hammering and she knew she sounded breathless when she asked for Eric North.

The woman behind the desk looked up immediately, noting Ivy's flushed face and the overnight bag. "You are...?"

"Ivy Enders, a friend of Eric North's. Is he here?"

"Of course, I should have guessed it was you." A wide smile curved the woman's cheerful face. "I'm Susan Mallory, Eric's secretary. Sit down, Ivy—may I call you Ivy?— I have something to tell you."

"He went to Denver?" Ivy asked when she had heard the story. "To talk to me?"

"I'm sure he'll be back when he discovers you're here." Susan gave Ivy the keys to Eric's house. "Probably the best thing to do is stay put and wait."

Handing someone the keys to another person's house would never have happened in a big city, Ivy knew, as she dropped the keys into her purse. She loved it here already.

"Thank you, Susan." She thought for a moment. "When is the last plane from Denver?"

"Gets in about midnight, I think."

"Thanks."

That gave her plenty of time to make a couple of stops before she went to Eric's house.

ERIC STOOD in front of her apartment door, listening to the silence on the other side. After a moment, he returned to the lobby and dialed Kevin's apartment from the pay phone. To his surprise, Kevin answered instead of Walter or the machine.

"Oh, it's you," Kevin said.

"I'd like to talk to Ivy. Is she there?"

"I'd like to talk to her, too. No, she isn't here. Walter saw her leaving about noon with an overnight bag. Maybe she went to Limon to visit her family. That's where she usually goes when she's in a sulk."

Noon was about the time he had phoned. It was possible she hadn't gotten his message. "Ivy isn't the type to sulk."

"You have your opinion, I have mine. I suppose you heard what happened."

The remark was so typically Kevin that Eric smiled. "I've moved to Wyoming, Kevin, remember? I haven't heard anything." And he didn't want to. He wanted to find Ivy.

"She caused a hugely embarrassing scene at a party I gave for Mike and Missy. You won't believe this, but she dumped a bowl of caviar on my head. Yvonne says I shouldn't forgive her, but I haven't decided yet. I'm very angry about this and about the way she's behaving. Returning the gifts and flowers, refusing to talk to me, as if this were all my fault. It's such a damned bore."

Eric's grin was so broad his mouth ached. "Ivy dumped a bowl of caviar on your head? Why would she do that?"

"Oh, Yvonne said something to her. I'm angry at Yvonne, too. Women are such a—"

"Wait a minute." Eric straightened abruptly. "When did this happen? Recently?"

"Right before you moved. Yvonne is so tacky when she drinks. She can't keep her—"

"Was Ivy wearing her fox coat when she dumped the caviar on you?"

"What the hell does that have to do with anything?"

"Was she?"

"I don't remember. She might have been but—"

Eric didn't wait for Kevin to remember. He hung up the phone and stood there, grinning like an idiot. When he could think straight again, he phoned Iris in Limon.

"Iris? This is Eric North. We've never met, but I'm a friend of Ivy's and I'm trying to find her. Is she with you?"

A voice delightfully like Ivy's laughed softly. "I'm pleased to meet you, Eric, I've heard a lot about you. No, Ivy isn't here. She's on her way to Jackson Hole."

"What?"

"I hope Ivy won't get angry with me for telling you this, but..."

When he hung up the telephone, he was grinning like a madman. He felt like running and shouting and leaping in the air.

"Taxi? Taxi!" Running forward, he jumped into the first vacant cab. "To the airport and hurry!"

IT WAS ALMOST MIDNIGHT when he stepped off the plane. A few snowflakes tumbled out of the dark sky. He threw his bag into the back of the pickup, then sat for a moment while the heater warmed up, trying to think where she would have gone. To a hotel, of course, but which hotel? A resort town was full of them.

Then he thought she might have left a message on his answering machine. Spinning gravel behind him, he sped out of the parking lot and burned up the road between the airport and his house. He had ceased to think of it as the Thayer place. It was the North place now. He couldn't wait for her to see it.

When he turned into the driveway, he noticed the lights were on. Had he forgotten to turn the lights off, or had Jim Henderson done it when he delivered the wood? Soft yellow light spilled into the night, illuminating the fat wet snowflakes twirling out of the midnight sky.

Then he saw a curl of smoke floating from the chimney over the bedroom roof. Someone might have forgotten to turn off the lights, but no one would have laid a fire in the bedroom fireplace.

Then he understood. He knew where Ivy was.

The moment he stepped inside, he smelled her perfume and heard soft music drifting from the stereo. Smiling, feeling his stomach tighten and his breath catch, he hung his coat in the hall closet. He didn't see the note until he closed the door.

Taped to the closet door, it said: "I love you, I love you, I love you. Please stop by the kitchen."

Laughing softly, wild with anticipation, he made himself go into the kitchen before he ran down the hallway to the master bedroom.

There he found a bottle of Dom Perignon chilling in a silver ice bucket. Two champagne flutes were also on the tray.

He wished he had known—he would have bought enough roses to cover the bed with petals. Silk roses would have to do. He grabbed a handful from an arrangement near the door and added them to the tray. Then, heart beating wildly, he followed the soft music to the bedroom.

The fire came into view first, the only light in the room. He still didn't believe what was happening. It was like a dream, a wonderful fantasy, coming true.

Then he saw the bowl of caviar sitting in ice on the table beside the bed. And he believed.

He stepped into the room and sucked in a breath when he saw her in his bed.

Her hair and face glowed in the firelight, her eyes were shy and warm and she held the blanket to her naked breasts.

"I've pictured you like this a million times," he whispered. "I love you, Ivy Enders."

"I've never been so nervous in my life," she said shyly. Then she remembered this was Eric, her friend, her confidant...her lover. And she relaxed and smiled and opened her arms, letting the blanket fall from her breasts. "I love you so much," she whispered. "Put down that tray and come here."

LATER, WHEN THE FIRE had died to embers and the champagne was gone and the caviar sampled, Ivy pillowed her curly head on his shoulder and smiled at the snow tumbling past the windows.

"Happy?" Eric asked, kissing the top of her head.

"I've never been happier in my life. You were wonderful." Turning her face against his chest, she hid a blush of contentment.

"So were you."

"I was beginning to think I was frigid."

"You?" His laugh of disbelief made her smile. "Darling, you are definitely not frigid. You were fabulous!"

"You know," she said, running her fingertips down his chest, smiling at the stirring she felt against her thigh. "Has it occurred to you that, this being a small town, everyone is going to know by this time tomorrow that the new banker is already involved in a scandal?"

"Good heavens!" He rolled his eyes in mock horror. "You're right. I've been here less than a week and already I'm entertaining a beautiful woman overnight."

"I suppose the only decent thing to do is marry you and save your reputation."

"Why, Cyrano, is this a proposal?"

Ivy grinned up at him and snuggled closer. "I hate to see a perfectly good sewing room go to waste."

"In that case, since my sewing room and reputation are at stake, I guess I'll have to accept."

"Good," she said, smiling against his mouth. His hands moved over her and she moaned softly. Then, as she slid beneath him and wrapped her arms around his neck, she grinned up at him. "You know something? I absolutely *love* caviar."

"I thought you might," he said, laughing.

Then there was just the snow and the fire and the music—and Eric, wonderful Eric.

Everything her heart desired.

Step into a world of pulsing adventure, gripping emotion and lush sensuality with these evocative love stories penned by today's best-selling authors in the highest romantic tradition. Pursuing their passionate dreams against a backdrop of the past's most colorful and dramatic moments, our vibrant heroines and dashing heroes will make history come alive for you.

Watch for two new Harlequin Historicals each month, available wherever Harlequin books are sold. History was never so much fun—you won't want to miss a single moment!

Harlequin American Romance

COMING NEXT MONTH

#273 TAYLOR HOUSE: CLARISSA'S WISH
by Leigh Anne Williams

Clarissa Taylor Cartwright was determined to rebuild the family home. But architect Barnaby Rhodes's terms were unusual. Make Clarissa fall in love with him. Don't miss the final book in the TAYLOR HOUSE trilogy.

#274 A FINE MADNESS by Barbara Bretton

Billionaire Max Steel's Florida island was so secure that even he couldn't come and go as he pleased. While Kelly plotted to rescue him, he and an island of PAX operatives plotted a riskier mission. A mission that was destined to make heroes of Kelly and Max—if it didn't kill them first.

#275 GIFTS OF THE SPIRIT by Anne McAllister

Chase Whitelaw wanted a wife and family—but he wasn't prepared to give Joanna another chance to fill the role. Five years ago she had left him at the altar; now she wanted back in his life. But this time, was *he* ready?

#276 WISH UPON A STAR by Emma Merritt

Along with her three children, Rachel March was finally making it on her own—until Lucas Brand demonstrated his devastating tenderness and Rachel realized she was up against a master. How could she resist the irresistible—and more importantly, did she even want to anymore?

**There was no hope in that time and place
But there would be another lifetime...**

The warrior died at her feet, his blood running out of the cave entrance and mingling with the waterfall. With his last breath he cursed the woman. Told her that her spirit would remain chained in the cave forever until a child was created and born there.

So goes the ancient legend of the Chained Lady and the curse that bound her throughout the ages—until destiny brought Diana Prentice and Colby Savagar together under the influence of forces beyond their understanding. Suddenly each was haunted by dreams that linked past and present, while their waking hours were fraught with danger. Only when Colby, Diana's modern-day warrior, learned to love could those dark forces be vanquished. Only then could Diana set the Chained Lady free....

Next month, Harlequin Temptation and the intrepid Jayne Ann Krentz bring you Harlequin's first true sequel—

DREAMS, Parts 1 and 2

Look for this two-part epic tale, the

Temptation

"Editors' Choice."

Harlequin Temptation dares to be different!

Once in a while, we Temptation editors spot a romance that's truly innovative. To make sure *you* don't miss any one of these outstanding selections, we'll mark them for you.

EDITOR'S CHOICE

When the "Editors' Choice" fold-back appears on a Temptation cover, you'll know we've found that extra-special page-turner!

THE *Temptation* EDITORS

ATTRACTIVE, SPACE SAVING BOOK RACK

Display your most prized novels on this handsome and sturdy book rack. The hand-rubbed walnut finish will blend into your library decor with quiet elegance, providing a practical organizer for your favorite hard-or soft-covered books.

Only $9.95

Approximately 16" x 8" when assembled

Assembles in seconds!

To order, rush your name, address and zip code, along with a check or money order for $10.70* ($9.95 plus 75¢ postage and handling) payable to *Harlequin Reader Service*:

> Harlequin Reader Service
> Book Rack Offer
> 901 Fuhrmann Blvd.
> P.O. Box 1396
> Buffalo, NY 14269-1396

Offer not available in Canada.

*New York and Iowa residents add appropriate sales tax.

BKR-1A